SENSING SECRETS

SUSAN C. DAFFRON

A JENNINGS & O'SHEA NOVEL

BOOK 2

Published by Magic Fur Press
An imprint of Logical Expressions, Inc.
P.O. Box 383
Ponderay, ID 83852

Sensing Secrets

ISBN: 978-1-61038-050-8 (paperback)
      978-1-61038-051-5 (EPUB)

Like all of my books, *Sensing Secrets* is dedicated to
my husband James Byrd,
my best friend and biggest supporter.
Thanks for everything!

<u>Books by Susan C. Daffron</u>
The Alpine Grove Romantic Comedies
Chez Stinky

Fuzzy Logic

The Art of Wag

Snow Furries

Bark to the Future

Howl at the Loon

The Good, the Bad, and the Pugly

The Treasure of the Hairy Cadre

The Luck of the Paw

Daydream Retriever

The Hound of Music

The Jennings & O'Shea Mysteries
Sensing Trouble

Sensing Secrets

Sensing Truth

Chapter 1

You Can't Be Too Careful

Maybe having people think you're dead isn't so bad. If nothing else, it keeps everyone guessing, which has advantages when you're hiding out.

These existential thoughts surfaced while I was perusing a news site on my spiffy new laptop and ran across an article speculating about Riley O'Shea's whereabouts and possible exit from this mortal coil. Although he was a private person, faking death was little extreme, even for Riley.

I knew the report wasn't accurate because Riley was walking up a long expanse of lawn toward me from the lakeshore with his dog Zelda who was leaping and cavorting around him in pure canine joy. Ironically, Riley appeared healthier than I'd seen him since we'd met a few weeks ago.

I was sitting at a table on the patio that faced the lake. I pushed my chair back and spread my arms wide to welcome Zelda from her walk. The fluffy white dog galloped up to me, waggling her whole body in greeting.

I gave Zelda a little affection and looked up at Riley as he sat down in the chair next to me. Pointing at the laptop, I said, "So when were you planning to tell me that you're dead?"

Riley flashed a sheepish grin. "Reports of my demise may be slightly exaggerated."

"Are you ever going to stop spawning these rumors?"

"Maybe when people start leaving me alone." He reached down to ruffle Zelda's ears. "When I sold my business and went on my road trip, the press started making up lies. If they're going to indulge in rampant speculation, I may as well give them something to talk about."

"You're enjoying this a little too much." I was probably overly sensitive to Riley's rumor mongering because I'd worked for so many years as a newspaper reporter. Yep, that's me: Meg Jennings, former reporter, current fugitive. My life had taken a few strange turns lately.

Riley may or may not be my stepbrother and for the last week, we've been sharing a gorgeous lakefront rental house with a guy named Dean Wolfe. Riley and I went to great lengths to get Dean away from some bad people, and now those bad people were after us too.

The reason they're so intent on carting us off is because we have special abilities. Tim O'Shea, Riley's father, is a retired engineer or "electrical specialist," and Tim coined the term "specialist" to describe people like us, who have sensory abnormalities. Although I rarely feel particularly special, it seemed appropriate to use Tim's moniker, given that the reason Riley and I met in the first place was because his father and my mother disappeared together.

While trying to find our parents, we met Dean, who had been abducted, drugged, and forced to travel with a circus. Riley and I still haven't found our parents, which distresses me. But when we rescued Dean from his big-top nightmare, he claimed our parents were happily doing research at a retreat somewhere. They may or may not have married, which is why I don't know if I'm actually Riley's stepsister or not.

Although Dean swears up and down that our parents are fine, he thinks his girlfriend Peggy is in danger from the people who abducted him. Somehow he managed to talk me and Riley into helping him find Peggy. Dean is convinced she's nearby so after some discussion, we decided to hang out in the small town of Alpine Grove while we wait for the heat to die down.

During this impromptu vacation, I have spent a lot of time grilling Dean for more information about our parents, but have learned almost nothing. Although Dean is generally a cheerful person, he's reached the point that he's barely willing to speak to me. It's been suggested that sometimes I can be a bit of a pest.

I glanced up from my laptop when Dean opened the French doors and walked outside to join Riley and me on the patio.

Dean sat down and placed a plate with a piece of plain dry toast in front of him. "We're running out of stuff to eat."

"Do you think the people chasing us have decided we've left Alpine Grove yet?" I asked.

"I dunno, but this is the last piece of bread in the house and we don't have anything to put on it. Naked toast isn't gonna cut it," Dean said. "We can't put off a store run much longer. Someone has to go to the grocery store or I'm going to starve."

"There's some granola left," Riley said.

A look of horror crossed Dean's face, as if Riley had suggested eating petrified ground squirrel. "Man, why do you buy that stuff? It tastes like dirt."

I chuckled. Riley's eating habits didn't match Dean's or mine, which had made our cohabitation more complicated.

Riley ate mostly fruits and vegetables, whereas I believed chocolate should be its own food group. Dean fell somewhere in the middle on the healthy eating scale.

Riley stood up. "Suit yourself. I'm going to make lunch."

Dean and I momentarily stared across the table at each other and simultaneously moved to get up. We followed Riley into the kitchen, accompanied by Zelda. Riley pulled a few items out of the refrigerator while the rest of us observed with interest. He dropped a bag of carrots on the counter and said, "What?"

"Are you making lunch? Please say you are." I said. Although I'd traveled with Riley for quite a while, we'd stayed in motels with nothing more than a microwave. Our rental house had a fully equipped kitchen and much to my delight, Riley's overdeveloped sense of smell meant he was the most amazing cook I'd ever met. Who would have guessed? My mouth watered at the thought of what he might create for lunch. Sure, he was a health nut, but his cooking made even vegetables taste good. It was a miracle.

Dean was just as eager and said, "Are you making a stir-fry again? The last one was great."

Riley held up the carrots. "You're not wrong about the food situation. We've eaten almost everything. Carrots and celery are a start, but that's pretty much all we have left."

Dean and I made noises of discontent and I said, "Can't you think of something?"

"I'll figure something out. But we're here for only a couple more days, so we can't go crazy buying a bunch of food," Riley said, turning back to the counter and grabbing a knife. "You could help by starting a batch of rice."

Although I'm not a chef, I can boil water, so I got busy with the rice program. If Riley was making food, I wanted to be in on it. I measured out the water and set the pot on the stove. "So where did you and Zelda go on your walk?"

Riley stopped chopping for a moment. "We found a place with the most amazing view. There's a rock that juts out over the lake, and when you sit out there, it feels like you're suspended over the water. You have to see it."

"Does this require hiking? You know how I feel about that type of activity," I said.

"Yes, but the view is worth the climb. You've been glued to that laptop, and you're going to resemble a red-haired marshmallow if you don't get some exercise."

"Says Mr. Toothpick. I love that with a laptop I don't have to sit at a desk anymore. I can be on the couch, the patio, in bed, or anywhere I want. It makes work seem less work-y."

"Doing that is bad for your neck, particularly if you never get any exercise," Riley said.

"I'm feeling great. No hallucinations. No headaches. Life is good." I gazed down at my rice water, which refused to boil. "As for exercise, my body and I have an agreement. I don't make it do anything it doesn't want to do, and in return, when I get overzealous and eat too much chocolate cake, the calories don't end up on my hips."

"For now," Riley said. "Returning to the point, you should come with me to check out the view before we leave. It's incredibly cool."

Dean said, "Hey, I think I know where you're talking about. That's Make-Out Rock."

Riley and I said, "What?" at the same time. I mumbled, "Jinx," because you can't be too careful. So far, 1997 had been a pretty bad year for me, and I figure it's best not to tempt fate.

Dean said, "Peggy told me about that overlook. She said the high school kids go there to make out. It's gotta be the same place."

The rich aroma of whatever spices Riley had put into the stir-fry wafted through the kitchen and I tried to refrain from drooling. Zelda had no such qualms and a little rivulet of saliva dripped off her tongue onto the floor.

As I watched Riley deftly create another mouthwatering meal, I tried not to think about the upcoming trip to town to get supplies. The anxious knot in my stomach wasn't from hunger. In the last few weeks, I'd been chased, attacked, almost blown up, and endured other bizarre experiences, most of which made me want to crawl under a warm blankie and never come out.

The last few days had been a welcome respite from the weirdness that had become my life. Part of me wished we could just stay in this comfy cocoon by the lake forever and forget about finding Peggy and our parents.

Soon reality was going to reassert itself and we'd need to venture out into the world again. But at least I'd be well fed when we did.

~

In the process of trying to track down Dean, Riley and I had talked to many people in the small town of Alpine Grove. Unfortunately, it's difficult to lay low in a small town once everybody knows your name.

Although Dean is fairly average looking, Riley is tall and extremely thin. My dyed hair has become an unusual and unnatural shade of red from too much time in the sun. Together, Riley and I are an odd and distinctive pair, so Dean offered to go to the store alone.

"I'm going with you," Riley said.

Riley's demand wasn't a huge surprise to me. When it comes to eating, Riley takes the word "finicky" to a Morris-the-Cat level, and I figured he wouldn't want Dean to be responsible for selecting food all by himself. But if Riley was going to the store, there was no way I wasn't going with them because the last time I let Riley and Dean out of my sight, they disappeared.

Although the two men made a compelling case for me to opt out of the journey, I played the trump card. Maybe if you've been married to a guy for twenty-five years you can talk with him about anything, no matter what. But in my experience, a sure way to make men uncomfortable is to throw out words like tampon and panty liner. Riley and Dean decided they didn't want to make difficult choices in the feminine-protection aisle, and said that perhaps it would be a good idea if I joined the grocery excursion after all.

We still had the issue of being recognized, so we compromised and decided to split up our shopping. I'd visit the pharmacy area while Riley grabbed the veggies. Meanwhile, Dean could pick up dry goods, like cereal for him and cookies for me. With any luck, we could get in and out of the store quickly before anyone who might be chasing us noticed our presence. We figured it would be better if I shopped with Dean and wore a big hat to cover my mutant hair. While I was in the pharmacy area, I also planned to pick up a box of Miss Clairol because I definitely wasn't feeling pretty these days.

Remaining incognito can be difficult in Riley's car, which is a cherry-red, souped-up classic convertible Mustang. The Mustang attracts automotive enthusiasts like nothing I've ever seen. More than once I've been waiting in the car for Riley when a gear-head has come up to ask about the specs. Of course, all I know is that Riley named the car Shelby, it goes fast, and he hardly ever lets me drive it.

Even though Dean's car is twenty or thirty years newer than Riley's, it's a lot less conspicuous. It's also way less fun to ride around in, partly because it's not a convertible and partly because it's been thwacked with an ugly stick.

Zelda seemed annoyed that we were leaving her at the house, but Dean whined that he didn't want dog hair sullying the delicate upholstery of his precious automobile. It was hard for me to believe we'd found someone more uptight about his car than Riley, but we had. Dean locked the windows, preferring to run the heat or air conditioning. I think he wouldn't let us put the windows down because it might mess up his hair. I figured he'd deny it if confronted though, so I laid low on the issue.

We loaded ourselves into the nondescript gray car and Dean drove north away from the lake toward Alpine Grove. He was quiet on the drive and I suspected he was hoping to hear Peggy again. Whereas Riley's special ability relates to his sense of smell and mine to vision, Dean's involves his hearing. If he gets too close to sources of electromagnetic radiation, he gets unbearable headaches, but when he isn't in agonizing pain, he sometimes can hear people like Peggy who aren't nearby.

In much the same way, my visual abilities become debilitating from radiation, but sometimes what I see can be helpful. And Riley has the amazing sniffer. In his case, when we're in an area with a lot of radiation and his sense of smell goes haywire, it's almost impossible for him to eat or sleep. There's no getting away from it. We're a weird bunch, and we're still trying to figure out how to manage what's going on with us.

According to Dean, Peggy also had sensory issues. Her sense of taste had gone nuts, so she's a specialist too. While we've been staying in Alpine Grove, Dean has tried driving around the area to listen for her, but so far he hasn't picked up even the tiniest of peeps, which I could tell was upsetting him.

When we arrived at the store, Dean grabbed a cart and leaned on it with one arm draped on the handle, shoving it forward. I've seen men pull this move before, as if they're trying to pretend they aren't really shopping. Poor Dean had to work harder to appear casual and cool because he needed to offset the fact that he was shopping with a woman wearing a dopey felt bucket hat adorned with a turkey feather.

He straightened, giving up on any pretense of coolness when one of the front wheels of the cart spun around like it was possessed. It's hard to be suave when you've got a bum cart. Meanwhile, Riley disappeared off into the land of produce so he could ponder the nuances of rabbit food.

Dean and I strolled down the cookie-and-cracker aisle. Although we couldn't stock up on many fresh items, we could buy munchies for the road. I grabbed a box of Triscuits and heaved it into the cart.

Dean said, "I like the plain ones better."

"No way. Rye Triscuits rule." I grabbed a box of Cheez-Its. "Don't tell Riley about these. He thinks they're the spawn of the devil."

At the sound of high heels clickety-clacketying along the tile floor, I turned my head. A woman in a tight black skirt was marching toward us. She had thick, black shoulder-length hair, and the blunt cut of her bangs gave her a resemblance to Marlo Thomas in *That Girl*. Except this woman was a lot burlier and surlier than Marlo. With a fake smile, she stretched out her arms and squawked, "Dean! Where have you been?"

Dean's broad shoulders slumped and he said, "Helen. It's a surprise to see you."

"Why? As you well know, I live here." Helen put her hand on her hip and pushed a lock of her thick black hair behind her ear. "So what happened to the lovely Peggy? Did you two break up already?"

In a glum voice Dean said, "This is Meg. She's, um, the sister of a friend. I don't know where Peggy is. Have you seen her?"

I piped up, "Nice to meet you."

Helen seemed unimpressed with my greeting, but managed to mumble, "Nice hat," before turning her attention back to Dean. "Why would I know about Peggy? After you dumped me, do you think I want to keep up with that trashy woman's whereabouts?"

I didn't know Peggy, but Dean had made it sound like the woman walked on water. Adding the word "trashy" into the conversation was an indicator that the exchange wasn't likely to end well. I said in my best reasonable placating reporter's voice, "Dean is worried about Peggy."

"Well, maybe he should go to the post office. I saw her there fifteen minutes ago. As usual, the line is out the door, so she could be there for hours."

Dean stood up straight. "You *saw* Peggy? I've been trying to find her! I've looked everywhere."

"Obviously, you didn't stop by the post office." A corner of Helen's mouth turned up. "Did you ever consider the possibility that maybe she doesn't *want* you to find her? She's probably dumped you. Considering how you treated me, who could blame the woman?"

Ooh, Helen was getting catty now. I moved the cart back slightly so Dean could step around it.

Dean strode up to Helen with his hands clenched into fists. "You know why you and I broke up, and I'm positive Peggy has not dumped me. Meg and I need to go. It's been real nice seeing you."

He turned on his heel and started for the exit. I noted the contents of our cart and lamented the loss of my Triscuits. Oh well. Dean was my ride and if he was about to jet off to the post office to find Peggy, I was going with him.

I caught up and yanked on his arm to slow him down. "Dean, what about Riley? You can't just ditch him."

Dean paused for a moment and scanned the store. "Oh yeah. Could you find him? I'll get the car."

I agreed and ran toward the far side of the store to the mysterious world of fruits and veggies. I found Riley studying a green pepper, took it from his hands, and put it back on the display. "We need to go."

He widened his eyes. "What's wrong? Did someone recognize you?"

"Not me. Dean. But we have a lead on Peggy." I grabbed his arm, yanking him along after me. "Dean's getting the car. Come on!"

One thing I like about Riley is that even though we may tease and gripe at each other sometimes, when I'm serious, he invariably listens to me. We ran out of the store and got into the car. Dean was already pulling away from the curb before we even slammed the doors shut.

"Dean, calm down. We'll find her," I said.

Dean shook his head, but didn't say anything.

Riley turned in his seat to catch my eye and said with a faint smile, "It's déjà vu all over again."

～

When we arrived at the post office, the parking lot was full. Granted, it wasn't a huge lot, but as Helen had said, the line was out the door.

"Why are so many people here? Was there a major postal event that I missed?" I asked.

Dean said, "There's always a bunch of people here. They have the slowest employee I've ever seen. Ethel is about a hundred-three years old and everyone keeps hoping she'll retire, but she never does."

Dean pulled the car over and double-parked so we could evaluate the situation. The people in line seemed happy enough and were chatting away. Some sat in folding chairs and were holding donuts or paper cups of coffee along with their packages, obviously settling in and making a morning out of their trip to the P.O.

"I don't know what Peggy looks like, other than what you told us. There's a tall woman with blonde hair over there toward the end." Riley said. "Is that her?"

Dean shook his head. "Peggy is shorter. I don't see her, but I can't think of any reason Helen would lie to me."

"Maybe Peggy made it to the front of the line and left. It has to happen eventually. Or maybe Helen did lie. She didn't seem to be the president of the Dean Wolfe fan club," I said. "So what did you do?"

"Nothing!" Dean said. "We went out a couple times and then she went all nutso on me. I would be out delivering my pies and then I'd notice her car behind me. Then one time when I was getting lunch at the diner, she stopped by to give me brownies. It was creepy and I threw them away."

"You threw away chocolate? What is wrong with you?" I said.

"I would have too." Riley said. "If she's as psycho as you say, they could have been poisoned."

"Maybe, but wasting perfectly good chocolate like that is just *wrong*." I gestured toward the line. "Should we ask around?"

Riley's expression was dubious. "I don't think that's a great idea. Maybe we should go."

"I'm wearing such a stupid hat no one will recognize me. I'll talk to a few people while you drive around the block." I opened the door to get out. "This won't take long."

I crossed the street to the line and went into low-key interrogation mode, chatting with a couple of people as if I were simply shooting the breeze, as opposed to grasping at our last feeble straw.

The tall blonde woman Riley had spotted earlier was cranky and let me know in no uncertain terms that her place in line was not to be trifled with and she didn't know who Peggy was. The petite woman with long wavy brown hair who was next to her shrugged, and her body language suggested she might not be best buddies with Ms. Tall-and-Cranky.

Spending much more time on even a cursory investigation was going to attract more attention than I wanted, and it was probably a big dead end anyway. I was pretty sure Helen had lied. People who bake poisoned brownies aren't usually known for their honesty.

I made a move toward the end of the line so I would look like I belonged while I waited for Dean and Riley to return from their journey around the block. I leaned sideways so I could see around the prodigious girth of an older man and see the cars coming down the street. Dean's gray sedan was trapped at a stop sign a couple of streets down.

I smiled at the man behind me in line, who smiled in response. He seemed friendly, so I went for one last question. "Did you happen to see Peggy Branson here today?"

"Yeah, she made it out. I was sittin' here and saw her cross the street. She went that way."

"Thank you!" I waved my hands in a game-show hostess maneuver to encourage him to take my place. "I think I'm giving up."

He hustled over, closing the space, and I walked to the curb. Because the post office was on a one-way street, I needed to cross so Dean could stop and pick me up. He'd be thrilled to hear that there had been a verified sighting of Peggy by someone who wasn't a potentially nefarious brownie baker.

Maybe we could cruise through a few side streets. If Peggy was on foot, she'd be easy to spot.

A dark-haired woman with oversized sunglasses was driving an old red Ford Econoline van at a glacial pace. It could take years before she finally reached the stop sign, so I boldly crossed in the middle of the street. Even in a small town, no one should drive like such a slug. I lived in Washington D.C. for years and jaywalking is in my blood.

I was about three-fourths of the way to the opposite curb when I sensed more than saw that the van was suddenly way, way too close to me. As I turned to see what was happening, a fist smashed across my jaw, knocking me over. I stumbled the last few steps onto the grass on the other side of the street and ended up on all fours.

Something silver flashed next to me, and then I had a jarring moment of complete confusion and disorientation as if all the air had been sucked out of my lungs. For a long second, I couldn't breathe and a jolt of pain seared across my back, causing my muscles to spasm. The red van's door slid open and hands gripped mine, hauling me inside. The door slammed shut and I lay motionless on my stomach as the unique zipping sound of a plastic cable tie came from behind my back.

Part of me was incredulous that I'd been captured. The other part was furious. Had someone used a Taser or stun gun on me? People in small towns were *supposed* to be friendly. My jaw hurt and I'd bashed my knees and scraped my palms when I fell. Blood was oozing into the web of flesh between my fingers.

Once I could feel my mouth again, I demanded, "Who are you? What do you want?"

A hand reached around my head and stuffed something that tasted like old gym sock into my mouth. I fervently hoped it wasn't truly an old gym sock and tried in vain to spit it out.

The person moved to the front of the van and the vehicle started up again. I turned my head, rubbing my face on the filthy floor in an effort to scrape the sock out of my mouth. When the van stopped, I wondered if it had finally reached the stop sign. I tried to remember what the driver looked like. Could it have been Helen?

I took a few deep breaths through my nose in an effort to remain calm and not dwell on the scent of old sock. Riley told me once that the reason his sensory overload was so hard to cope with was because if something smells bad, it's all you can think about. He'd pointed out that humans can't smell without judgment. I was gaining a much better understanding of what he had meant by that comment.

After I finally managed to get the sock out of my mouth, I focused my attention on my surroundings. It was a typical panel van like the kind used for moving with no seats, wall covering, carpet, or upholstery. No one was in the back of the van with me, so it was just me and the woman driving. Every time the van turned, I rolled around like a sausage on a grill.

Although the rolling was annoying, I could use it to my advantage. After I had a little momentum from a turn, I was able to roll all the way onto my back. Then I was able to curl my feet under me and use my hands to help push myself into a sitting position. I laboriously scooted on my butt closer to the sliding door and leaned on it so I could use the door to help lever myself to my feet. As quietly as possible, I bent to pull the door lock with my teeth and gave it a good yank upward. My hands were tied behind me, but I was able to grab the sliding door handle. I gazed out the window. It appeared we were cruising through the same residential area of Alpine Grove where Riley and I had found Dean. Interesting. I scrutinized the driver closely and was positive it was Helen.

The sight of a couple of kids playing in a yard gave me an idea. Because of where I was standing, Helen couldn't see me in the rearview mirror. If she bothered to look behind her, she'd know I wasn't on the floor where she'd dumped me, but so far I'd been lucky.

I gripped the door handle more tightly, took a deep breath, and screamed as loud as I could, "Watch out for that little boy—you're going to hit him!"

Helen slammed on the brakes and I braced myself for the impact. My weight and the inertia helped me yank the door handle and slide the door open. I let go, leaped out of the van, and ran.

Although Helen was shouting, I didn't look back because it didn't matter where I ended up. Anywhere had to be better than the inside of that van.

~

Behind me, Helen shrieked obscenities about the injustice of the world, mutants with sensory problems, Peggy, and me, but I kept my focus on running. Being completely terrified is a big motivator, and even though I'm horribly out of shape, I shot across backyards, front yards, and over and through hedges like a track star.

Although it's great at first, the combination of fear and adrenaline can only take you so far. Because my body is mostly composed of flab, after a point, my leg muscles and lungs were in agony. I desperately needed to rest, and finally took a moment to glance behind me. I'd been so terrified, I didn't know if Helen was chasing me, but now she wasn't yelling or anywhere in sight.

Many of the cute little residential cottages in the neighborhood didn't have fenced yards, so I was able to go diagonally across blocks. If Helen had returned to the van, it would take her a while to circle around to where I was. The house I'd ended up at was well-maintained and had a tall privacy fence. I needed a few moments to catch my breath and pull myself together.

The house had the tidy appearance of being owned by people who worked all day and could afford a gardener. No toys, no swing set. Just neat, weed-free flower beds. With a small plea to the pet-loving gods that the owners didn't have a huge mean dog, I used my teeth to pull open the gate latch. The metal tasted disgusting and I didn't want to think about the layers of bird droppings, lead-based paint, and germs it might have accumulated. I spat a few times to get the metallic taste out of my mouth before I crept into the backyard. No snarling three-hundred-pound Rottweiler attacked me, which I viewed as a win.

I walked across the grass to a small patio and sat down on the concrete steps that led to the back door of the pretty cedar-sided house. I pulled my knees up close and curled over, resting my forehead on them trying to catch my breath. My physically unfit body wasn't used to this type of complete exhaustion and my muscles and lungs were burning. Mentally, I was also spent. Helen had said, or more accurately screamed, that she was after me, removing any uncertainty about that question. I'd held out a tiny glimmer of hope that maybe bad people were only after Dean and that I was exempt from being kidnapped. So much for that idea.

I closed my eyes so I could listen for Helen. I've never understood why people do that, as if not seeing might improve their hearing. But it did seem to help me focus on something other than my aches and pains. The only sound was the twittering of birds happily flitting through the branches of the huge maple tree above my head.

At the distinctive creaking sound of the gate opening, I jerked myself upright and assumed a defensive stance, my bound hands raised behind my back, as if that might help anything.

Riley closed the gate and pressed his index finger to his lips. My entire body melted with relief to see a friendly face, and I slumped back down to the steps.

He sat down beside me and leaned down to whisper, "Are you all right?"

I threw myself onto his chest. "Mmmph…fine."

Riley pushed me away and fingered the zip tie around my wrists. "We need to get that off you."

Somehow the clarity and simplicity of the statement overwhelmed my tattered emotions and tears started streaming down my face. He wiped my cheek with his thumb. "Hey, don't do that. It's going to be all right. With a garden like this one, I bet they have pruners or scissors sitting around somewhere."

He stood up, walked to a little wooden shed that sat on one side of the patio, and returned with a scary saw-like implement.

My eyes widened. "What is that for?"

"I have no idea, but it's sharp."

He cut the zip tie and I flapped my hands, trying to restore the circulation all the way back down to the tips of my fingers. I contemplated the state of my palms, which had scrapes on them with little bits of asphalt embedded in the dried blood. Ouch.

After putting the gardening tool back, Riley sat down next to me again. "We need to get you back to the house."

"Where is Dean?"

"Driving around the block and not encountering that red van, I hope." He put his hand on my shoulder and gazed into my eyes. "Are you sure you're all right?"

I stared down at my damaged hands again and nodded. Riley patted my shoulder, stood up, and walked to the gate.

He waved to me, encouraging me to get up, but I didn't budge. I knew I had to leave this pretty little yard on this pretty little street, but my legs refused to move. Why didn't I have a calm, serene life like these people evidently did? Why was I being chased by people all the time? Normal law-abiding people weren't zapped by Tasers or stun guns or whatever that thing was. They didn't have their wrists zip-tied behind them. I was a good person and I hadn't done anything wrong. Why was this happening to me?

Riley turned and theatrically widened his eyes and raised his eyebrows in a silent "What is your problem?" query.

I closed my eyes and shook my head. When I opened my eyes again, Riley was sitting next to me. He said softly, "What's wrong? You know we need to go."

A few silent tears dribbled down my cheeks and I mumbled, "I'm not a criminal. This isn't fair!"

Riley put his arm around me. "I know. If life were fair, you wouldn't have visions either. You'd still be happily reporting the news in Maryland, and I'd still be an entrepreneur with a thriving company."

"Why does this keep happening to me? I hate it."

"I'm not thrilled with what's going on either, but we can talk about it later. Right now, we need to leave this yard."

"I want a little house like this one. Isn't it cute? Why can't I have a normal life with a normal house? With a pretty garden." I pointed at a ceramic toad that was perched on a rock next to the steps. "They even have cute garden art. I don't have garden art. Why is that?"

"Meg, please. We need to go."

"I'm scared and my whole body hurts. I want to live in a safe little house in a quaint small town where I never have to think about how my mother is missing and people are trying to kidnap me."

"Maybe you can work on that later." Riley gently cupped one of my hands and turned it over to examine the scrapes on my palm. "But first you have to come with me."

With a heavy sigh, I shook off my fear-induced immobilization and followed Riley to the fence. We waited until we saw Dean's gray car before we opened the gate and rushed across the lawn to get in.

I crawled into the backseat, put on my seatbelt, and flopped down on my side. I was wiped out.

Dean said, "What happened to her? Is she okay?"

"Just a small post-kidnapping emotional meltdown. Maybe we can stop at a gas station on the way back to the house and pick up some chocolate," Riley replied.

"I heard that!" I retorted. Chocolate did sound good though. "I'd like M&Ms if they've got them. Plain, not peanut, please."

"I think she's going to be fine," Riley said as Dean pulled away from the curb.

Chapter 2

Sweets and Nothings

I polished off my bag of M&Ms on the way back to the house. When we returned to our home away from home, I made a beeline for the bathroom and took a long, hot shower to wash off stress sweat and blood from my various abrasions. Afterward, I put on my coziest sweatpants and curled up on the cushy sofa next to Zelda.

Riley sat down on the other side of the dog, and Zelda put her muzzle on his thigh with a big sigh. He grabbed a brush from the coffee table and ran it along the fur between her ears. Settling his feet on the coffee table, he turned to give me an appraising look. "You seem more relaxed. Are you feeling better?"

"I am, although I'm thinking maybe you were right about getting more exercise. Wonder Woman doesn't gas out when she's being pursued by a psycho super-villain."

"Wonder Woman also could have used the Lasso of Truth to find out where Peggy is."

"No kidding." I began petting Zelda's back and reflected on my lame efforts at interrogation at the post office before everything fell apart. "No one had seen Peggy, except the last guy I talked to."

"Someone actually saw her?" Riley stopped brushing Zelda, who snorted in dismay. "Dean didn't hear anything."

"That's what the guy in line told me. Maybe he was just being overly agreeable, but he said he saw Peggy cross the street after she got through the line. I was going to tell Dean to drive around the block and look for her, but then Helen, the Wicked Witch of Alpine Grove, showed up and almost ran me over."

"I'm glad she didn't succeed."

"Well, if she had, I'd be dead and I don't think that's what she wants. The people in line might have noticed if I'd been squished too. Instead, she whacked me across the jaw."

Riley leaned forward over Zelda to examine my chin. "That's turning into a nice bruise."

"She also zapped me with some kind of Taser or stun gun. I don't know what it was, but it hurt."

"I saw you hit the dirt and get dragged into the van."

"That reminds me. How did you know I was in that yard? It had a tall fence."

Riley tapped the side of his nose. "I had a feeling. We were following the van and I saw you leap out. I got out of the car and tracked you down to that backyard."

"Zelda would be proud of your scent-following skills. I'm glad you found me before Helen did."

"I can't believe none of those people sitting in line at the post office saw anything."

Dean walked into the room and sat across from us in a plush recliner. "No one saw what?"

"Me getting punched and zapped by your ex-girlfriend," I said.

"She hit you?" Dean crossed his arms across his chest. "I don't believe that. Helen Yana may not be the nicest woman I've ever met, but she's not violent."

"I beg to differ." I pointed at my chin. "I have facial evidence. I think there are also two zap marks on my back from the prongs of whatever electrocution device she used on me."

"Are you sure it was Helen?" Dean asked.

"Of course I am. I was in the van with her. She was trying to kidnap me!" I paused. "I just thought of something. When I got away, Helen was yelling at me."

Riley lifted his hand from Zelda's head. "How *did* you get away?"

"I used my body weight to open the van door when she stopped. And then I ran." I shrugged. "It wasn't the most thought-out plan. And now, I realize maybe I shouldn't have done that. Helen mentioned Peggy."

Riley and Dean both started talking at once and I waved my hands. "Both of you be quiet for a second. I just remembered what she said. I was so freaked out and scared that I didn't think about what she was yelling at me when I ran away."

"What *did* she say?" Riley asked.

"Well, minus the bad words, it was essentially that she'd used Peggy as bait, and we hadn't been cooperative about taking it. Dean was supposed to follow her, but it was taking too long. Oh, and by the way, we're a bunch of filthy mutants." I shrugged. "Fill in a bunch of f-bombs and scatological language and that's more or less it."

Dean leaned back. "Peggy is still here? I've driven everywhere and heard nothing. I don't understand. I was so sure she was in Alpine Grove."

"I think I know what happened." Riley leaned back and scrubbed his face with his palms. "I can't believe I didn't think of this before. Being here, I've been enjoying feeling good for a change, but it's making me stupid."

"Think of what?" I said. "What are you talking about? You're a lot of things, but stupid isn't one of them."

"An enclosed car like Dean's acts as a Faraday cage." At my blank expression Riley continued, "A Faraday cage shields whatever is inside it from electric fields. A car or airplane can act as a Faraday cage and protect the people in it."

"Okay, I'm not seeing where you're going with this," I said. "So what?"

Riley turned to Dean. "I'm guessing that when you were driving around, you didn't get out of your car, did you?"

"No, I never heard Peggy, so I figured she wasn't nearby." Dean said. "It's been so frustrating cruising all over Alpine Grove and not hearing anything. Nothing at all. I was so sure she was here, but I started to doubt myself."

"Riley, you and I spent weeks driving all over the western United States. What does driving have to do with anything?" I asked.

"You've probably heard that if there's a lightning storm, it's a good idea to be inside a car, right?" Riley said.

"Because the tires are rubber it's supposed to be safer," I said. "Everyone knows that."

"Except that's not the reason. It has nothing to do with the tires. The reason it's safer is because the car acts as Faraday cage. It picks up the lightning's discharge of energy and conducts it around the people in the car and down to the ground," Riley said. "If you wear rubber-soled shoes or are riding a bicycle with rubber tires and lightning strikes, you'll be toast. Being in a convertible isn't good either, because it's not enclosed."

I sat up straight and put my hand on Zelda's back. "Right after I met you, we were in your car next to a cell tower during a lightning storm. You're saying we could have been killed?"

"Don't remind me. I stopped because you were screaming your head off. Because Shelby is a convertible, we never were shielded from electromagnetic radiation. But in his car, Dean was, which may have affected his ability to hear Peggy," Riley said.

Dean stood up. "Can I borrow your car?"

I chuckled, knowing that wasn't going to happen. Riley had allowed me to drive his precious car only under duress and had been in a state of quasi-panic the entire time I was behind the wheel.

Riley said, "I know we'd all like more time to rest, but I think what happened to Meg indicates we're not safe here."

"But we haven't found Peggy," Dean said. "We need to find her and figure out what these people want."

"I think they want *us*." I said. "I don't know why, and the reasons I've invented are disturbing. Maybe they want to do experiments on us. Or perhaps they want to eliminate us, so we don't blab about how all their creepy electromagnetic radiation makes us sick."

"They wouldn't have dragged me around with that circus if they wanted me dead." Dean retorted.

"True," Riley said. "Meg and I also need to focus on finding our parents and learn more about this retreat where they are supposedly staying."

"I'm pissed off and almost ready to publish my first article about what we've learned so far." I turned to Riley. "Can you show me again what I need to do to put it in the thingie you created?"

"It's a web site." Riley said.

"I know that, but you did something so I don't have to write a bunch of gobbledygook crap to make it show up."

"HTML code."

"Yeah, that. What do I need to do?"

"You log in, type in a title, then copy and paste your article. The software I wrote figures out the rest and puts it online."

"Cool. These people are going down. I want Helen to pay for what she did to me."

~

"Hey, where did my fonts go?" I pointed at the laptop screen. "That's not what it looked like before."

Riley tore his gaze from his laptop. "On the web, you can select from two fonts. I told you that before."

"It's not as pretty as it was in my document. I want my fonts back."

"You're supposed to be all about informing the public. Power to the people and all that. No one cares that the *New York Times* hasn't changed its typeface in a hundred years."

"I suppose. But the way I had it was pretty."

Dean came into the room. "Are you done yet? I want to go."

Riley and I shut down our laptops. The deed was done. I'd written my first scathing exposé and it felt good. Now it was time to go find Peggy. I was looking forward to packing up and getting the heck out of Alpine Grove.

We tromped out to the Mustang, got in, and Riley drove us back to town. If nothing else, Dean could get his need to listen for Peggy out of his system. Because of our speedy exit from the grocery store, we had no food for dinner, so the secondary plan was to stop by a deli in town and pick up sandwiches.

I told Riley that if we stopped anywhere I was staying in the car next to Zelda with the engine running. I wanted to avoid any possibility of being snatched off the street again, and I knew from past experience that Zelda could be quite ferocious when suitably provoked.

It was a beautiful afternoon with gardens bursting forth with spring blooms. The smell of lilacs perfumed the air, and although my scraped hands hurt and my face ached, at least riding around in the convertible was enjoyable. I didn't have to drive and I didn't have Dean's super hearing, so I wasn't going to hear Peggy. I'd never seen her, so I didn't know what she looked like either. I had no responsibilities, so Zelda and I could just hang out in the backseat watching the world go by.

The warmth of the late afternoon sun was relaxing. I leaned my head back and closed my eyes. The sound of a car door slamming woke me up. When I opened my eyes, the car was stopped and Dean wasn't in the passenger seat anymore, although Riley was still behind the wheel.

"Where's Dean?" I asked.

Riley pointed toward the house across from us. "Over there."

"Is that Peggy talking to him?"

"I think so. She matches the description. Short, blonde hair, kind of rounded around the edges."

"You mean stacked." I nudged his shoulder. "Is it just me or does she not seem happy to see him?"

In addition to being well-endowed, Peggy had a round face and a rosy, clear, almost pearlescent complexion that was reminiscent of a porcelain doll. The illusion of the perfect pink girlfriend fell apart when she hauled back an arm and slapped Dean across the face hard enough that the whacking noise echoed through the maple leaves.

Riley said, "I think they might have a few things to work out."

Peggy moved to close the door and Dean shoved his foot in front of it, turned, and waved at us.

I waved back and thumped Riley's shoulder with my palm. "Now what are we supposed to do? Wait here? Follow him inside? What if we lose him again?"

"We can hang out for a few minutes. It looks like they need to talk."

"Unbelievable." I crossed my arms across my chest. "Maybe she's not as *smitten* as Dean thinks she is."

The door swung open and Peggy and Dean emerged, followed by Helen. I sat up straight in my seat. "Oh crap! What's *she* doing here?"

Riley looked equally alarmed, and Zelda growled low in her throat. It was one of those moments when I had absolutely no idea what to do. Stay? Run? What?

I could tell Peggy and Dean weren't happy to have Helen there either, so my assumption was that she was threatening them in some way. I reached around the passenger seat, tilted the seat and opened the door so I could get out of the Mustang. If I had hackles, they'd have been rising on the back of my neck. I was not going to let Helen get the best of me this time.

After I opened the passenger door, Riley exited the driver's side of the Mustang. Zelda leaped out after me and we all stood in front of the car.

Dean said, "You probably remember Helen."

"Lovely to see you again." I said as the trio drew closer. "Why are you here?"

Helen smiled smugly as she stopped about a foot from us. Zelda's growls were getting louder and more intense. Zelda liked me, but Riley had once mentioned that the dog was selective in her affections. Apparently, Helen didn't rate.

Helen said, "Peggy and I are roommates."

My jaw dropped. "You have *got* to be kidding."

"It's true. She really helped me out," Peggy said and turned to Dean. "You, on the other hand, dumped me. Why are you here?"

Dean's expression crumpled and he said, "I didn't dump you. I thought you dumped *me*."

Poor Dean. I felt bad for him. He was a nice guy and deserved the chance to explain himself. I raised my eyebrows at Riley as an unspoken, "Should I?" He gave me a small smile of encouragement, and I said to Helen, "I believe I owe you something."

Helen smirked. "And what's that?"

Under normal circumstances, I'm not a violent person. But nothing about this circumstance was normal. All the anger I'd been repressing coalesced as I curled my hand into a fist. I stepped forward and at the same time, drew my arm back and punched Helen in the jaw as hard as I could.

Helen's hands flew to her face and she staggered backward. Zelda growled and moved closer to Helen. All of the fur on Zelda's back was standing straight up, which made her seem far larger than she really was, more like a white wolf than a dog.

The noises coming from Zelda were vicious and threatening, and Helen waved at us. "Do something! If that dog bites me, I'm calling the sheriff. Or the police. Or animal control. I'm calling somebody! You need to call off that mutt."

Dean was focused on Peggy, clutching one of her hands with both of his. "Please, please come with us. I need to talk to you. I'm telling you, Helen isn't your friend. She's *really* not."

Peggy glanced down at Zelda, then at Helen, then Dean. "Yes, she is."

Riley moved his hand slightly, indicating to Zelda that he wanted her to settle down. He said, "Maybe I'm more selective, but my friends don't use stun guns and drag people into vans without their consent."

"He's got a point." I turned and lifted my shirt to show Peggy the marks on my back. "Helen did this to me earlier today."

The expression on Peggy's face clouded and she turned back to Helen. "I need to talk to Dean privately."

Dean's face lit up. "I promise I'll explain everything. You won't be sorry."

Helen said in a low voice, "Oh yes, you will. Sorry doesn't begin to cover it."

Peggy allowed Dean to lead her to the car, and I thought he might keel over with joy. Smitten wasn't the right word. He was utterly besotted with the woman.

Zelda and I returned to our positions in the back of the Mustang. After the dog's fierce performance, Peggy had no interest in sitting next to Zelda, so Dean got in the back seat with us. He was unwilling to let go of Peggy's hand and leaned forward so he was practically wrapped around the passenger seat.

Riley started the car and pulled away from the curb. As we drove past Helen, I stuck my hand out of the car and flipped her the bird.

I glanced at the rearview mirror and grinned at Riley. He was wearing sunglasses, but I could tell he was amused by my farewell.

Score one for us.

∼

Dean spent most of the drive back to the lake house whispering what I could only assume were sweet nothings into Peggy's ear. By the time we arrived, he was practically panting on her neck.

We all got out of the car, and Dean led Peggy to the house. Riley said he was going to take Zelda for a walk. As noted, I'm not big on exercise, but I asked to go with him.

Riley said, "You're kidding, right?"

"I mean it. Show me that place you found."

"It's going to be getting dark before too long." He turned to survey the view of the lake. "But sunset from that spot could be incredible. Could you get a flashlight?"

I ran inside the house to grab the flashlight, a coat, and different shoes. It would be a relief to get away from Dean and Peggy. It had become quite obvious that they really needed to get a room. Fortunately, the house had quite a few of them.

Riley was standing outside with his hands clasped behind his back, facing the lake. Zelda was leaping around him, obviously impatient to get on with her walk.

I walked up to them and bent to ruffle Zelda's furry ears. "Thanks for being my brave defender, Zee. I'm glad you didn't bite Helen, though, because the Alpine Grove cops don't like me much."

Riley chuckled. "Zelda seems to take issue with people who attack you."

"I know, and I have to say that I like that in a dog. How far away is this rock?"

"It's a bit of a walk, and then you have to clamber up a few boulders to get up to the point. Maybe a half hour or forty-five minutes?"

As we walked along the rocky shoreline, Zelda galloped ahead of us and then returned to us at a run. It was easy to see why she usually took such long naps after her walks. What a nut.

Riley said, "You had a long day, and I figured you'd curl up on the sofa with your laptop. What prompted this sudden urge for exercise?"

"Dean was fawning all over Peggy, and I thought I might throw up."

"Love is in the air."

"And horniness."

"That too." He stopped, picked up a rock, and skipped it across the water. "You seem to be slowing down. Are you all right?"

Getting attacked had worn me out more than I wanted to admit, and various muscles hurt from falling and being yanked around. "It's okay, but I need to pace myself on this whole exercise thing."

"The trail to get up to the rock is over there."

"How did you find this place?"

"I didn't. Zelda did. I followed her and that's where we ended up. We're probably trespassing, but it's a well-worn trail, so I think a lot of people do. You'll see."

We walked down a path through a copse of trees that ended at an enormous rock outcropping. Zelda leaped up onto the first boulder and wagged her tail. I could see the path ascending through the crags. That was a whole lot of up.

I'm not particularly good at up and I glanced at Riley. "So we have to go there? I've already been damaged today. How hard is it to get to this overlook?"

"I promise the view is worth it." Riley moved ahead of me and held out his hand. "Come on."

I took Riley's offer of assistance and he helped me clamber up the rocky path. I tried not to pant and grunt too audibly during the ascent. He grabbed my hand again at the points where I might plummet to my doom, which just showed how much time we'd spent together. He was well aware that I'm not always a graceful gazelle.

Finally, we reached the end of the trail, and Riley stepped aside to let me through the last craggy pass. I stepped out onto a flat granite slab that jutted out over the lake, far above the water. It was like we were suspended over the lake with the most amazing one-hundred-and-eighty-degree panorama I'd ever seen.

I stood, momentarily stunned into silence, drinking in the breathtaking view. Finally I said, "Holy crap."

Riley laughed. "I told you. Isn't it incredible?"

The sun was low in the sky, and the way the light hit the water made it sparkle as if millions of fireflies were dancing on the surface of the lake. The scene was positively magical.

Zelda had parked herself near a huge boulder and was lying down, contentedly panting. Riley gestured toward her. "We sat over there in that spot for ages the other day. I didn't want to leave."

"I'm all for sitting down." I walked over near the edge of the rocky promontory and sat down cross-legged so I could gaze at the vista in front of me.

The lake was gigantic, stretching for miles. A few islands dotted the water, and along the perimeter other outcroppings of rocks sloped toward the shoreline. Beyond the rocks was the forest, which was an unbroken span of deep, dense green, with the exception of a few clearings where houses had been built, including the house where we were staying.

Riley sat next to me, and we stared at the lake for a while in silence. The only sound was Zelda's panting and the breeze rustling the evergreen boughs behind us.

I pulled my knees up and wrapped my arms around my legs. "I can see why this is called Make-Out Rock. This view of the sunset is about as romantic as you can get. It's kind of a drag that I'm here with you."

Riley turned his head to squint at me and I grimaced. "Sorry. I didn't mean that the way it sounded. It's just been a long time since I've even had a date."

"It's all right. I knew what you meant."

"Dean and Peggy should come up here. He was practically drooling on her when we were riding back in the Mustang." I let go of my knees and straightened my legs so my feet could dangle off the edge of the rock. "So what's Erin like? You never talk about her."

Riley leaned back and propped himself up on his elbows. "Well, I haven't seen her for a while. I've been focused on other things. Finding our parents, for example."

"I know. But what's she like? Don't you miss her?"

"In certain ways, yes. Why do you want to know?"

I pointed the index fingers of both hands toward myself. "No date in who knows how long, remember? And as you know, my last boyfriend was quite possibly evil."

Riley chuckled. "Matt sounded like a jerk. But evil? That's harsh."

"If he's really wrapped up in the whole kidnapping of specialists, that counts as evil in my book. You didn't answer my question. What's your girlfriend like? Is she pretty? How did you meet? When did you meet? Did you fall madly in love?"

"You're interrogating again."

"I can't help it. Curiosity is part of who I am. So answer the question."

"That was five questions."

"I told you about Matt and he's not even current. At this rate, I may never have sex again, so I need to live vicariously through others."

"All right. Erin is smart and did well in school. She graduated summa cum laude from Harvard Law."

"She's a *lawyer*? I didn't know that. Wow, I just...I can't quite imagine you with a lawyer." I pulled my knees up to my chest again. "Wait. Is she *your* lawyer? Is that who you called to get your new company set up?"

"No, but she works at the same firm."

"What does she look like?"

"Tall, blue eyes, long blonde hair. Or the last time I saw her, it was long. She might have cut it by now I guess."

I shoved his shoulder. "Hey, you haven't cut your hair. Are you worried your hair is longer than hers now?"

"Very funny."

"How did you meet?"

Riley stood up. "We should probably head back. It's going to get dark here soon."

"Okay, but you have to tell me how you met while you keep me from falling on my head."

Apparently realizing that the humans were mobilizing, Zelda got up and joined us for the descent down the trail. She went ahead and Riley took my hand as we started climbing back over the rocks.

A few minutes passed, and I was breathing heavily again. The trip down wasn't as bad as coming up, but defying the pull of gravity was still hard work. In between embarrassing gulps for air I managed to sputter, "I haven't forgotten, you know. You're supposed to be telling me how you and Erin met."

"All right. You saw my high school in Thousand Oaks. She went to the rival school."

"You've been together since high school? I had no idea. That's remarkable. I'm impressed."

"Don't be. She didn't know I existed then. I knew of her, I guess you'd say. She was the homecoming queen, prom queen, cheerleader."

"What an overachiever."

"You'd hate each other."

"Thanks."

"I didn't mean it like that." Riley grabbed my hand to help me over a boulder. "We met again later."

"And was it love at first sight?"

"No."

"Oh, come on. Spill it. What happened?"

"I went to the law offices for a meeting with my lawyer and she recognized me." Riley stopped and waited for me to catch my breath.

I managed to wheeze, "From high school?"

"No, from an article about me." He shrugged. "I recognized her from school, though. To be honest, I was shocked she knew who I was."

"Awww, this is getting cute!"

"Jeez, you really do need a date. Give me the flashlight."

I pulled the little Maglite out of my pocket and handed it to him. "So what happened?"

"We were in a meeting together, and afterward she asked me out."

"She asked *you* out?"

"That's what I said. She's not shy. Definitely not shy."

"Oooh, I want details about *how* she's not shy."

"No way." Riley grabbed me around the waist, lifted me over the last rock, and plopped me on the ground. "I answered all five questions. I'm done."

We walked down the trail back to the lakeshore toward the house. I took Riley's hand again and swung it between us. "Tell me more. How long have you been together?"

"It was around four years. Then I got sick and, well, you pretty much know what happened after that."

I dropped his hand and walked backward a few steps so I could see his face. "I guess I do. So have you talked to her?"

"Not lately."

"Didn't you call her from here?"

"No."

"She knows you're alive, right? All those rumors…I mean, she doesn't think you're dead, does she?"

"I doubt it. My lawyer knows I'm alive, and she works there."

"But you haven't called her?"

Riley stopped before opening the French doors leading into the house. "Meg, I don't want to talk about this anymore."

Oops. Guess he'd had enough. Riley was one of those people who would talk for a while then abruptly stop. It was one of those introvert things that I didn't completely understand. He'd reach a threshold of conversation, then shut down and disappear for a while. He called it needing "alone time."

We went inside and the house was quiet. I glanced at Riley, who shrugged and wandered off into the kitchen, trailed by Zelda. A burst of female laughter came from upstairs. Okay, now I knew where Dean and Peggy were.

It wasn't fair that everyone had a significant other except me. Riley might be sort of down on his relationship with Erin at the moment, but at least he *had* a girlfriend out there somewhere. I was alone and had been for quite some time.

What was so wrong with me, anyway? I was smart. Maybe not Harvard Law smart, but I did okay. Was I ever going to have a normal life with normal relationships again? Or was I doomed to spend the rest of my days trying to figure out where my mother had gone?

Chapter 3

Not Quite Empty

The next morning, I was awakened by the sound of a fist pounding on my bedroom door. Riley yelled, "Meg, get up!"

I stumbled out of bed and opened the door. Riley was walking away from me down the hallway and I called after him, "What's your problem?"

"If you want breakfast, you need to move it."

I slammed the door and yanked on a pair of jeans, grumbling. Riley could be such a crank. But I did want breakfast, so I wasn't going to complain too loudly.

I walked into the kitchen, where Riley and Peggy were at the stove debating esoteric nuances of food. Peggy was convinced that the pancakes needed nutmeg and Riley wasn't having any of it. I was too asleep to get involved. I needed coffee. A pancake might be good too.

I proffered a plate and Riley tossed a pancake on it.

Peggy said, "Let me know what you think. They're supposed to be *spiced* pancakes and it's not the same without nutmeg."

I was focused on coffee, not nutmeg, and I settled into a spot at the table so I could ease into the idea of being awake. The pancake tasted fine to me and I wasn't getting in the middle of an argument, particularly since Riley was undoubtedly still annoyed about the interrogation I'd given him on our walk. Although I liked eating, I wasn't into cooking. Mr. Scent Meister could fight it out with Ms. Taste Meister without my help.

Dean walked into the kitchen all showered, scrubbed, and happier than I'd ever seen him. He wrapped his arms around Peggy, kissed her neck, and nibbled his way around to her lips. I averted my eyes, lest my pancake end up all over my shoes. Why was it necessary for people in love to slobber all over each other?

Adding to the slobber factor, Zelda plopped her muzzle on my thigh to indicate that she would like to share my pancake. I tore off a piece and gave it to her, which she gobbled down.

Riley sat next to me and set a plate with a stack of pancakes in the middle of the table. Zelda moved her head from my thigh to his as he grabbed a pancake off the top of the stack. He gave her a piece and she moved her muzzle back to my thigh. Canine loyalty clearly took a back seat to food.

Dean and Peggy sat down across from us, and we all focused on eating for a few minutes. I noticed that Dean was holding Peggy's hand under the table, which slowed them down. I snatched another pancake off the stack. If we ran out of pancakes, it wasn't my fault if the lovebirds couldn't keep up.

Dean set down his fork and said, "Peggy and I were talking last night."

I doubted they'd just been talking and I didn't want to hear the details. I took a swig of coffee to wash down the last of my pancake.

Peggy said, "Helen mentioned the retreat where your parents are. I think it's in the Northwest."

Riley and I both started asking questions at once, and then stopped to stare at each other. I silently waved my hand to indicate he should go first.

"Where is this place?" Riley said.

"What are they doing there?" I asked. "Dean said the retreat was owned by a group called Enviro Freedom. I haven't been able to find anything about them online. I need to get to a library."

"Helen said they keep a low profile, and the people she was, well, working with are trying to find them too," Peggy said.

"Do you know where the retreat is?" Riley repeated. "The Northwest is a large area."

"She just said something about them being a bunch of tree huggers in the Northwest," Peggy said.

I scowled. That wasn't much to go on. "Do you remember anything else Helen said?"

"No, that was it. Pookie and I were just talking about where we could go." Peggy replied.

Dean blurted out, "We're getting married!"

My mouth opened involuntarily and I snapped it shut. *Pookie?* Barf. I composed myself and managed to muster, "Congratulations, you two. That's wonderful. I'm happy for you."

"We're going to run off to Las Vegas! I'm so excited," Peggy said.

Riley poked his fork into a piece of pancake, swished it around, and said, without even trying to fake enthusiasm, "You might think about how being there is going to affect you."

Vegas had been the site of some of my most terrifying visions, and I chimed in, "Dean, you'll probably get bad headaches again. I hope you'll be careful."

"We'll just run in, get married, and run out. Then find a place to settle down. We want to start over somewhere else." Dean raised their clasped hands to his mouth and kissed the top of Peggy's fingers. "I lost my job and sweetums is thinking about doing something different too."

"Our week here is up tomorrow, so we'll have to leave anyway," Riley said. "I hope you'll be happy together, wherever you end up."

"Now that we helped you find Peggy, our job here is done," I added. Frankly, it was going to be nice to be away from this love fest. I had no interest in being a third wheel and if a guy ever called me 'sweetums' I'd probably smack him.

After breakfast Dean and Peggy went off to their room to pack up and probably have more sex. I didn't want to think about all the action I wasn't getting, so I ate the last pancake instead. Riley was still sitting next to me. He'd pulled out his laptop and was undoubtedly committing acts of mysterious geekitude.

I gave Zelda the last piece of pancake and pushed my plate forward. "What are you up to over there?"

"Mindless surfing of news sites."

"Well, that's not anywhere near the techie answer I was expecting."

He glowered at the screen. "Hmmm. That's weird."

"What's weird?"

"There was a fire at Hector's circus. It was at a fairground in California and they had to evacuate the animals to a temporary shelter."

"Fire?" I tugged the corner of the laptop toward me, so I could see the screen. "This says it isn't the first time the circus has been plagued by arson."

"Given your visions, that's disturbing. We wrote off the fires in your visions as something more symbolic than literal. Maybe we shouldn't have."

I put my elbows on the table and rested my forehead on my palms. I gazed down at the wood grain of the table. "I don't want to think about the fire I saw being real."

"I know."

I was silent for a few moments, trying to quell the overriding thought that was never far from my mind. A tear splashed on the wood and I wiped my eyes. "Riley, do you think our parents are still alive?"

"I hope so, but I don't know any more than you do."

"I *want* to think they're at that retreat, happily doing research like Dean says. Maybe the place really exists in the Northwest somewhere, but I'm having trouble believing it. Unless something happened to them, what are the odds they'd leave the house they were renting here without saying anything to us?" Brushing another errant tear from my cheek, I sat up in the chair. "Before we leave Alpine Grove, I'd like to check my mom's house again. It's probably silly, but I want to stop by there one more time."

"I don't have anything else to do."

The sound of Peggy giggling came from upstairs and I pointed at the ceiling. "I wouldn't mind getting away from that, either."

"Me too." Riley shut down his laptop and stood up. "Hey Zee, you want to go for a drive?"

Zelda wagged and ran to the door, which I took as a *yes*.

⁓

We parked in front of the cute cottage where Riley and I had met about a month earlier. The place was just as quiet and empty as ever. It was strange that when our parents disappeared, all of my mother's furniture went with them. Kidnapping is one thing, but taking a house full of furniture hostage is just plain bizarre. Dean claimed that the retreat people took everything.

I walked up the short concrete path to the door and knocked. As we'd experienced before, no one answered. When Riley and I found out our parents were gone, we'd contacted the local police, who had investigated. No one in the neighborhood had seen a trace of our parents. It was like they'd disappeared into thin air.

Riley told Zelda to wait in the car and walked around to the side of the house, peering in the windows. I joined him in snooping. With any luck no one would notice us behaving like criminals. That was an awkward conversation I'd rather avoid.

I made my way around to the back and peeked in the kitchen window. There was a round wooden table sitting in the middle of the room with a framed photograph on it. I waved to Riley. "Check this out. I think that's my mom's old table."

"That wasn't there before. Is someone moving in?"

"With Mom's table?"

Riley put his hands in a circle and squinted through them. "Is that a photograph of you?"

I turned back to see what he was talking about. "It looks like me when I was about nine. Okay, that's creepy."

Riley stepped back, away from the window. "Wait! Maybe they're moving back in. Problem solved. Wouldn't that be fantastic?"

I walked to the back door and gazed up at the neighboring houses to see if anyone was watching us out the windows. I tried the door handle and it was locked. I tugged it a little harder. Still locked.

Riley came up beside me. "What are you doing?"

"I want to examine that photograph more closely."

"You're not thinking what I think you're thinking, are you?"

"I want to get in there."

"No."

"The house is empty. Or almost empty. I'm not stealing. I just want to look. I won't even touch anything, but I need to see that photograph." I shook on the knob again with both hands this time. "I don't suppose your mechanical engineering skills include lock-picking, do they?"

"Sorry, but when I was in college, breaking and entering wasn't part of the curriculum."

I dropped my hands. "Dean said he helped our parents find this place. Maybe he knows who owns it or the rental company. I want to see that photograph."

"Maybe someone else rented the house. It has been a while."

"And the only thing they moved in is Mom's table and a photograph of me? I'm sorry, but that's too weird. Let's go home, extract Dean from Peggy's embrace, and ask him."

Riley shrugged. "All right. That seems reasonable..."

As I turned to return to the car, I came face-to-face with a short, burly woman with curly permed brown hair. She had buggy eyes that appeared distorted behind her huge, round glasses. Her hands were fisted on her hips and her brows converged, indicating that perhaps she wasn't pleased to meet us.

She bellowed, "Excuse me, but who are you people and what are you doing here?"

I recoiled from her extreme animosity, and then recovered my composure. Sure, I'd thought about breaking in, but I hadn't done anything. "My name is Meg Jennings and my mother rented this house. Who are you?"

"I'm the owner, Irene Hollingsworth. You have no business being here. The last tenants moved out."

I pointed at the door. "I know. They're missing. But I'd really like to look at that photograph. I think it's my mother's."

"The house is empty." Irene said. "I don't know what the deal was, but they're paid up for six months, so the place isn't available. Get off my property."

"Technically, it's my mother's rental, so I have a right to be here, particularly if she's dead, which she could be, for all I know." I glanced at Riley. "His father was the other person living here, so he has a right to be here too."

Riley nodded but didn't say anything. He stood with his hands in his pockets, seemingly content to let me fight it out with this unpleasant woman.

Time for me to go on the offensive. I jabbed my index finger more emphatically toward the door. "Could you let us in? That's my mother's table and a picture of me is sitting on it. If she has died, I want that photograph. It may be all I have left."

My comments about us possibly being orphaned seemed to have an impact on Irene and she pulled a huge key ring out of her jacket pocket. "I guess if I'm with you, it wouldn't hurt anything."

"Thank you," Riley added as we followed her inside.

I rushed to the table and picked up the photograph. It was a five-by-seven black-and-white photograph in a wooden frame. It was definitely little-girl me in the picture, but I'd never seen it before. I handed it to Riley.

He examined it and passed it back to me. "Is that really you?"

"It is, and that's my dog, Buster, with me."

"You were cute."

Irene said. "Is that all you need? I've got things to do."

"Since we're here, could you walk us through the rest of the house?" Riley asked.

"Yes, please! If there's anything else of my mother's here, I'd like to see it." I added.

Irene said, "Okay, but you need to be quick about it. I've got other stuff I need to get done today, you know."

We walked through the house and poked around. I inspected the medicine cabinets and closets. Riley examined windowsills, built-in bookshelves, and door frames. We found nothing except dust. Why would anyone bring back only a kitchen table and a photo?

After wandering around, we returned to the kitchen. I picked up the photo again and was holding it in my hands when a teenaged boy with stringy brown hair burst in through the back door.

Irene turned around. "Mikey, what are you doing here?"

"Don't call me that. It's Mike."

"Don't be smart with me. Why aren't you in school?"

Mike shoved straggly lock of hair off his forehead and stared at his sneakers. Irene said more forcefully, "Well, answer me! You'd better not have been suspended again."

Mike's eyes widened in alarm. "I wasn't! It's…uh…the other day a guy was here and I was hoping I might meet up with him again."

"Why?" Irene demanded.

"He gave me money."

"If you're selling drugs, so help me, you'll be grounded until you're thirty-five. Your father is going to skin you alive."

Mike straightened his shoulders and made an effort to appear mortally offended. "I would never do that. I moved that table in here, that's all."

I held out the photograph. "Did the person give you this photograph too?"

"Yeah, I don't know why. I mean, it's ancient. Who takes black-and-white photos anymore? That kid probably is, like, a hundred years old now."

"I assure you, she's not." I said.

Riley asked, "What did the guy look like?"

"I don't know. He was just a guy. Black hair. Shorter than me," Mike said.

"Did you steal my keys?" Irene said.

"Uh, maybe a little."

"You are in such big trouble."

I held up the photograph. "Could I keep this?"

Irene moved her hands in a shooing motion. "I don't care. Everyone get out of this house right now. I've had enough of all of you. Right now! Mikey and I need to go have a chat with his father about how he's stealing again."

"I didn't steal nothing!" Mike said.

"Anything." I said involuntarily and wished I hadn't. I glanced at Riley, who was still trying to maintain a serious expression, but had a telltale glimmer of amusement in his dark eyes.

Irene herded everyone out the back door and locked the house. She pointed toward the front yard and told Mike to get in the truck. His shoulders slumped and he slithered off in the uniquely surly manner of a recalcitrant teen.

Riley and I thanked Irene and returned to the Mustang, where we were greeted enthusiastically by Zelda. On the drive home, I mostly stared at the photograph. It had been taken such a long time ago and it was strange to me that I'd never seen it before.

Riley momentarily pulled his eyes away from the road to look at me. "Is something wrong?"

"I think my grandfather took this photograph."

"Was your hair really blonde? You look like Cindy Brady on the Brady Bunch."

"It got darker when I got older, so I started dying it. I guess that makes you Bobby Brady."

"Very funny."

"The thing that's strange is that I haven't seen my grandfather since that time. I've never seen this photo, but I know he had a darkroom with an enlarger. He's the only person I can think of who ever took black-and-white photographs of me."

"Do photographers sign prints like artists do? Maybe it says something on the back."

"If nothing else, it might have the date. I'm guessing 1972 or 1973." I pulled the little metal tabs up along the frame and pulled out the backing. A business card fluttered to the floor of the Mustang and I bent to retrieve it.

When I examined the small head shot on the card, I couldn't believe my eyes. "Lars Lindeman. He's a real estate agent in Seattle."

"Do you mean Lars, as in the clown that you made out with at the circus?"

"I don't think he was always a clown."

~

Riley was merciless in his teasing on the way home, which I didn't appreciate. He continued to find my make-out session with Lars at the fairgrounds endlessly amusing. I still found the encounter with Lars and my response embarrassing and mildly creepy.

After discussing the experience with Riley multiple times, our theory was that Lars had a sensory disorder like we did, but his was related to touch. It made Lars virtually irresistible to me, and our little interlude had been one of the strangest experiences of my life. I'm not normally in the habit of throwing myself on random men, much less clowns. Ugh.

At the house, I tucked the photograph and business card into my bag and got out of the car. "Have you gotten all the clown jokes out of your system yet? I'd rather not have Dean and Peggy share in that joy."

Riley flashed an evil grin. "I think I'm done now. Zelda and I are going for a walk, so you can tell them whatever you want."

Zelda was running around in circles, having focused her attention on the magical word 'walk.' I couldn't blame her. The lake was gorgeous, and it was a sunny spring day.

I pondered the wood grain of the front door. The fact was I didn't really want to deal with Dean and Peggy at all. They were probably holed up in their room having nonstop sex anyway. I turned back to Riley. "Would it be okay if I join you on your walk?"

"You might hear more about Lars."

"That's fine. Forgetting the whole 'you made out with a clown' thing for a moment, we should talk about what's next. Now we know Lars is in Seattle. Maybe that relates to the retreat somehow."

"Well, he *was* in Seattle. These days, he's hanging out being a clown at Hector's circus and making out with unsuspecting redheads."

"Unless he got away. Maybe he's like Dean and wasn't there voluntarily either."

Riley stopped and picked up a rock from the beach. "This one has lots of sparkles."

"You're not listening."

"Sure I am, but you haven't said anything that makes sense, so I'm checking out the cool rocks. You think Lars was at the circus under duress. But he wasn't drugged like Dean was. If that's the case, why did he stay? Why would *anyone* stay?"

"Okay, I suppose you have a point." I picked up a rock, inspected it, and dropped it back on the ground. I didn't get Riley's fascination with them. Rocks are inherently dull.

Riley said, "You didn't answer my question. Why did he stay?"

"I don't know." I stopped and picked up a stick and threw it for Zelda, who ran after it, sniffed, and then found something better to do. She wasn't much of a retriever. "What if Lars was spying on the circus people?"

"All right, now you're getting somewhere. I could buy that as a reasonable hypothesis."

"So, this outrageously sexy real estate agent who looks like a male model for Coppertone decides to join the circus? I thought this up and even *I* think it's a stupid theory."

Riley picked up a rock and skipped it across the lake surface. "What if he's an environmentalist working with the people who own the retreat? Enviro Freedom or whatever they're called?"

"Maybe. I don't know."

Riley skipped another rock. "Tomorrow, do you want to head north toward Seattle?"

"I don't have any other ideas—do you?"

"Nope. Have you ever been to Yosemite National Park?"

I shook my head. "Not even close. Is it nice?"

"It's incredible. If we go the back way up 395, we could visit Yosemite and avoid a whole lot of large cities with radiation. Being around you is a lot easier when you're not screaming."

I shoved him in the arm and knocked him off balance. "You're a lot more pleasant to be around when you eat, you know."

"So I've been told."

Our last evening at the house was enjoyable. Dean and Peggy had taken a break from their amorous adventures to run out to the store and get a couple of frozen pizzas. The food was remarkably good, and we all had fun eating up the last of our snacks before going our separate ways.

I was pleased that Riley and I had fulfilled our promise of finding Peggy. She thanked us many times for finding Dean too. Apparently, Dean had been successful in convincing her that Helen was not perhaps the greatest roommate. I certainly agreed with that assessment and was eager to put a whole lot of miles between me and Helen the Shrew. Dean and Peggy were giddy with excitement about their impending wedding, and it was easy to get caught up in their happiness and anticipation.

By the time I went to bed I was physically tired from the unaccustomed walking, but my brain didn't share the fatigue. It was busy trying to assimilate and make sense of the new information I'd learned today. The idea of Lars somehow knowing a member of my family was strange. But how else would his business card be in with a photo of me if he didn't put it there?

Lars was definitely not the person who had asked Irene's son to move the table either. The kid had said the guy he talked to had black hair. But Lars had dark blonde hair and the most gorgeous dreamy, warm, brown eyes I'd ever seen. Yummy.

My limbic system took an enjoyable side trip to the land of sexy Lars memories before the annoying logical part of my brain piped back up. I hadn't seen my grandfather since my dad walked out on my mom. Or Mom threw him out. I was never completely clear about what happened exactly, but whatever it was, Dad left and I never saw any relatives on that side of my family again.

After years of telling me only that my father "had problems," once I was an adult, Mom had finally confessed that Dad hadn't been the same after he came back from Vietnam. He was an alcoholic and drug user who I now realized probably was suffering from a severe case of post-traumatic stress disorder. The arguments he had with Mom were all I remembered about my father. They'd had world-class fights until one day he simply wasn't there anymore. Mom, in her efficient way, moved on and refused to discuss it beyond saying, "Dad has gone away for a while."

A while turned out to be forever. So why was I now in possession of a photograph taken by my grandfather? Was my father still alive? I may be nosy, but I'm not good with rejection. After I found out that my father left my mother with nothing, I didn't want anything to do with the man. I mean come on, not even child support? What kind of creep does that? Certainly not someone that I wanted to know. But maybe my indignation wasn't fair. Maybe he'd gone to AA. I had no idea, so I hadn't tried to find him. Of course, he'd never tried to get in contact with me either.

My thoughts swirled around going nowhere until I finally fell into a fitful sleep. I woke to the sound of pounding on my door and Riley yelling, "Meg, get up!"

I slowly packed the last of my things into my suitcase. Our little vacation in this idyllic lakeside home was over, and I was going to miss it. But now it was time to hit the road and return to the business of finding my mother and Riley's father. Even though we didn't have much information to go on, we had to keep trying.

~

I dragged my suitcase and laptop bag down the stairs to the kitchen where Dean, Peggy, and Riley were sitting at the table. Riley and Peggy were discussing arcane spicing options again, and Zelda was monitoring the breakfast activities, sitting next to one person, then moving to the next, seeking possible handouts.

I had a bizarre pang of melancholy, wondering if I'd ever have a family of my own who would argue at the breakfast table. My focus had always been on my career, and I'd never indulged in weepy, sentimental thoughts about motherhood. I was probably just tired. Riley was right; not sleeping really screws with your mind.

After breakfast, we did our final clean-up and loaded the cars. I gave Dean and Peggy big hugs and wished them well in their new life together. Now that I wasn't going to be subjected to their romantic goo-goo eyes, it was a lot easier to be happy for them.

Zelda hopped into the backseat of the Mustang, ready to hit the road. Riley latched her doggie seat belt, we waved goodbye, and headed north out of Alpine Grove. The weather was iffy and Riley had put the convertible top up.

One of my favorite things about riding in the car was being able to see the sky above. I'd never willingly get on a motorcycle, but the Mustang was the next best thing. Most of the time Riley and I had been on the road before, we'd been in the Southwest, so I'd gotten used to catching rays. Having the convertible up was claustrophobic.

Riley seemed subdued for some reason too. Maybe all the time we'd spent socializing with other people had worn him out. Or he'd realized he was stuck driving me around again.

I unfolded a map and pondered our route. California is a huge state and we had a long day ahead of us. In my sleep-deprived condition, the noise of the car's gigantic engine acted like a tranquilizer and after my head had involuntarily bobbed forward a few times, I folded up the map and closed my eyes.

I woke when the car stopped. Zelda was making grumbly rrr-ing noises in the back seat, and I turned around to see what the problem was. The red and blue lights of a highway patrol car flashed behind us.

Riley reached over in front of me to the glove compartment and pulled something out.

"Well, I guess it was inevitable. You finally got nailed for speeding," I said.

"I was going fifty-eight in a fifty-five. Nobody stops you for that."

Given the extreme speed violations Riley had committed in the past, it did seem like small potatoes. "*Sure* you were. Face it, you're so busted."

Riley rolled down the window as a uniformed patrolman walked up to the car. At the demand for license and registration, he handed the documents over to the man without comment.

The officer examined the documents and said, "Mr. O'Shea, do you realize you were speeding?"

"I was going fifty-eight."

"I have you clocked at eighty-five."

"That's impossible. I was going fifty-eight."

I didn't say anything, but it was easy for me to believe Riley had been going eighty-five. And *impossible* wasn't the word I'd use, since I knew the car could go a whole lot faster than that without any trouble at all.

The officer said, "All I know is what the machine says. If it says eighty-five, you were going eighty-five."

"May I see the reading?" Riley said.

"What?"

"You said you have a machine. May I see what it recorded, please?" Riley repeated. "If there's something wrong with my speedometer, I'd like to know. I did the restoration work on this Mustang, so I need to fix it."

"Really? I gotta say, she's a beaut. What year is it?"

"1968 Shelby GT500KR."

"Is it V-8?

"It has a 428 V-8 Cobra Jet engine."

"Nice. I suppose I can let you see it. I gotta write up the ticket. You stay right here and I'll be right back."

The officer walked back to the car and I nudged Riley. "What are you doing?"

"I wasn't going eighty-five."

"Is the speedometer broken?"

"I doubt it."

The officer returned and handed Riley a piece of paper. "This is a warning. You need to sign here. Press hard. There's carbons."

Riley took the pen and examined the warning ticket. "It says I was going fifty-eight."

"I read the display wrong. Sorry." The officer looked a little sheepish for a second, and then the radio on his hip squawked loudly and announced something unintelligible was in progress with a circus. He reached toward Riley with a gimme gesture, took the small clipboard, and gave Riley a copy of the warning. "I gotta go. Have a nice day."

"What's happening?" Riley asked.

"Accident and fire up ahead. You might wanna turn around. Drive safe, you hear?" The office hustled back to his patrol car and zoomed around us.

Riley put his registration back in the glove compartment and turned to me. "Did the radio say circus?"

"It was kind of garbled, but that's what it sounded like to me." I'd been hoping that I'd misheard the word circus. After the visions I'd had, fire and circus were two words I didn't like to hear in the same sentence.

"I think we should take a look."

"Do we have to?"

Riley started the car. "If it's Hector's circus, I want to know. We already know they've had issues with fire. Maybe this is another one."

As we returned to the two-lane highway, smoke was billowing in the sky, so I wasn't optimistic about what we might find up ahead.

Traffic ground to a halt and we pulled over to the side so fire trucks could go by. Police officers were directing cars into a single lane, alternating between northbound and southbound traffic.

We got close enough that I could see flames coming out of the windows of a trailer. The emergency services were spraying water on it and getting it under control, but it was likely only a charred hull would be left.

Riley looked over at me and our gazes locked. I said, "That crispy trailer is awfully familiar."

We inched forward. As we got closer Riley said, "I think this might be the end of Hector's circus."

The side of the road was littered with blackened trailers. When we'd seen them last, they'd been covered with faded paint advertising Hector's Traveling Big Top Circus. Now they were piles of twisted metal, plastic, and wood. The air was filled with chemical-infused acrid smoke that wafted across the highway. Many of the trucks that had been hauling the trailers had been de-coupled and were strung along the highway, surrounded by people. Some of the people might be circus personnel we'd encountered before, but they were mixed in with a whole lot of lookie-loos.

The grass was blackened and debris was everywhere. Riley and I drove though the mess in silence. Once we were clear and waved into the other lane again, traffic sped up. I released a long breath, relieved to be away from the site of such devastation. I turned to take one last look at what was happening behind us as one of the trailers burst into flames.

I tapped the back of Riley's hand on the gearshift to get his attention. "At first I thought it was an accident, but another trailer just exploded. It's weird that the trailers were torched, but the trucks were fine."

He nodded. "I thought the same thing. All the people I saw seemed to be all right. Just the trailers were affected."

"And you said the animals were evacuated after the last fire, so we know they're okay."

"I think this might be another case of arson."

I shrugged. "It could be the same people who tried to blow me up at that rest stop."

"At the time, we thought it was people working with the circus, but something else must be going on."

"Maybe we're not the only ones who don't like Hector's circus."

"Maybe."

Chapter 4

Stinkville

In my travels with Riley, I had learned that he preferred to stay at motels in the Motel 6 chain because they take dogs without complaint. Since we certainly weren't leaving Zelda behind, we'd stayed in many rooms that were similar. Same layout, same bedspreads, same carpet. They were functional, but not exactly opulent.

Early on, Riley and I had agreed to stay in the same room, which, given that we're not romantically involved could be construed as slightly odd, but it worked for us. And after a few acts of canine heroism by Zelda, I felt safer being in the same room with her at night. Riley also claimed he sleeps better with me nearby, which relates to his extraordinary sense of smell in some way I prefer not to dwell upon too much. After so much time on the road together, we had developed little routines for things like loading and unloading all of our junk from the Mustang so that it had become almost second nature.

Because of the circus fire and resulting traffic jam, we didn't get as far as we'd hoped on our first day of driving northward. We only made it to a crummy manufacturing town called Windiberg. I wasn't sure what the problem was, but the air quality was awful. Maybe it was the nasty pesticides and chemicals being sprayed on the fields, but the whole place smelled like decomposing food with a dash of manure as a garnish. Because of the rank odor, Riley was cranky about stopping, but past Windiberg was a whole lot of nothing, so we didn't have much of a choice.

After picking up food at a seedy grocery store, we settled into our room and I turned on the air conditioner to help filter out the stench. I fiddled with the knob and the unit made a loud groaning noise, like a geriatric elephant with arthritis settling into a Barcalounger.

Riley peered over my shoulder. "What are you doing?"

"I turned the thingamabob over here. And then that doohickey made a noise from the whatchamacallit down there at the bottom."

"If you break the AC, I could expire. This town stinks. Literally."

"I'm not breaking it. All I did was turn it on." I stepped back. "If you're so smart, you figure out how to make it quit doing that."

Riley leaned over and fiddled with a couple of knobs and the ancient air conditioner made a higher-pitched squeal.

"Stop that!" I kicked the bottom with my foot and the noise subsided. "There. I fixed it."

"I doubt that, but hey, whatever works."

I grabbed the remote control from the desk, sat down on the end of my bed, and turned on the TV. The traffic on the highway had been backed up so badly, I figured the circus accident must have made the local news. I flipped through the channels and found the news report. Riley sat next to me and we watched footage of the scene we'd driven by earlier. Traffic had not improved in the interim. In fact, it had gotten considerably worse.

According to the report, arson was suspected and a person had died in the accident. Eyewitnesses said that one of the circus trailers had exploded, and the truck pulling it had swerved into oncoming traffic and was hit by a car going the other way. The car had spun off the highway and rolled, but the driver was fine. The driver of the circus truck had gone through the windshield and later died at a local hospital. Other circus trailers had subsequently exploded and caught fire. Traffic had been backed up for hours and there was an interview with Hector, who said that the circus was a total loss.

I frowned at Riley. "That's horrible. I mean, we were there, so I knew it was bad, but from what he said, it sounds like all of the trailers caught fire. *All* of them."

"Well, we saw one catch on fire, so I think we can do more than just suspect arson."

"Either someone was running around there with matches or they used bombs. Maybe on timers?" Suddenly chilled, I clicked off the TV, chucked the remote onto the bed, and wrapped my arms around my waist. "I've never been Hector's biggest fan, but this is alarming. Someone died."

"At least we finally know what Hector looks like."

"I wonder if Lars is okay. I hope he wasn't the one driving the truck. We know he had another life in Seattle, so maybe he escaped before this happened."

Riley mimed a few smoochie faces at me and was laughing so hard at my response that when I shoved him, he fell off the bed onto the floor. Zelda stood up and licked his face. I peered over the side of the bed. "Don't be a jerk."

"All right, fine. I sincerely hope all parts of your *lover* continue to be fully functional." Riley was still chuckling as he got up and patted Zelda's head. "Hey, Zee, want some food?"

I heated up a frozen dinner in the microwave and typed a few notes into my laptop. I also checked out more news reports online. It had been a long day and I was distressed to note that the ache in my temple had returned. The feeling was like the beginnings of a headache, and it was an indicator that we were in an area with electromagnetic radiation. When the pain got bad, sometimes I had hallucinations that ranged in intensity from mild to terrifying, and were inevitably bizarre. The dread that I might end up screaming was another unpleasant side effect of my sensory problem.

I fell into another fitful sleep, and when I woke up for the twenty-fifth time, I reached over to the nightstand to check Riley's watch. It was two twenty-three in the morning. Why did insomnia always hit between two and three? If it were earlier, I could turn on the light and read a book. If it were later, maybe I'd get up. But no one wants to do anything between two and three. If you're sharing a room and don't want to wake everyone else up, you end up staring into the darkness, thinking about burned-up circus trailers.

I could hear the sound of Riley's breathing and Zelda's snoring from the other bed. For a dog, Zelda snored remarkably loudly. Normally I found her snorty, snuffly sleep noises comforting, but at the moment the sounds were annoying me enough that I could use her snoring as an excuse for being awake.

The light from headlights in the parking lot flashed around the curtains, presumably from a late-night check-in. The beams hit the ceiling and flicked across it like tendrils of flame. The white-yellow rays twisted into swirling orange fire that sent showers of red and gold sparks raining onto my head. Thick black smoke began to engulf the room, and I struggled to breathe, gulping and choking for air. Sounds of screaming and barking surrounded me and the blackness of the heavy smoke closed in like a shroud. Was I really going to suffocate and die in a Motel 6?

I felt the pressure of hands on my shoulders and opened my eyes. Riley was sitting on the side of my bed and Zelda had her nose in my face. She stuck out her tongue for a big slurp and I quickly averted my head. "No, Zee, don't. Ick."

Riley let go of me and moved to sit on the floor next to Zelda. He sat cross-legged with his arm around the dog, keeping her from moving in for another tongue bath. "I guess I'm not the only one affected by the radiation here."

"Sorry. I had trouble sleeping and I was thinking about fire."

"That rarely ends well."

All of our faces were inches apart and I could see Zelda's white eyelashes as she blinked and the tension and worry clouding Riley's dark eyes. I pulled the covers over my shoulder. "The lights from outside turned into fire, then there was all this black smoke. I thought I was dying."

"Are you going to be all right?"

"Does it smell like smoke in here to you?"

"No."

"Okay, that's a relief." I took a deep breath now that I was fairly sure I wasn't going to asphyxiate. "I shouldn't have spent so much time thinking about arson. Do you think they know we're here?"

"Who?" Riley let go of Zelda and leaned back on side of the other bed. "I'm confused. We had the guys in the suits who dropped off people with the circus to be transported somewhere. The circus is owned by Archetypal Media Systems, so we think they might be in on the abductions somehow. But who would want to blow up the circus? I mean, they were the ones after us. Is someone after *them* too?"

"I don't know, but I don't like it. The last time I had fire visions, it turned out they were right."

"I don't like it either, but at least we'll be out of this disgusting town tomorrow. How does anyone stand to live here? It smells like the inside of a sewage-treatment plant."

I chuckled, relieved that Riley had recovered his equilibrium. "Not everyone has your keen sense of smell."

Riley stood up, crawled back into his bed, and grumbled. "It's not just me. This place is gross."

I got up to go wash my face and stopped by his bed. I touched his shoulder and said, "Thanks for pulling me back from the scary abyss. I'm glad you're here."

He patted my hand and closed his eyes. "I always am."

∽

We got up early the next morning. Riley was motivated to leave Windiberg, or Stinkville, as he referred to it. I felt lousy partly because of the lack of sleep, but also because of what I thought of as 'hallucination hangover.' Much like a regular hangover, I sometimes felt strung out after an unpleasant vision. My eyesight was strangely dulled, so it was as if much of the color had been drained out of the world.

I also was feeling anxious because I hadn't been able to do any digging to get answers to my many questions. I wanted to find out more about the real estate office where

Lars had worked and the Enviro Freedom group that owned the retreat.

The information I could find online was negligible and the odds were low that I'd be able to convince Riley to stay one moment longer than necessary in the land of bad smells. So I had to be patient. Unfortunately, I'm not particularly good at patience. After Riley and Zelda left for their morning walk, I decided to call my former boss, Leo.

Leonard Olson, otherwise known as Leo, had been my mentor and friend at the newspaper where I used to work. We'd all been laid off from the paper, and although I'd been furious about getting canned, I knew that in many ways Leo was thrilled to have an excuse to retire at last. I missed his no-nonsense personality and my life back in the newsroom, but there was no going back. His last day was coming up, and I thought I'd see how he was doing as things wound down.

I smiled at the sound of his gruff voice. "Hi, Leo. It's Meg."

"Hey there. What's up? Where *are* you?"

"A stinky town in central California. You don't want to know. But we're heading north."

"You following a lead?"

"Maybe. Have you heard anything more about the merger?" The newspaper I used to work for had been sold to Archetypal Media, which then merged with Online Systems United. The new Archetypal Online Systems would involve every form of communications, online and off.

"Nothing much going on, except I can tell you that your ex, Matt What-His-Face, remains a prick."

"That doesn't surprise me. Are you looking forward to retirement?"

"Oh yeah, I guess you don't know, but we're moving. Mrs. O is thrilled. We got a little windfall, so we're selling our house and getting a place out on the Eastern Shore. I want to do some fishing."

"That's great. I guess you'll have a lot more honey-dos getting the house ready for sale."

"You don't know the half of it. Hopefully, retirement won't kill me."

I laughed. "I'm sure you'll be fine."

"If you ever come back East again, you need to come see us at our new place. Keep in touch."

"I will. Promise."

We said our goodbyes and I sat on the bed staring at the phone. Everyone was moving on and happy. I still hadn't found Mom and remained on the road with Riley in a strange state of limbo. Even though I'd made a deal with Riley to commit to finding our parents and report any wrongdoing we discovered, I couldn't help missing my old life.

Nostalgia is a funny thing. I always knew I loved my job, but at the time I was so wrapped up in day-to-day stresses and deadlines that I didn't think about how much I'd miss it when it was over.

Riley opened the door to the room and Zelda launched inside, obviously fired up from her outing. She jumped up on the bed next to me and I ruffled her ears. "Hey you. I guess you feel better."

"That makes one of us. Let's get out of this disgusting town." Riley threw a t-shirt into his suitcase. "Heading for the hills is appealing."

I stood up and embarked on my packing process, trying to rid myself of the melancholy mood left over from talking to Leo. Something about the conversation bothered me, and I felt mean for being jealous of Leo and begrudging his upcoming retirement and new home. What kind of rotten person was I? Maybe I was just sad because I'd probably never see him again. People always said they'd keep in touch, but it never happened.

Once we were on the road again, Riley turned on some loud music, which helped us both shake off the morning gloom. After we were away from the vast farmlands, Riley turned down the volume and asked if I was ready to stop for lunch. He didn't need to ask, because I was always hungry.

We pulled over at a rest stop that was surrounded by pretty trees. After miles upon miles of flat empty fields, it was nice to see different vegetation at last.

I pulled out sandwich-makings and chips from the trunk and we leaned on the back of the Mustang snacking. I tossed a corner of crust to Zelda, who snapped it out of the air. "When was the last time you ate before now?"

"I don't remember, but I guess it was before we got to Sewage City."

"Are you okay?"

"I'll be fine. But I've been thinking that before we get to Seattle, I need to make a modification to Shelby's convertible top."

"What kind of modification?"

"Shielding."

"Is this a geeky Star Trek reference I don't get or something?"

Riley smiled. "No, but it's the same idea. I need to get some copper woven screen."

"I'm guessing this isn't like the regular window screens you buy at a hardware store."

"It's kind of specialized. It's used to protect MRI rooms. I called a few companies while you were in the shower this morning."

I tossed another piece of bread to Zelda. "I guess while we're in cities, we'll have to drive around with the top up. What a drag." After logging thousands of miles in the Mustang throughout the Southwest, I'd found I liked riding around with the wind in my hair.

"We're heading to the Northwest, where it rains all the time, so we'd have the top up anyway. And it might keep you from having screaming hallucinations."

"I do like that idea." I stretched my arms over my head and splayed my fingers, enjoying being out of the car for the time being. "And you might eat more than once every few days."

"That too."

Late in the afternoon, we found a motel outside of Yosemite Park that allowed pets. I'd really wanted to stay at the Ahwhanee, but dogs weren't permitted at any of the swanky places in the park. Riley said that some of the campgrounds might allow dogs, but I vetoed that idea. We'd already established that I'm a big fan of indoor plumbing and walls that aren't made out of fabric.

The next morning, we drove into the park and cruised around. Like most people, I'd seen photographs of Half Dome and El Capitan, but even the famous Ansel Adams photos don't do justice to the beauty of the Yosemite Valley. John Muir was onto something. The place was stunning and

I mostly just sat and stared at the scenery as we drove through the area.

Riley had mentioned that the Merced River had flooded that past January and the park had been closed for three months. A number of areas he'd seen before had simply washed away.

We drove over a bridge and Riley said, "There used to be a campground next to the river. We camped in a tent there and nearly froze to death."

"Good thing Zelda has so much fur."

"It was before I got Zee. I came here with Erin a long time ago. I wonder if the Mist Trail was damaged too."

"The Mist Trail?"

"It's a three-mile hike that goes up next to Vernal Falls, which is probably flowing like crazy. Half the time the trail isn't even open at this time of year."

The craggy granite peaks were covered with snow, and the river and waterfalls I could see without doing anything radical like hiking were certainly flowing. Water was everywhere, probably because it was a gloriously sunny day and snow was busy melting up above us in the higher elevations. I found myself mildly annoyed that the mysterious Erin got to see the top of Vernal Falls and I hadn't.

As we cruised out through Tuolumne Meadows back toward highway 140, Riley was unusually quiet, even for him. Maybe he was overwhelmed by the grandeur of the scenery or remembering all the fun times he'd had with Erin.

"What are you thinking about?" I asked.

"Nothing."

"No one thinks about nothing, unless you're a Zen monk or something. I doubt you're gaining inner peace over there."

"I'm not."

"Then what are you thinking about?"

Riley glanced at me. "What difference does it make?"

"I'm curious." And bored.

"Fine. I'm thinking about how I have a cramp in the arch of my foot and I can't use the cruise because this road winds around too much."

"That's it?"

"My butt is tired from driving."

"Have your thoughts ventured beyond a physical inventory?"

Riley shifted gears and shot me a glare. "If you must know, I was thinking about what I need to do to disassemble Shelby's convertible top to add screening. I don't have my tools, which means I'll have to find a garage or work space somewhere. And the modification might not work."

"Why not?"

I regretted asking the question almost as soon as Riley methodically started going through the properties of copper screening and all the parts of the Mustang that were going to have to be removed, modified, or otherwise touched to add the screen.

By the time he finished explaining, I was utterly lost, but we were back at the motel, so it was easy to end the conversation and focus on more important matters like letting Zelda out of the car. She leaped with joy, ran to a grassy spot, relieved herself, and galloped back to join us at the door to the motel room.

"Somebody is ready for dinner," Riley said as he opened the door.

"She's not the only one. I'm starving."

After Riley fed Zelda, they went for a walk. I stayed in the room and snacked while I reviewed my notes. Talking to Leo reminded me of something Riley had said a long time ago. Before I'd had the spectacular hallucination that cost me my job, Leo had assigned me a story about Online Systems United, which later merged with Archetypal Media and subsequently laid me off.

Riley had gently suggested that maybe Leo knew more about the impending merger than he'd let on. I still couldn't quite buy into that idea, but I typed a few notes concerning what I could remember about that period of time. Leo had also given me a cellular phone, which I now knew aggravated my little headaches that sometimes led to screaming hallucinations. Had he known what a cell phone would do to me?

The walk among all the pretty trees dramatically improved Riley's mood and settled Zelda down. After she ate her kibble, the dog curled up into a furry white ball on my bed and fell asleep. Riley and I amused ourselves by selecting and microwaving our frozen dinners.

After dinner, we moved on to reading. I tucked my toes under Zelda's tail to keep them warm and dug into a romance novel that I'd picked up at a cute little bookstore in Alpine Grove. Riley was reading a book with a title so nerdy that I couldn't remember it. He'd been reading it for weeks, and it seemed to be a great sleep aid.

The book I was reading had a classic 'second chance at love' storyline about a couple that had met when they were young and then rekindled their romance when they were older. They'd met in elementary school and played on the playground together. I wasn't quite believing it, but maybe that was because the boys I'd met on the playground when I was six were truly loathsome.

"So when you were six, did you play with girls?"

Riley looked up from his book. "No. At the time, the prevailing theory was that girls had cooties and should be avoided."

"I know! I'm having trouble with the premise of this book. I never played with boys at that age. The girls were all on one side of the playground and the boys on the other. And it was by choice. We said boys were creepy and they said girls were stupid."

"Not much has changed. Men and women continue to have communication problems."

"This sounds like a statement based on personal experience."

"I plead the Fifth."

"You know, if our parents had met earlier and we'd grown up together, I'd know a lot more about you."

Riley closed the book. "Like what? That I didn't like broccoli when I was six? I still don't like it."

"Okay, that's not particularly interesting. But I'd know stuff like whether or not you're ticklish."

"Why is that important?"

"I bet you are."

"Pleading the Fifth again."

I leaped off the bed and jabbed my fingers into his ribs, tickling madly. Riley crumpled up into a fetal position and I yelped, "Aha! You are!"

Zelda jumped onto the bed, joining the fray as Riley feebly tried to push me away. But I was relentless in my tickling torture. Through his laughter, Riley managed to gasp, "What is wrong with you? Would you cut it out?"

There was pounding on the wall and someone from the next room yelled, "Keep it down in there!"

Having successfully proven my point, I stopped. "I knew it."

I returned to my bed and Zelda leaped up to reclaim her warm sleep spot.

Riley collected himself, sat up, and wiped the tears from his eyes with the back of his hand. "Jeez, that was exhausting. I can't remember the last time I laughed that hard."

"Me neither."

"What got into you?"

"You were so serious today. I thought it might be good to lighten you up a little."

"We still haven't found our parents though, and I feel guilty."

"Was that what you were really thinking about?" I picked up my book and set it on my lap. "No one thinks that much about disassembling a car."

"You're right, that's not all I was thinking about. But I figured if I described my automotive plans, you might fall asleep and forget about it."

I chuckled. "It was touch and go there for a while. So what *were* you thinking about so hard?"

"The last time I went to Yosemite."

"With your girlfriend," I added. "You probably have lots of great memories. I know you got to see a cool waterfall."

"We did. I'm not sure how to say this, but even when we were there, I thought the trip should have been more fun. I was thinking about that."

"What do you mean by 'more fun'?"

Riley heaved a big sigh. "I don't know why I'm telling you this, but it was basically that we were in this gorgeous place and still not really connecting. It's hard to explain."

"What happened?"

"It was like I never seemed to do the right thing. I always felt like I was a klutz in an antique store, breaking things and embarrassing her."

"Unless she was worried about impressing grizzly bears, I don't know what you could have done. I think that says more about her than you."

"Maybe, but I felt bad that the trip wasn't better. We never took another vacation like that together."

"Well, it takes two." I shrugged. "I think every relationship has events you reflect upon and wish you could change. I wish I'd treated my friends better when I was with Matt. They said he was a jerk and I didn't believe them."

"From what you've said, he *was* a jerk. And still is."

"I know, but at the time I thought he was the be-all and end-all. I thought those people were just jealous of me. In retrospect, I know I treated some of my friends badly. I apologized later, but it wasn't ever the same."

"Relationships are hard."

I slumped down on my pillow. "No kidding."

～

The next day we were back on the road heading toward the great Northwest. Unfortunately, first we were going to have to go to Sacramento, which was significantly less appealing because it was another large city surrounded by a whole lot of flatness. The good news was that Riley had found a supplier of copper screening located in an industrial park, and they were willing to sell him the stuff he needed to modify the car. I was silently hoping that I wouldn't succumb to a mortifying hallucination during the transaction.

California is a huge state, and it feels even larger when you're driving the length of it. There was no way around the situation. We were facing major road time to get where we needed to go. The other somewhat distressing issue was that we didn't really know where we were going. I still needed access to a library that was large enough to have business or legal databases that might have listings with information about Enviro Freedom. An address would be a good start, and we didn't even have that yet.

After the glorious day in Yosemite, the weather took a nosedive and the skies became gloomy as we drove north. We stopped for lunch in a little town called Angels Camp, which refers to itself as "Frogtown USA" in homage to Mark Twain's short story "The Notorious Jumping Frog of Calaveras County." A small stone statue of a frog perched on top of a pile of rocks had a plaque about Twain and the story, which is the tale of a Gold-Rush era frog-jumping contest. I was pretty sure I'd read it in high school.

After we ate, Riley put the convertible top up and we cruised on. The clouds coalesced into storms and I was lulled into drowsiness by the monotonous sound of the windshield wipers flapping back and forth.

Riley kept a thermos of coffee with us at all times because he'd vowed never to get so sleepy that I would have to drive his car again. I hadn't thought my driving was that bad, but he got all persnickety about things like shifting gears at the right time. What a car geek.

I took a sip from the coffee and Riley glared at me. "Hey, that's mine."

"I'm not sick, just sleepy."

"You could be getting sick and not showing symptoms yet."

"Don't be weird. It's just coffee. And if I'm getting sick, you're getting it too because we're traveling together. Consider yourself doomed to share my germs."

"I suppose. My mother was always a stickler about that type of thing."

I glanced at Riley. He'd never mentioned his mother before. "So, I was wondering…"

"Uh-oh."

"Because of my visions, you know all about how my parents' marriage flamed out."

"Emphasis on flames."

"Yeah, yeah, let's not talk about fire again. I know your Dad isn't with your mom anymore, since he's with my mom, but did your parents get divorced too?"

Riley studied the road intently. "No."

"Where is your mother?"

"She died when I was eight."

I put my hand on Riley's forearm. "I'm sorry. You never said anything."

"It was a long time ago."

"What was she like?"

"I don't know. She was Mom. Nice, I guess."

"What did she look like?"

Riley turned his head to give me an irritated glare. "Why do you want to know? She's been gone for years. It has no bearing on our current situation. We're trying to find *your* mother, not mine."

"Don't get touchy. I'm curious because I know you—more than you probably want me to know you, but I do."

"Not really." Riley lifted his hand off the steering wheel to gesture toward the flat landscape. "We've spent a lot of time driving around."

"Of course I do. At this point, I bet I know you better than almost anyone."

"Is this a contest?"

"I know you walk around while you're brushing your teeth. You're always wandering around motel rooms with a toothbrush sticking out of your mouth."

"That's some vital intel right there. Call the CIA."

"I know you turn your dirty t-shirts inside out. I know your second toe is longer than your big toe."

"That's true of a lot of people."

"You finger-comb your hair after you get out of the shower to pull the knots out. And you never remember to put your hair into a ponytail before you get into this car."

"Wow, this is fascinating stuff."

"I know that even though you're a slob and throw your clothes all over motel rooms, you're kind of obsessive about the trunk of the Mustang and pack it neatly like a puzzle."

"Why are you telling me this?"

"Because you need to get over this idea that we don't know each other. I hate to break it to you, but we do. And I think you must have figured out by now that I'm curious by nature."

"You mean nosy."

"Okay, nosy. Call it what you want. What did your mom look like?"

Riley let out a long breath. "All right. She had long brown wavy hair and pretty dark brown eyes. I remember her being a kind person, but I suppose every little kid thinks that about their parents."

"Not necessarily. I don't remember my father that way. What happened to her?"

"She was going out Christmas shopping and she was killed by a semi that sideswiped her car on the freeway."

"Oh Riley, that's awful."

"I always think about it when I go by bad traffic accidents. Some family out there is about to be changed forever."

He had been quiet while we'd gone by the circus accident, but so had I. Another thought occurred to me. "What happened to Bubba's mom?"

"I never really knew her. She was a flight attendant, and as Dad used to say, she flew away."

"She just ditched her kid?"

"Dad didn't say much about it other than they had problems and she wanted to travel. I think that having Bubba wasn't planned, and in the fifties you had to get married."

"Ah, I see."

"Dad was the ultimate family man. He never really said it, but I think he was relieved she bailed."

"Your father sounds like a warmhearted person."

"He is. I hope I get to see him again."

"I know what you mean. I keep thinking about what it would be like when I finally get to talk to my mother. I go back and forth between wanting to hug her and yelling at her for just disappearing like this."

We slowed down for a traffic light, and it was like I felt, more than I actually saw, something swoop low next to the Mustang out of nowhere. Once my brain assimilated what I was seeing, I determined it was a gigantic black bird, which flapped manically for a few seconds before it hovered over the hood of the car and barfed all over it.

Zelda barked and Riley punctuated her commentary with a derivative f-bomb that might have made me blush if I hadn't heard the term so many times in the newsroom. The massive bird flew off and Riley pulled over to the curb. That was when the odor arrived.

I said, "Gross! What is that horrendous smell?"

Fortunately we had the top up, so whatever the bird had horked up did not roll up and over the windshield into my lap. But a considerable quantity of foul residue remained on the hood of the car.

Zelda was standing up, tugging on her seatbelt trying to get a closer look at the vile substance.

Riley said, "An awful stink like that means the bird must have been something like a vulture that eats dead stuff. Turkey buzzard maybe? Whatever it was, we need to find a hose as soon as possible. Anything that smells that bad could eat through the paint."

We were on the outskirts of Sacramento, and I could feel the twinge of a headache that meant we were near cellular towers and radiation again. That would make the stench from the buzzard barf riding on the hood of the car with us even worse for Riley.

I pointed. "There's a nursery up there. Maybe they have a hose we can borrow."

Riley slowed to turn into the driveway and I looked up at a twenty-five-foot-tall statue of an Old West cowboy that bore a striking resemblance to Kevin Costner.

I nudged Riley's arm. "Why is the West filled with large weird statues? It's like Bob's Big Boy came out here and sired a race of giants. These things are everywhere."

Riley smiled as he got out of the car. "I'll be right back. Watch out for Cowboy Bob."

Chapter 5

Not-so Random Effect

We checked into the local Motel 6, and after we unloaded the car, the first thing I did was take a shower. Even though the buzzard had not literally vomited on me, the smell was so pervasive that I felt as if it had adhered to me like a horrifying stinky leech.

The next morning we agreed that Riley would drop me off at the California State University library, and then he would go to the industrial park and modify the car while Zelda supervised. From what Riley had said, it sounded like Zelda had years of experience sleeping in garages while he worked on the Mustang. The library was an absolutely gigantic multi-story building that acted as the central library for the campus of California State University in Sacramento. If I couldn't find the information I needed there, I wasn't going to find it.

I have a particular affection for reference librarians because they are almost universally nice people who love helping patrons find answers. When I was a reporter, most of the librarians in the Washington D.C. area knew who I was. It was probably because I often sent a gift basket filled with chocolate and other goodies as a thank you after the librarian had ferreted out helpful facts for me.

After Riley dropped me off, I went straight to the reference desk and made my request. I wanted to find everything anyone could find on a group called Enviro Freedom. The reference librarian was named Nancy, and she was thrilled to help me out. I settled in next to her, opened my laptop, and we got to work. The library had subscriptions to countless databases that you can't access using a regular online search.

Nancy had pretty, long brown hair, which she occasionally swished behind her shoulder as her fingers flew across the keyboard. I was envious of her typing speed and when she found entries with any information about Enviro Freedom, we chatted about them as I typed notes into my laptop. It took a while to find much of anything because the EF folks were clearly working hard to keep a low profile. However, every nonprofit has to file certain forms, so it's almost impossible to be completely invisible. After a couple of hours, Nancy and I were pleased that we'd managed to verify that the group truly did exist. I even had a couple of names of the people involved. I couldn't wait to tell Riley.

I thanked Nancy profusely, went outside to grab a sandwich for lunch, and returned to the library to scan news reports. Riley had warned me that I'd need to amuse myself all day because retrofitting the Mustang was going to take him quite a while. Fortunately, the library had a number of computers connected to the Internet, so I figured I could spend more research time looking for follow-up reports about the circus accident.

I often get distracted doing online research and end up falling down a cyber-rabbit hole that leads me to unexpected information. Somehow I ended up reading about the 1996 Telecommunications Act, which was enacted to open other communications markets to competition.

According to the Federal Communications Commission, the goal of this new law was to let anyone enter any communications business and let any communications business compete in any market against any other. The FCC claimed that the Telecommunications Act of 1996 had the potential to change the way we "work, live and learn." It would affect telephone service—local and long distance, cable programming, and other video services. The text said it was an act "To promote competition and reduce regulation in order to secure lower prices and higher quality services for American telecommunications consumers and encourage the rapid deployment of new telecommunications technologies."

I leaned back in the chair, trying to absorb all the governmentalese. This law was part of the reason the electromagnetic radiation was affecting me and Riley now. Within the last year, companies like Archetypal had become free to compete with everybody. And they were taking advantage of that new freedom. The only thing that could stop them was proof that people might be harmed by their activities. No wonder they were trying to track down specialists who were affected in odd ways. We were bad PR for them.

After my detour into government sites, I returned to the news. There wasn't much I hadn't already seen about the circus accident. Most of the write-ups were from the day of the incident, which didn't tell me anything I didn't already know. I idly clicked through the search results and yawned. Riley wasn't going to pick me up for another hour or so and my researching mojo was petering out.

My eyes widened at a remarkably close-up photo of the accident scene that prominently featured Lars. He was still gorgeous if a little blackened, but it was the person with him that caught my attention.

I frantically clicked around the computer screen to see if there was a way to print it. Apparently the printers were monitored and I would have to pay for a printout. What a pain. I leaped out of the chair and ran back to the reception desk to talk to my new friend Nancy. She smiled and asked if I needed more help.

"Yes! I found a photo that I really need to print." I pointed back at the row of computers. "Could you help me? It's important."

Nancy came over to the computer I'd been using and typed a magical code that made the printer go. I thanked her again and after I collected my printout, I relinquished my coveted computer spot to a college student. My brain couldn't handle any more hard news, so I settled into one of the comfy reading chairs with a magazine to wait for Riley.

According to the cover, *Cosmo* wanted to know if I was sexually satisfied. The answer to that was a big "no," so I opted to flip past that article because it would only depress me. They also wanted to share dating survival secrets. Lately I'd been more worried about survival than dating, so it was difficult to get too worked up about that piece either. I idly flipped through an article about a "Melrose Place Workout" that I would never willingly perform.

I jumped and my eyes flew open at a touch on my shoulder. Riley was in the chair next to me holding the magazine. He grinned, "So before you fell asleep, did you find out what men think when they first see you naked?"

I snatched the magazine from him and stood up. "Hey, you tell *me*. What do you think when Erin gets naked?"

"That information is classified." He pointed toward the exit. "Are you ready to get out of here?"

I nodded. "Did you bathe in motor oil or something? You look like a coal miner."

"Working on cars can be messy."

"Does the Mustang still run?"

Riley gave me an indignant glare. "Of course Shelby runs. All I did was take apart the convertible top."

"Does that still work?"

"It's not quite as automated as it used to be because it's heavier and I didn't have the parts to modify the motor. But it's fine." He gestured toward vast stacks of books and said, "Did you learn anything interesting here?"

I stopped and grabbed his arm so he'd look at me. "Yes! I have so much to tell you."

"That sounds promising."

"I don't know what it all means, but at least it's something to go on."

"Any information would be more than we had before."

～

On the way back to the motel, I regaled Riley with the information I'd found about Enviro Freedom and how strange it was that they were so difficult to track down. He agreed that it was odd.

After I'd exhausted that topic, I added, "There's something else I found that I think explains something."

"What's that?"

"Lars has a son. There's a photo from the accident and he's with a little boy."

"You're sure it's his son?"

"They're holding hands and the kid is like a miniature version of Lars. Mom's genes definitely took a backseat to his."

"Do you suppose the kid has the same touch sensitivity that Lars does?"

I turned in my seat to face Riley. "Are you suggesting that whatever is wrong with us is genetic?"

"I don't know, but it could be, couldn't it? Haven't you ever thought about that possibility? Certain cancers have a genetic component. Maybe this does too."

"I thought of our weird problems as a random effect, not something genetic. But if it is, would that mean my children would have screaming hallucinations?" I put my hands over my eyes. "I would never wish that on anyone, particularly my own child."

"Maybe that's something that our parents are researching."

"I hope so." I hadn't thought much about having kids, but the idea that I could pass on my problem shook me. If it were true, maybe I shouldn't have children. My stomach tied itself into a tight knot and by the time we got back to the room, I felt mildly ill.

Unlike me, Zelda obviously felt fine and leaped around, eager for her dinner. After Riley fed her, I showed him the printout of the photo of Lars.

He held it in his hands for a moment, and then set it in his lap. "Do you think Lars was with the circus because they threatened his kid?"

"Can you think of any other reason he'd stay?"

Riley scratched the stubble on his chin. "It's a reasonable explanation. Or maybe his wife or significant other was working there."

"I'd rather not think about the possibility of Lars being married. But maybe his son being there explains why Lars wasn't drugged. The boy or maybe his entire family kept him from leaving."

"If it's true, it's not making me feel more love for Hector." Riley frowned at the photo. "Lars might not be my favorite person, but if Hector was using a kid as leverage, that's cruel."

"Given what Hector said about the accident, it sounds like the circus is a total loss. Maybe Lars and the little boy are free now."

"Maybe."

I leaned back against the pillows. "I have an old friend that I should probably talk to about Enviro Freedom."

"Why am I getting the impression you don't want to do that?"

"Because she hates me."

"That sounds more like an enemy than a friend. Why does she hate you?"

"I behaved badly and called Rachel some, well, names that I probably shouldn't have."

"Why?"

I put my arm over my eyes. My huge blowout with Rachel had not been my finest hour. "She was critical of Matt. I think I told you I lost a few friends over him. Rachel was one of them."

"You could apologize."

"That would involve picking up the phone first." I sat up again and put the pillow in my lap. "What if she hangs up on me?"

"You're asking *me*? I'm the introvert, remember? You're the one who says she's willing to talk to anyone."

I laughed and threw the pillow at him. "Good point. You'd go off on a road trip and never be seen again."

"See?" Riley tucked the pillow behind his back with a smug smile.

"Okay, I get your point. I suppose it's better than telling me to suck it up and get over it, which is more or less what I'm saying to myself."

"No comment. We'll go for a walk." Riley got up off his bed and waved at Zelda. "C'mon Zee. Meg has to make a call."

After they left, I stared at the telephone for a long minute. Riley was right. Normally I didn't have trouble talking to anyone about anything. But this wasn't like ferreting out information from recalcitrant people when I felt like I had truth on my side. In my giddy state of love-induced stupidity, I'd been horrible to Rachel. And then after my humiliating vision at work and subsequent medical leave, Rachel, along with everyone else, gave me a wide berth.

I rooted through my luggage to find my address book and dug up Rachel's number. It was three hours later there, so she'd probably be home from work by now.

Rachel is a little bit younger and a lot prettier than I am. When we used to go out together after work, she'd attracted a lot of attention. If I were completely honest, I'd have to admit that I'd been jealous of her for a long time. So when the utterly gorgeous and charming Matt Eskridge had taken an interest in me, it felt good to be the one with the hot boyfriend for a change. Of course, it turned out he was a lying, evil snake, but I hadn't known that at first.

I picked up the handset and dialed Rachel's number. As the phone rang, I frantically scanned my mind for an opening that wouldn't make me seem like a nut. My mind was still blank when Rachel answered.

"Hi Rachel, it's Meg Jennings."

There was a long pause and for a moment I thought she was going to hang up on me. At last Rachel said, "I'm surprised to hear from you."

"I'm sorry about what I said before. I was wrong."

"Are you calling because you're in some kind of twelve-step program?"

"No, it's not that. And you know I don't drink much."

"So is it a different addiction? Drugs? Sex? You tell me. Why are you calling me?"

"Well, first to apologize, but I also have a question."

"Okay, here it comes."

This wasn't going well. I tried to collect my thoughts before proceeding. "I know you were involved with a lot of environmental groups. I remember you said that you did volunteer work writing grants."

"I still do. Why do you care?"

"I am wondering if you've heard of a group called Enviro Freedom."

"I've heard of them. Do you have a point, Meg? Because if you don't, I'm hanging up now."

"No, wait! Please, this is important. My mother is missing and I think she might be involved with the group. I'm having trouble finding out anything about them."

Rachel said in a softer voice, "What do you mean, she's *missing?*"

"I was supposed to meet her at her new house and she never showed up. I've been trying to find her ever since. We think she's at a retreat run by Enviro Freedom."

"We? Who is we?"

"Me and my, uh, maybe stepbrother. I've been traveling with him because I can't drive."

"Because of your so-called health problems, I suppose?"

I could hear the sneer in Rachel's tone and I said, "I know more about what is wrong with me now. And if it makes you feel better, the last time I talked to Matt I called him a slimeball."

"That's because he is."

"I know. And like I said, I'm really sorry. Can you tell me anything about Enviro Freedom? I'm afraid something terrible has happened to my mother and I need to find them."

After another long pause, finally Rachel said, "I'm sorry about your mom. From what you told me, she sounds like a nice person. I've heard that EF is an ultra-secretive group. Some people say they're like a cult or maybe even eco-terrorists."

"You mean these people might be dangerous?"

"It depends on who you believe. There are lots of petty squabbles among nonprofits. One group will say you need to take massive action, even if it involves violence. Then other groups are pacifists that engage only in lobbying and marches. And everything in between."

"Okay, but what did they do? When you say cult do you mean like a religious thing?"

"The EF people have a few unusual ideas about nature and they have, I guess you'd say, an almost religious zeal toward saving the environment. There are rumors about fires being set, bombing, and stuff like that."

At the word fire I gasped. Maybe Rachel hadn't heard me. I cleared my throat. "Do you know how I can find them?"

"The only thing I know is that they're based in Seattle somewhere. I have more information about them on my computer, but I'm about to go out, so I have to go."

"Maybe you could call me with the information and leave a message?"

"I thought you said you're on a trip."

"I am, and we're headed to the Northwest. But I still have my answering machine at home. If you don't want to call me, would it be okay if I call you again once we get closer to Seattle?"

"I suppose that's okay if it helps you find your mother."

"Thanks Rachel."

I hung up the phone and curled up on the bed, trying to assimilate what Rachel had just told me. No matter how I looked at it, from what Rachel said, it sounded like Mom was being held by a bunch of fire-loving lunatics with bombs. This revelation did not make me feel warm and fuzzy about her safety at all.

~

By the time Riley and Zelda came back from their walk, I'd more or less collected my thoughts and was typing notes into my laptop. I closed the computer, set it aside, and patted the bed to encourage Zelda to curl up next to me. I needed some furry consolation.

Riley grabbed a yogurt out of the mini-fridge and sat down at the desk. He poked at the contents of the container with a spoon, and gave it a half-hearted stir. "You seem depressed. Did your friend hang up on you?"

"No, but the call was definitely depressing." I stroked the soft fur on Zelda's head as I explained what Rachel had told me about Enviro Freedom.

When I was done, Riley said, "They sound like a bunch of whackos."

"I'm wondering if they caused the circus accident."

"Given that they might like bombs, it's certainly possible."

I scrunched down next to Zelda. "I feel sick."

"Maybe you should start going on the walks with us. A little fresh air might help."

"I get plenty of fresh air driving around. And if I go on the walks with you, you don't get your alone time."

Riley took a bite of yogurt and grimaced. "Well, you could try being quiet."

"Oh, come on. This is me we're talking about."

He set the yogurt aside. "Treat it like meditation. Instead of talking, focus on breathing and being in the moment."

"Yeah, right. Like that's going to happen."

"It couldn't hurt."

The next morning, I was still more than a little bit surly, partly because I was afraid I was going to have another vision. Stupid cities. I couldn't go anywhere near civilization anymore and it was bringing me down. My foul humor did not go unnoticed by the other occupants of the tiny motel room. Even Zelda was giving me extra space as I stomped around the room packing my stuff back into various suitcases and bags for what felt like the ninety-fifth time.

When I was done, I sprawled out on the bed to wait for Riley to get out of the shower. He took absurdly long showers. What the heck was he doing in there? Scratch that. I didn't want to know.

At last the bathroom door opened and Riley emerged, along with a cloud of steam. He rubbed the towel on his head and stopped in front of me, assessing my appearance. "What's wrong with you this morning?"

"Nothing."

He threw the towel over the back of the desk chair. "Yes, there is. You're getting all mopey again."

"I'm not mopey. We have big problems here." I stood up and grabbed my clothes. "Yesterday I found out my mom is being held by nutballs. That's *not* good, you know."

"I know, but you're being mopey about it."

"I'm taking a shower." I called over my shoulder before I closed the door, "And I'm *not* mopey."

I get many of my best ideas while I'm in the shower, and this morning's epiphany was that I should do an online news search to see if there had been any unsolved bombings lately. As someone who had almost been blown up in a rest stop bathroom, I didn't have to take a huge mental leap to come to this conclusion. I'd assumed the people in the gray suits who had been chasing us were the ones who bombed the place, but maybe it was the environmental nuts.

I closed my eyes and let the warm water wash over my face, enjoying a few minutes of peace and quiet. If the EF people were the ones who had tried to blow me up, that meant two groups of people were after me and Riley, not just one. Why was this happening to me?

By the time I was done with my shower, Riley and Zelda were off on their morning constitutional, so I took the opportunity to do some web surfing. I settled myself in at the desk and after only a few clicks discovered that the circus wasn't the only thing that had been bombed or set on fire lately. Since the accident happened, a couple cellular towers had been targeted. I doubted that was a coincidence.

When Riley returned with Zelda, she ran around the room a few times, leaping over luggage as if she were running a steeplechase.

I motioned for Riley to come look at my laptop screen. "I don't like this."

He leaned over my shoulder and his long hair flapped in my face. I shoved it aside. "Hey."

"Sorry." He stood up. "That's not good news for the cellular provider, although I have to say part of me doesn't care."

"Blowing up cell towers is not the way to bring about change."

"They got a big one near Sacramento, which is good news for us in the short term, but somebody is out a whole lot of expensive technology."

I gazed up at him. "You're not a closet terrorist, are you?"

"No, and I think by now you would have noticed if I were running around blowing things up every night."

"Who knows what you do on those walks of yours? You and Zelda could be up to no good."

Riley ignored my comment and continued, "I'm not too excited that the bombers were so close by recently. I'm ready to get out of here. We should be able to get to Bend before nightfall. Or maybe even a little farther from civilization, if you would get moving."

"You're the one who took forever getting your act together this morning. It's not my fault."

He gave me a dismissive gesture and picked up a suitcase. "You always say that when you're the one screwing around. Grab your stuff."

After we loaded up the car, Riley checked out of the motel, and we blazed out of Sacramento via Interstate 5 north toward Redding. The plan was to take a route north that would avoid large metropolitan areas like Portland. Instead we were going to go inland near Mount Shasta, through Klamath Falls, past Crater Lake, and stay somewhere outside of Bend, Oregon.

Riley had put the new and improved convertible top up, and after a while, the little ache in my head went away. Maybe he was on to something with this cage thingie and copper screening.

I folded up the map and set it my lap. "How do you feel?"

Riley glanced at me. "Fine, why?"

"Do you feel better than you did at the motel?"

"I guess I do."

"Does that mean we could stop for lunch and eat at a normal restaurant like normal people?" I stuffed the map into the glove compartment. "I'm tired of sandwiches made from stuff in the cooler."

"All right, I suppose we could find a place. Does the Triple-A guide have anything in Redding?"

I dug out the book and amused myself by searching for dining possibilities, idly flipping through pages. The options were limited.

A tiny clang noise came from under the car and Riley looked at the rearview mirror, then down at the dashboard. He mumbled what sounded like a remarkably explicit scatological string of words, which wasn't like him. We'd gone through some pretty hairy experiences and he almost never lost his cool, even when things got weird.

"What's wrong?" I asked.

He hit the turn signal, changed lanes, and moved the car to the right. As he pulled off to the side of the road, he said, "We've got a big problem."

"Worse than buzzard barf?"

"A lot worse."

Chapter 6

Under the Hood

Riley pulled the car way off the road so that it was sitting on the gravel strip that ran alongside the paved shoulder of the highway. He handed me Zelda's leash. "Take her and get out of the car now."

"What's your problem?"

"Someone messed with Shelby. Get out of the car!"

I grabbed my bag, turned around, clipped the leash on Zelda, and we got out. Traffic was whizzing by and I was glad we were as far off the road as we were. Riley pointed toward a clump of scrubby trees. "Go over there."

"What are you doing?"

"Meg, don't argue with me for once. Get away from the car. I'm serious."

My heart thundered in my chest, but I tugged on Zelda's leash and we tromped over into the shade. Was the car about to blow up?

Riley crawled underneath the Mustang, so all I could see were his sneakers sticking out. What was he doing under there?

I clutched the leash, staring at Riley's shoes, waiting for something awful to happen, for what felt like forever. At last his feet moved and he crawled back out. When he stood up again, I could see he was unbelievably grimy. Redding certainly was a filthy place.

He popped the hood and spent some more time peering inside and poking at the engine. I had no idea what he was up to.

When he put the hood down, I held out my arms away from my body and waved them at him. "What is going *on*?"

Riley walked over and sat down next to Zelda under the tree. "Someone unscrewed the oil plug on the drain pan. The noise we heard was the plug falling off and hitting the pavement. I saw a stream of oil on the road, the pressure gauge was dropping, and the temperature gauge was rising. And now what's left of the oil is draining out. If we drive any farther, the engine will seize."

"The car isn't going to blow up, is it?"

"I don't think so. I checked it over pretty carefully. I've spent a lot of time staring at Shelby's insides, so I think I would be able to tell."

"But we're stranded here?"

"Yes."

"What are we going to do?" I waved my arms in exasperation. "This is why people have cell phones."

He rubbed at his chin, leaving a greasy oil stain behind. "Cell phones aren't the greatest idea for us. But I can walk over to that farmhouse and see if they'll let me use a phone to call for roadside assistance."

"You look like you bathed in motor oil."

"At least they'll believe me when I say I have car trouble."

"What am I supposed to do?"

"Stay here with Zelda and keep an eye on Shelby. Everything we own is in that car."

I sat down and leaned on the tree. "Hurry, okay? If someone messed with the car, they might come back."

"I was thinking the same thing." He bent to pet Zelda. "Take care of Meg and Shelby, Zee."

Riley jogged off toward the farm and I stared at his retreating form. The driveway to get to the house had to be a half-mile long. On the one hand, I was scared. If someone was following us, I didn't want to be alone when they turned up. On the other hand, if no one showed up, sitting here was going to be boring. I pulled my book out of my bag and Zelda settled in next to me, seemingly content to watch the cars zoom by on the freeway in front of us.

I read my romance novel for a while, until the gray skies let loose a fine drizzle. The tree sheltered me somewhat, but I didn't want my book to get soaked, particularly before I found out what happened to the troubled couple in the story. I tucked my book back into my tote bag and wrapped my arms around my knees, joining Zelda in freeway traffic observation.

I'd discovered on my long road trip with Riley that in California, drivers seem to lose any semblance of rational thought when it rains. The unaccustomed moisture has a detrimental effect on their driving skills and they commit acts of unreasonable stupidity.

A blue van veered toward the side of the freeway and for a horrible instant, I thought it was going to crash into the Mustang. It managed to swerve and miss the car and pulled in front of it, then backed up, so that it was parked far off the shoulder in the weeds.

Two men jumped out of the van and Zelda launched away from me, yanking the leash out of my hands. She was barking in the menacing way that made me forget that I had spent so much time with her fluffy white form placidly snoozing next to me.

The misty drizzle had evolved into a more significant rain, which muffled and distorted the sounds around me. I stood up and clutched the straps of my bag in my fist as I started toward the van. I knew those men. Although they'd taken off their gray suit jackets, I recognized them as the same people who had been following me and Riley off and on for weeks.

I increased my pace to an all-out run, yelling Zelda's name as loudly as I possibly could. She was lunging at the men, trying to grab onto various appendages as they swatted her away. The traffic sped by and the sound of the cars, coupled with the rain and Zelda's barking, made it difficult to hear what the men were saying. I made out a deep voice from the shorter man saying, "Get the goddamn net!"

The taller of the two opened the sliding side door of the van and reached inside. His hand emerged with a huge fishing net, which he flailed at Zelda. The dog dodged successfully a few times, but then the net swished over her. The man stepped backward away from the highway and into the weeds, pulling Zelda back with him.

The short man ran behind the Mustang. He shook his head and shoved his sopping black hair off his face. His gaze locked with mine, and I changed course away from Zelda and toward him. She was struggling to free herself, which was keeping the tall man busy.

The short man stopped in front of me. "I've been waiting a long time for this."

"Me too," I said, gripping my tote bag with both hands. I swung it around and slammed him across the face. The huge hardback Nora Roberts novel I'd been reading must have crashed into his nose, because his palms flew to his face and he staggered backward a few steps until he collided with the side of the Mustang.

I turned and ran back toward Zelda who, although confined, wasn't going quietly. I pulled the heavy book out of my bag and whirled it like a Frisbee. The book fluttered a little, but made contact with the tall guy's gut. He bent over and dropped the net.

I shouted, "Zelda, *come!*" and the dog whirled around toward me, dragging the net along with her.

I yanked off the net and faced the man who was approaching me, poking the net toward him like a weapon. Zelda growled threateningly and I said, "Get away from us."

The two men turned when a tow truck pulled up behind the Mustang. They paused to stare at each other for a moment and then ran back to their van. Zelda barked incessantly, her fur standing straight up off her back as the van pulled back onto the highway.

A hand grabbed mine and spun me around like a swing dancer. I found myself with my ear pressed to Riley's chest and his arms wrapped tightly around me. For a long moment, all I could hear was his heart beating loudly. His voice reverberated in my ear. "Meg, are you all right?"

I wrapped my arms around him, returning the hug. My fingertips ran along his ribs, which felt like a ladder. Because I spent so much time with Riley, most of the time I didn't think about how skinny he was. He was just Riley. But yeesh, the phrase *skin and bones* had new meaning for me.

I leaned back so I could look up into his face and soggy strands of my hair plastered to my cheeks. "It's okay. I'm fine."

A man wearing navy coveralls and a yellow rain slicker walked up. "You two got a little car trouble here? My name's Jim, and we got a call from someone named Riley O'Shea."

"That's me." Riley released me with one arm and pointed at the Mustang. "Like I told the guy on the phone, we need an oil plug and a whole lot of oil."

I let go of Riley and stepped back so he could deal with the car guy, who was examining the Mustang with admiration.

Jim said, "Would you look at that beauty! The dispatcher told me it was a classic Mustang. So what is she? A sixty-seven? Sixty-eight? You sure it's just oil? Maybe I should check under the hood."

"I already did, but you can if you like," Riley said.

Even though the air temperature wasn't particularly cold, the spring rain felt like shards of ice on my skin. I was freezing and started to shiver uncontrollably.

Riley pushed a thick clump of dripping hair behind my shoulder. "Are you sure you're all right?"

I said through chattering teeth, "Just cold."

Riley stepped forward and put his arms around me again, so I could share more of his body heat. He rested his chin on the top of my head and sighed. "I was afraid you and Zelda were going to get captured or killed on the highway. I'm sorry I didn't get here more quickly. I don't run very fast."

"It's okay. Zelda held her own."

Riley leaned back so he could see my face. "From what I saw, so did you. But you scared the crap out of me."

He wasn't the only one who'd been scared. Score one for literature. Who knows where I'd be if it weren't for Nora Roberts and her thick, juicy romance novels.

~

Riley went to get a towel out of the trunk, and I walked over to pick my book up out of the mud. It had crash-landed facedown with the pages open, and I tried to smooth them before tucking it into my tote bag. The book, the tote bag, and I were all utterly sodden, so it wasn't like the bag was going to keep the novel dry, but after the book saved us, I wasn't going to leave it to die an ignoble death as roadside litter.

Riley put the towel on the backseat of the Mustang and Zelda shook herself vigorously before hopping inside. He handed me a huge navy blue sweatshirt of his, which I pulled over my head before curling up in the front seat to get warm. I didn't slip my arms into the sleeves, opting to keep them wrapped around my body. I was chilled to the bone and closed my eyes as if it might help me stop shivering. I could hear the low tones of male voices outside the car as Riley discussed automotive matters with Jim.

I felt more than heard rattling from the undercarriage of the car, and I opened my eyes when I heard the tow truck start up behind us. Riley got into the car and reached around the seat to grab Zelda's towel.

I rearranged myself and poked my arms out of the sleeves of the enormous sweatshirt. "Is everything okay now?"

Riley started the car. "It should be. We both checked Shelby over, and I think I pulled over before any damage was done to the engine."

"We'd better not blow up."

Riley put a greasy palm on my arm. "It's going to be fine, Meg."

"Excuse me if I'm a little freaked out. What are we going to do now? Every time we leave the car, I'm going to be worried that someone might sabotage it."

"I was thinking about that, but first I'd like to get out of here."

"Okay." I let out a heavy breath as we pulled onto the highway. It was good to be moving again. "Thanks for the sweatshirt. I was cold and freaked out. To be honest, I'm not cut out for confrontations like this."

"Me neither. Once Shelby warms up, I'll turn on the heat."

After driving for a while with the heat running full blast, I felt a bit better. Riley was less drenched, although still filthy. His clothes were covered with dirt and oil and he'd even managed to get oil in his hair, so he looked like a bedraggled water bird that had been caught in an industrial oil spill.

In Redding, we stopped at a deli. I took off the sweatshirt, combed my hair, slapped a hat on my head, and ran inside to get sandwiches. I'd been wearing a hat because of the unnatural color of my hair, but thanks to our recent adventures I was even less presentable than usual. Because Riley's appearance was even worse than mine at the moment, we agreed that I was more suitable for public viewing.

I returned to the car with the food and wolfed down my sandwich in silence. I grabbed a potato chip from the bag and handed it back to Zelda, who appreciated my largess. She rested her muzzle on the seat to make sure I knew she would like more chips should they become available.

I chomped on another chip and rearranged myself in the seat so that I was facing Riley. "Okay, so how are we supposed to keep the car and us from getting attacked? I'd like to avoid having that experience ever again."

"It pains me to say this, but I think I need to install a car alarm with motion sensors. I hate those things."

"You mean the ones that always go off accidentally in parking lots?"

"Exactly. We can be a public nuisance."

"Great."

"It also means we need to find another garage."

"This idea gets better all the time."

Riley took a bite of his sandwich and raised his eyebrows at me in a way that silently asked, "Do you have any better ideas?"

I said with a sigh, "I suppose you want to install this thing today?"

He extracted a pickle from the sandwich and passed it back to Zelda. "We probably should deal with it while we're still in an area that's populated enough to have a store where I can buy an alarm."

"But I want to crawl into a nice, warm motel room and take a shower."

"How do you think I feel?"

I grinned. "Probably better than you look."

"Thanks. Let's find a motel. I'll take a shower while Zee guards the car. You can hang out while I get an alarm."

I liked that plan and we found a local Motel 6. Riley claimed that when he checked in, the guy at the front desk didn't even blink at his appearance.

Riley left to buy the alarm and after a lovely warm shower, I curled up on my bed with my laptop. Zelda joined me on the bed for a nap. Apparently, when you're an exceptionally furry dog, drying off is an exhausting process.

I ignored the lingering wet-dog smell and tapped away at my laptop, surfing news sites and running my typical searches on Enviro Freedom and Hector's circus to see if anything new had come up. I glanced through another news report that had the same quote from Hector saying that the circus would have to fold.

An obvious thought occurred to me. The guys in the suits were still trying to capture us, but what were they going to do with us if the circus was disbanded?

Hector's circus has been used as a way to move people around the country without being noticed. But where were the guys in suits taking people if there was no circus to dump them at? It was a good question and one for which I hadn't even the slightest glimmer of a guess. I'd seen the photo of Lars after the accident. Was he still with the circus people now? If not, where was he? I couldn't think of any way to find out.

I gave up on the Internet and went back to my slightly soggy romance novel. It was a little battered after the rough morning, but still readable, so I settled in for a relaxing reading session.

Riley entered the room as I was closing the book. The novel had a great ending, and I was sad it was over. Why couldn't I live happily ever after with the outrageously sexy love of my life?

Zelda launched off my bed when Riley closed the door behind him. He strode the three steps to my bed and thrust a flyer in my face. "You aren't going to believe this."

"What is it?" I scanned the piece of paper. "The Specter of Hector?"

Riley sat on the other bed. "The circus is now a traveling rock band."

"They mean specter as in ghost? Ick. That's creepy." I shook the flyer. "I'm sorry, but I think Hector has some serious issues."

"I know."

"While you were gone, I was wondering where the guys in the suits were planning to take us, since the circus is defunct."

"I think we know now."

"Well, at least if they catch us again there won't be clowns."

"Look at the picture, Meg. It's a Kiss tribute band."

I studied the flyer. The man in front was Hector clad in leather armor and plastic boots. "That's a grotesque photo. And what is it with these guys and makeup?"

"I don't know, but I'm pretty sure Gene Simmons wouldn't be impressed."

∼

The next morning while loading our stuff into the Mustang, Riley somehow managed to set off the new car alarm three times, thoroughly irritating the remaining residents of the Motel 6 and me. One of the alarming events happened while I was standing next to the Mustang, and I almost keeled over. The thing was unbelievably loud.

If nothing else, the awful alarm would certainly get our attention. And if anyone crawled under the car again and the alarm went off, the perpetrator would end up stone deaf. Riley was as grumpy as I was about the unwelcome modification to his precious car, but it had to be done. Now it was time to get back on the road. Maybe today we could go more than two hundred miles. I was ready to leave populated areas and return to the wide open spaces, so the twinge in my head would go away and we could consider putting the convertible top down again.

I jammed my toiletry case into my suitcase and looked at Zelda, who was going through her usual routine of running back and forth between the car and the motel room while we packed up. She stopped in front of me, and made an rrr-ing noise low in her throat.

What sounded like an air-raid siren went off and Zelda's body moved sideways as if the room were tilting. I had a sensation of vertigo and it occurred to me that we were in California, the land of earthquakes. Were we near the San Andreas Fault?

I peered out the door of the motel room, and beyond the red Mustang a strange gold glow was expanding like a miniature sunrise. Lars and his son emerged from the light, running away from the motel toward the highway. The trees were swaying and something, maybe a folding chair, flew off a second-floor balcony. It landed near the little boy, and I heard a woman's voice yelling, "You need to save him!" I screamed and ran out of the room after the pair.

I kept screaming as I ran toward the retreating forms. Cars were whizzing in both directions on the divided highway that ran in front of the motel. Wasn't it bad to drive during an earthquake? The only earthquakes I'd seen were on film. In *Superman*, Lois Lane almost fell into a crevasse, but did that type of thing really happen? I had no idea.

I kept screaming, but it seemed like Lars and his son were getting farther away from me. Somehow I wasn't covering any distance and it was like space had compressed.

I fell and hit the ground with a thud that knocked the wind out of me. When I opened my eyes, Zelda was licking my face and Riley was lying on my back with his arms around my waist.

Once I caught my breath, I squirmed and shoved myself out from underneath him, "Get off me! What are you doing?"

Riley sat up and rubbed his knees. "What am *I* doing? What are *you* doing?"

"Where is Lars?"

"Lars? How the heck should I know? I was turning off the stupid alarm again and the next thing I know Zee is barking like crazy because you're about to run into traffic and kill yourself. What is *wrong* with you?"

"I guess it wasn't real." I put my arms around Zelda's furry neck and hugged her. "Zee went all sideways. I thought it was an earthquake. People were yelling and I saw Lars running with his little boy. There was stuff flying through the air and I thought they'd get hurt."

Riley rubbed his eyes with his palms and mumbled. "Jeez, Meg."

"I didn't realize what I was doing."

A gray-haired couple holding hands walked up to us. The man said, "Are you okay?"

The woman added, "We heard screaming and came to see what was going on."

I stood up and brushed the dirt off my pants. "I'm fine. I, uh, thought I saw something, but it's okay now."

A few more residents of the motel who were packing up their cars stopped by to make sure that the screamer, aka me, had calmed down. I assured everyone that I was fine and apologized for the noise from me and the car alarm.

After the crowd dispersed, Riley took my hand and practically dragged me back to the motel room. We grabbed the rest of our things and finished packing the car in silence. He was more upset than I'd ever seen him, which was saying something, given everything we'd been through together.

We headed north out of Redding, which I was glad to see disappear behind us in the rearview mirror. I'd managed to get attacked once and almost run over twice in as many days. It was hard to blame Riley for being a little disturbed by recent events.

A quiet hour later, we stopped for gas in a little town called Weed, which had a stunning view of Mount Shasta and fewer than three-thousand residents, according to the sign. The sign proclaimed that Weed was a lumber town, but I was betting teenagers weren't buying the souvenir "I love Weed!" t-shirts because of the trees.

After gassing up the Mustang, Riley got back in and started the car. He pulled out onto the main drag through town and turned to take Route 97 north toward Klamath Falls.

I touched the back of his hand on the gear shift. "So are you ever going to talk to me again? Because it's going to be a long ride to Oregon if you don't."

"I'm getting there."

"Get there faster." I waved my hands in exasperation. "I mean, what am I supposed to do? If I could make these awful visions stop, don't you think I would? I would have done it months ago. You know better than anyone how bad I felt about losing my job because of this."

"Technically, you were on medical leave."

"And then I was laid off. Whatever. You know what I mean. How can you be mad at me? You *know* this isn't my fault."

He glanced at me. "I do know. But like you said, excuse me if I'm a little freaked out. Having you run and play in traffic is not generally part of my morning routine. I almost watched you die a horrible death, and I don't know what to do to keep it from happening again."

"I don't know either. Tackling me worked this time. Are you sure you weren't a football star in high school?"

"Very sure." Riley shifted gears and gunned the engine to pass a semi. "What if I hadn't been there to stop you?"

"This is the second time I acted out what I was seeing in a hallucination, but it's not like I know what I'm doing or when it might happen again. I agree that my visions are worse when I'm running around, though."

"I'll say." He took a deep breath. "There's nothing we can do about this right now, except hope that there's less radiation in rural Oregon. Is there anything we can learn from what you saw?"

"That maybe Lars is with his son?"

"We already know that."

"Was there an earthquake somewhere? If there was, maybe I saw it."

"There wasn't one in Redding. The ground wasn't moving under anyone's feet except yours."

"But maybe Lars is somewhere that did have a quake. Is that possible?" I tugged on my earring, trying to remember anything else. "I don't know what's real and what's not. But I had a vision about Lars, and I think that's important."

"It would be easy enough to find out online if there was an earthquake somewhere this morning, assuming it was large enough to make the news."

"When we get to Bend, I'll look."

"Did you see anything or anyone else?"

"No, but I heard a woman yelling."

"Do you know who it was?"

"I didn't recognize the voice, but I'm sure it wasn't my mom." I slumped down in the seat. "We're not getting anywhere with this, are we?"

"Not really."

"In Seattle we can visit the real estate office and find out what happened with Lars. Maybe Lars is important."

"Maybe."

I gave up on conversation and let Riley return to his silent troubled state. My thoughts were tangled and muddled and I couldn't bear to think about it anymore, so I opted to stare vacantly out the window at the scenery going by. It was going to be a long day.

~

By the time we arrived in Bend, Oregon, the repercussions of my morning hallucination had subsided somewhat. I was feeling better, and Riley was communicating again. Bend is located on the eastern side of the Cascade mountain range, and I was relieved to find it wasn't a particularly huge metropolis. The thirty-thousand or so souls who chose to live in the town along the Deschutes River apparently didn't need to have cell phones glued to their ears at all times, so I felt better than I had since we left Alpine Grove.

We found a motel along Highway 97, the north-south highway that divides Bend. Like many of the places we'd been, a swath of motels, big-box stores, and other retail outlets lined the highway. Because of all the outdoor recreation opportunities in the area, fishing and hunting shops were interspersed with the typical array of grocery stores and fast-food joints. All of the cutesy shops, restaurants, and trendy coffee shops were located in the original downtown that was off the highway.

After we got settled into our motel room, we went to the grocery store to replenish our stash of road food. Our shopping journeys had settled into a routine, with Riley collecting healthy items like fruits, nuts, and vegetables from the perimeter of the store while I scouted the center aisles for easy-to-transport packaged goods. Then we'd meet in the frozen-food aisle and collect a few microwavable dinners.

On my way to forage for crackers, I got distracted by the beauty aisle. Because of our adventures with Helen the Horrible in Alpine Grove, I'd never dealt with my multicolored hair. My unattractive tresses gave me the appearance of a mutant skunk crossed with a fox that was having an unbelievably bad hair day. I wasn't fond of wearing hats and it was way past time to return my hair to a monochromatic state.

I didn't see the familiar box of Miss Clairol that I'd been using for years, so I pulled a few boxes from the shelf and explored uncharted coloring frontiers. Choosing a hair color is complicated. After a few unfortunate experiences, I'd found that you should never believe the image on the front of the box. Those women in the photos are always blessed with unbelievably great hair that has no resemblance to mine. The reality of hair dye is revealed on the other side of the box, where you can ponder how your true hair color will blend with the tint. The chart of "expected results" for a given shade showed a wide range of color, and a number of them would definitely not be flattering. Of course, given the current state of my hair, how much worse could it get?

I returned the box I was holding to the shelf as Riley walked up.

He deposited a bunch of vegetables into the cart and wrinkled his nose. "What is that horrible smell?"

"I should know better than to ask you this, but what smell?"

He leaned toward the rows of hair-dye boxes. "It smells like ammonia. Gross. Do people willingly put that on their hair?"

"No one ever said dye smells great."

"You're not seriously going to do that in our motel room, are you? Please say you're not."

I took off my hat. "I'm sorry, but I can't stand looking like this anymore."

"Like what? You look the same to me."

"Are you blind? My hair is twenty-five different shades of weird."

"Why don't you go to a salon?"

"I don't like them."

"I thought all women loved going to get their hair cut. Pampering and beauty treatments and all that stuff."

"Not this one." I didn't want to divulge that one reason I'd always worn my hair long is because I avoid hair salons as much as possible. When I was six, I had done what every mother tells you not to do. That old rule about not playing with scissors is probably a good one and something I'd ignored. I gave myself a haircut, and when my mother found a trail of hair along the floor with me at the end of it, she'd shrieked and hauled me off to the beauty parlor for professional intervention.

Having a room full of women laugh at me and witnessing a hushed consultation among five hairdressers to figure out how to salvage the horrifying hair debacle that I'd caused was a humiliating memory that had stayed with me. Even my worst home-hair-dye jobs were better than subjecting myself to the condescending style appraisal of a snooty beautician.

Riley picked up a box and studied it. "This has dire warnings about skin irritation and allergic reactions."

"I don't have those. It's fine."

"Why don't you just let the color grow out?"

"No way. That would take forever and I'd have to get my hair cut. I don't like how I look with short hair or my true hair color."

"All those chemicals can't be good for you." He crouched down and examined the lower shelves. "Is there anything that doesn't contain poison or generate noxious fumes?"

"I've never found a hair dye that doesn't smell bad. I suppose there might be something at a health-food store, I guess."

He held up a plastic jar. "What about this stuff? It's red and it passes the sniff test."

"Henna?"

"It smells like dirt. I can handle dirt."

I read the label and threw it into the cart. "Okay, fine. I'll put dirt on my head. But if my hair becomes even more of a freak show than it already is, I'm blaming you."

"You can always shave your head and start over."

I ignored the comment, yanked my hat down farther on my forehead, and pushed the cart down the aisle. "Let's get out of here."

Back at the motel, I studied the directions on the jar of henna. It wasn't that different from hair dye, but it took a while. I gathered all my supplies in the bathroom, boiled water in the microwave, and mixed up the henna according to the instructions.

Riley and Zelda watched the proceedings with interest. Zelda followed me into the bathroom and I pushed her back. "It's not food, Zee. Go away."

I'd purchased rubber gloves and a shower cap at the grocery store, but I still wasn't prepared for the messiness factor. When you mix up henna, it gets everywhere and stains everything. The Motel 6 wasn't going to be too pleased at the state of their towels when I was done. Oh well.

I crouched naked in the bathtub, glopped the henna onto my scalp, and mushed it around into my hair. When I was done, I felt like my head had been the big loser in a mud-wrestling match, but I was committed to the process now. After I covered my gooey hair with the shower cap, I wrapped it in a towel turban.

I put on the cozy sweatpants I typically wore while lounging in motel rooms and when I opened the door, Zelda ran up and sniffed me furiously. I shooed her away and carefully sat down on my bed, trying not to dislodge the turban precariously perched on my head.

Riley put down his book and raised his eyebrows at me. "Why are you wearing my shirt?"

"I can't get a t-shirt over the towel. I needed something I could button up. This is all your fault anyway."

"Don't get that gunk on my shirt." He pointed at me. "I think it's oozing."

I wiped a drip of henna off my neck that had seeped out from under my towel. "It should wash out." Maybe. Probably not.

The directions said I needed to let the henna sit for at least an hour. I carefully reached for my book on the nightstand and settled back against the headboard.

One positive aspect of this long, strange road trip with Riley had been my return to reading for pleasure. When I was a reporter, I'd spent so much time reading and researching that I'd stopped reading anything else. After work, I'd usually just crashed on my sofa and watched re-runs on TV.

While we'd been on the road, most nights Riley read something, whether it was a novel or a horrifyingly geeky book. Over time, I'd started joining him in evening reading. I still had a few paperbacks from the Alpine Grove bookstore and I found I enjoyed hanging out with just the sound of pages turning and Zelda snoring.

After a stressful day like I'd had today, I didn't mind behaving like a boring old woman. I'd had far too much excitement in my life lately and a girl needed a little down time. My mind wandered and I reflected on my vision.

Riley and I had agreed to take my visions more seriously, so even though I felt a little silly about it, I planned to investigate where Lars had been in the past. One of the notable elements in the vision had been the folding chair flying by. It was like the chair had been caught on the wind. But earthquakes didn't cause wind, so it didn't make sense.

"Windfall!" I blurted out.

Riley looked up from his book. "What?"

"Leo said he had a windfall. That's how he's buying a new house. He didn't say where the money came from, but who gets a windfall right before being laid off?"

"What are you talking about?"

"Maybe you were right and Leo knows more about the merger than he let on." I wiped another glob of henna off my neck and rubbed it on the towel. "What if he was paid off for something?"

"I thought he was your friend."

"He was, but how well did I know him? I mean, how well do you really know anyone you work with?"

"You are the one who said 'follow the money.'"

"I know!" I leaned forward and a glob of henna plopped onto the long shirttails in my lap. "Oops."

"Maybe you should just keep the shirt."

Chapter 7

Birthday Wish

When I woke up the next morning, Riley was taking a shower and Zelda was sprawled out flat on his bed, taking advantage of the extra space.

The door to the bathroom opened with a gust of steam and Riley walked out with a towel draped over his head. He pointed at me, "Hey, check out your hair…"

I touched my head. "I knew it! That nasty stuff turned it green, didn't it? I'm going to kill you for this!" I jumped out of bed and ran to the bathroom. After rinsing out the henna the night before, I'd fallen asleep. My hair hadn't appeared to be green, but it had still been wet. I hurriedly rubbed the condensation off the mirror and leaned in close to see the damage. My racing heartbeat slowed. My hair was an auburn color. Thank God.

Riley walked up behind me, threw his towel on my shoulder, and grinned at me in the mirror. "You need to relax."

"This is my hair we're talking about! If I'd been forced to shave my head, you'd be in deep trouble."

He tugged on a strand. "It's nice. This color is better."

"At least it's a natural color again, which was the goal." I shoved him toward the door. "Get out. It's my turn for the bathroom."

After my shower, I perched on the edge of my bed and picked up the phone to call my answering machine and find out if Rachel had left a message about Enviro Freedom. Every few days, I checked in with my machine. It was probably ridiculous to continue paying rent and utilities on my apartment while I was on this marathon road trip, but I didn't want to let it go. I had to believe that eventually I'd find my mother and be able to return to my life. I'd probably have to move from DC because of the radiation level, but in the meantime, I still had my apartment and people could contact me. Not that anyone I wanted to contact me actually had, but I was hoping Rachel had dug up something good by now.

I called my number and typed my passcode. A smooth-talking gentleman wanted to see if I was happy with my long-distance provider and another smarmy voice wanted to know if I was getting the lowest rates on my credit card. Delete. Delete. Crap. I was going to have to call Rachel again, since she obviously wasn't going to bother to call. I sighed at the prospect of another acrimonious conversation with my not-so-friendly friend.

There was a pause before the next recording began and my jaw dropped when I heard a familiar voice.

I waved frantically at Riley, who raised his eyebrows and said, "What?"

I ran to sit next to him on his bed and held up the phone receiver so he could hear. "It's my mom!"

He leaned over and grabbed the handset to pull it closer to his ear. I pressed the button to replay the message and we held the receiver between us and listened.

For the first time in what seemed like forever, I heard my mother say, "Hi Meg. I was thinking I should call, but I, well, I couldn't. It's a long story. But Saturday is your birthday and I couldn't just let that go by without saying anything. I miss you. Oh, oh, dear, someone's coming…I need to go now. But happy birthday, honey. I miss you and I love you."

I moved away to press the button on the phone to save the message, then turned back to give Riley a hug. I released him and pressed my hand to my chest, feeling the thump of my heart pounding. "She's okay. Oh my God, Riley, I can't believe it was her. She's really *okay*!"

"That's a relief. She has a nice voice." He closed his book and set it aside. "Although it does concern me that someone isn't letting her use the phone. If our parents are truly at this retreat, what kind of place doesn't let you call your daughter on her birthday?"

"I know. It sounded like she got caught sneaking a call. And she didn't leave a number. I still don't know where she is."

Riley smiled. "Happy birthday, by the way."

I returned the smile and held out my hands. "It's not until tomorrow, but check it out, my hands are still shaking. Hearing my mom's voice is probably the best birthday present I've ever gotten."

"If we can figure out where this retreat is and find her, maybe you'll get a chance to say thank you."

I got up and returned to my own bed. "I need to call Rachel again."

"Normally, we'd go for a walk, but given your recent hallucination, I don't know…" Riley nudged Zelda with his foot and she rolled over onto her back, going for a lethargic upside-down pose with her front paws curled against her chest.

"It's okay. She's happy and you don't need to disturb her nap." Zelda thumped her tail a couple of times to acknowledge my comment.

I glanced at the clock and wondered if Rachel had gotten a new job yet. Like me, she'd been laid off. Even if she was at work I could leave a message, so I still should call. But I was trying to find any excuse not to. This was pathetic. I needed to get over myself and talk to her again. But my thoughts and emotions were scattered and I couldn't think of a way to open the conversation. "Hi Rachel. You still hate me, right? Did you find out anything about that retreat? No? Well, uh, bye." Ugh.

Because procrastination is always a good option for those times you are supposed to do something you don't want to do, I opened my laptop to see if I could determine where the Specter of Hector was playing next.

The flyer Riley had found had been promoting a show they were doing in Redding, but unlike their old circus flyers, it didn't say where they'd be playing in the future. Given that Hector's latest endeavor was brand new, it was possible they were desperately trying to land gigs.

After our automotive disaster in Redding, Riley and I had fled the area, but I kept thinking about Lars. If we were near one of Hector's shows, I wanted to check it out and see if Lars was there. Now that I'd seen him in my vision with his son, I wondered if Lars knew more about what Hector was up to than I'd originally believed.

Zelda rolled over so she was upright again and Riley got up. "I thought you were going to call Rachel."

"I wanted to check on the Hector situation."

"Wimping out?"

"I need to do more research on Hector. If Hector is doing a show, you'd think they'd promote it online."

"Maybe. Although if you ask me, finding out where that retreat is located is more important."

"I've been trolling the Kiss bulletin boards. There are some hard-core fans out there in the world. If Hector is performing, they'll know about it."

Riley grabbed his sneakers. "You're making excuses not to call Rachel, aren't you? If you're not ready to deal with it, why don't you go for a walk with us?"

"Maybe that's a good idea." I closed the laptop. "I'm not seeing anything new here and my emotions are scrambled from hearing my mom's voice. I need to clear my head and come up with decent questions to ask Rachel, so I don't sound like an idiot again."

Zelda leaped off the bed and ran around the room, apparently having realized that both humans were attending the morning excursion.

Riley clipped the leash onto Zelda's collar and we walked out into the crisp morning air. The Cascade Mountains were still snow-capped and the morning light on the landscape was sparkly and bright.

We strolled to a coffee shop and Riley and Zelda waited outside while I went in. I chatted with a squirrelly dude with tattoos, multiple body piercings, and baggy clothes about the merits of the various designer coffee options. He then whipped me up a latte with a little heart swirl in the cream.

I carried my prize back outside and handed a to-go cup of boring black coffee to Riley.

He took a sip from the cup and gestured toward a sign. "There's a trail over there that ends up near the river, I think."

"Is this going to be one of your marathon walks? Because you know I'm not up for that kind of thing."

"It's good for you." Riley took another sip of coffee. "Plus, we should talk."

At the serious tone, I glanced up at his face. "Is something wrong?"

"Since you almost ran into traffic, I've been worried we're not doing enough, and hearing your mom this morning reinforced that feeling."

I stopped and faced Riley. "I know! I feel the same way, but I don't know what to do. I feel like we're constantly grasping at straws."

"We can't keep doing this forever and now I'm worried something is going to happen to you."

"I'm fine."

"You are now. But what if something happens to you? I don't want to be responsible for that."

"You're not responsible for me."

Riley made a dubious face. "How can I not be? And I don't want to feel this way, Meg. I want my life back."

"I feel the same way."

"After getting attacked, the natural response is to run away. But maybe we shouldn't have done that. Maybe you're right and we should go find Hector and get some answers."

"What about the retreat? And Lars."

"That too. All of it." Riley waved his arms in a gesture of helplessness and spilled coffee on the sidewalk, which Zelda sniffed. "We need to figure out what's going on. Now we know your mom is out there at a place where they aren't even letting her use the phone. That can't be good."

"What are you saying we should do?"

"I don't know and it's driving me insane." He shook his head. "There are too many different possibilities and I'm not sure how they fit together. But we need to move faster. Do *something.*"

"Something other than run away, you mean."

"Pretty much."

~

Riley and I strolled down the forested trail drinking coffee and going over the various things we knew. Our route descended into a shady area, and the boughs of huge trees hung over the trail so it was like we were in a leafy tunnel. Zelda stopped to attend to a few personal needs. Riley leaned against a tree, holding his hand with the leash out in front of him, as the dog walked back and forth.

"This process takes a while," I said.

"I refer to it as endless pacing. For some reason, it's a necessary preamble to the big event."

I took a sip of my latte. "Okay, so we know that Helen was in league with the guys in suits who we think are in league with Hector. We also think Lars and his son are with Hector."

"And Hector's circus has something to do with Archetypal Online Systems, which wants to provide cellular service to everyone in the known universe and make bazillions of dollars. But now Hector and his band of wackos have formed a Kiss tribute band."

"And we know that somehow someone put a photograph of me in my mother's house. We don't know who or why, but the person included a business card that indicates Lars used to be a real estate agent in Seattle."

"Which is handy because it's in the Northwest," Riley said as he followed Zelda to a tree. "And that's where we are headed, because we think that this mysterious Enviro Freedom retreat is there. Somewhere."

"The Northwest is big."

"I know. Seattle is a place to start, but I'm worried that we don't know where this retreat is located." Riley resumed walking behind Zelda, who had indicated she was ready to continue the excursion. "We might never find your mom and my dad. It's like a parental needle in a haystack. We need help."

"What do you mean by *help*?"

"I don't know exactly. Maybe someone who is better at looking for things than we are."

I stopped and put my hand out to grab Riley's arm to stop him. "Exactly! Sometimes reporters use private investigators to find people or information because PIs have better access to cool databases."

"Can we do that?"

"Sure! Why not? You've got the money to pay someone."

Riley laughed. "Why yes I do, don't I?"

"I just need to figure out how to find someone good. Leo was too cheap to ever let me hire a PI. I'd ask him for a recommendation, but now I don't know. I hate thinking that he might be involved somehow, but I don't know who I can trust."

"Maybe we can find someone located in the Northwest. They'd know the right people to talk to. I can call my lawyer and set him on the task. Certain types of lawyers use private investigators too. Maybe he can get a referral to a person in Seattle."

I sucked down the last of my coffee. "What's your lawyer's name? I don't think you've ever mentioned it."

Riley made a wry face. "Elmer Flood. I just…he doesn't look like an Elmer. And when I say it out loud, I'm always afraid I'm going to say Elmer Fudd by accident."

"Wow, that must have been a tough name to grow up with."

"Everyone calls him Mel, so I guess it didn't scar him for life. When I started my company, everyone said I should get the best lawyer and accountant possible. I couldn't really afford it, but everyone said Mel's firm was the best and it turned out to be a good decision. That feels like a million years ago, but things he helped me with early on, like the patents, paid off later."

"I'll say." At a movement below me, I looked down. "Zelda, what are you doing?"

The dog gave me a satisfied canine smile and Riley said, "Uh-oh."

"What do you mean uh-oh?"

"That's her smug 'I just ate something while you weren't paying attention' face, which rarely ends well."

I crouched down and ruffled Zelda's pointy ears. "You would never eat something bad, would you?" Zelda belched so forcefully that her lips rippled and I was enveloped in a foul cloud of rotting-garbage stink.

I recoiled with a horrified squeal as Riley stepped backward away from the smell. He waved his hands. "Oh jeez, Zee. What did you do?"

I stood up and Zelda tugged on the leash, ready to move on. I said, "She seems remarkably unfazed by whatever she ate."

"I wish I had a longer leash. That's disgusting. Let's go."

We increased our pace along the trail leaving the evil smell behind and hustled back to the motel. After we returned to the room, I had a nice chat with Rachel's answering machine, and Riley called Mel to ask about private detectives.

I typed notes into my laptop and listened to Riley's conversation with his lawyer. When he hung up the phone, I said, "That sounded promising."

"He's going to make some calls. Are you about ready to get out of here?

"Five more minutes."

Riley started throwing things into his suitcase while I typed. He leaned over my shoulder to see the screen. "That's remarkably organized."

"Hey, I was a good reporter. This thingie you made to put the information online is cool. It's like I have a journal there, with everything all in chronological order."

"I should probably log into the server and see if any email showed up about what you posted the other day."

"Why can't I just get email the normal way?"

"Too easy to track." Riley tucked a shirt under his chin and folded it against his chest. "Hmmm. This is the shirt you destroyed. It's yours."

He threw the shirt, which fluttered over my head, blocking my view of the monitor. I yanked the shirt down into my lap. "Do whatever you do to get at the email."

He shooed me out of the desk chair and tapped at the keyboard. I leaned over his shoulder to see what he was typing. "What's *su?*"

"Superuser."

"Superuser? Are you kidding me? Is this some geek ego thing?"

"It's an operating system thing."

"Way to go all justice league, Batman." I folded up the shirt and put it in my suitcase.

"I'm logging in as the administrator."

"In an unbelievably geeky way, Batman."

"Holy crap."

I turned back to look. "What?"

"There are seven hundred and forty-one emails in here."

"Wow, when you get mail, you *really* get mail."

"Very funny. It seems more than a few people read the article you posted." He looked over his shoulder at me. "Your job will be to go through the emails and see if there's anything useful mixed in with all the junk and loony ranting from low lives hanging out in their parents' basement."

"Why is doing that *my* job?"

"You write the stuff; you get the fallout from the weirdos." He shut down the laptop and slid it into the laptop case. "Plus, I'm dead, remember?"

"You're not really going to play the death card with me here, are you?"

He grinned. "You bet I am."

I tried not to roll my eyes so hard that they fell out of my head, and instead concentrated on packing.

Riley gave Zelda a dirty look. "Don't give me that innocent face. I know what you just did. It's a good thing we can put the convertible top down."

I waved my hand in front of my face. "Oh Zee, that's nasty."

"Let's get out of here."

~

Riley put the top down on the Mustang and we packed up the car. Zelda was sitting in the backseat, having been instructed to hang out in her own smelly space. She seemed a little put out about being ostracized and not allowed to join in the parade of dragging stuff from the motel room to the car, but I knew she'd get over it once we hit the road.

Riley and I got into the car, and before he could start it I said, "We're not going to get all the way to Seattle today, are we?"

"Not unless you want to."

"It's my birthday tomorrow, and it might sound a little pathetic, but I don't want to spend the day worrying that I'm going to have a screaming hallucination."

"I'm glad you feel that way." He reached for the map and opened it up. "I was thinking that we should stay on this road and go north to Ellensburg, Washington. You'll see a whole lot of farmland, but probably not too many cell towers."

"Ellensburg? I've never heard of it. How big is it?"

"It's this little dot." He patted my hand and folded up the map again. "Happy birthday."

"Honestly, if people had told me a few months ago that I'd be spending my thirty-third birthday in a tiny town in Washington State, I never would have believed them."

"Sometimes life takes you places you would never expect."

"So does my mother." I shook my fist at the sky. "Mom, why didn't you leave a number when you called me? *That* would have been a great present too, you know."

Riley laughed as he started the car. "Mel should have the phone numbers of private investigators by the time we get to Ellensburg. Since we're about to have help, we don't have to feel guilty about doing something fun tomorrow to celebrate your birthday."

"Like what?"

"I don't know. What do you want to do?"

I pulled out the Triple-A guide and thumbed through it. "I guess going to a five-star restaurant and trendy nightclub is out."

"Is that really what you want to do?"

"No. And it's a good thing too. Apparently, Ellensburg is a college town. Unless I'm up for fast food and a sports bar, it doesn't look promising." I flipped through a few more pages. "There's a guest ranch nearby."

"Fun with horses."

"Horses like me. My experience with the circus horse is proof of that."

"That's true. At the circus, Dolly the Wonder Unicorn thought you were hot stuff."

"Oh, be still my heart. The guest ranch has cottages with kitchens." I pressed the book to my chest with both hands. "I know what I want for my birthday."

Riley glanced at me and raised his eyebrows. "What?"

"Food and square footage! If we stay in a place with a kitchen that's larger than a ten-by-ten room, you could cook again. I know you brought all those spices with you when we left Alpine Grove." I held up the guide. "They allow pets. Can we go there instead of another motel? You could create yummy food and we could pet horses. Please, please, please!"

"All right. Although honestly, I'm not sure what the big deal is. I'm not that great at cooking."

"Are you kidding me? You make vegetables taste good, and let's face it, generally I'm not a fan of vegetables. Well, other than potatoes that have been deep fried to crispy perfection, of course."

"I just throw in spices until whatever I'm cooking smells like something I want to eat."

"Whatever you do, it ends up tasting incredible." I dropped the Triple-A guide on the floor and raised my hands over my head to wave them in the wind. "Happy birthday to me!"

Compared to some of our marathon driving days, the drive from Bend to Ellensburg was easy. We went through miles and miles of open scrubby areas with more sagebrush than I ever thought could possibly exist.

We stopped for lunch in Yakima, and it occurred to me that unlike a Motel 6, we probably needed a reservation to stay at the ranch. With motels, you can just stagger in at any time, day or night, and ask for a room. Places like bed-and-breakfasts, resorts, and guest ranches tended to be a little more uptight about planning ahead.

At a gas station I found a pay phone and called the ranch. The woman I talked to informed me that April is mud season so things were slow. She was delighted that we were interested in late spring lodging and reassured me that the road was okay. She claimed the Mustang wouldn't get stuck in a gigantic mud bog, which would make Riley happy too.

The gas station had a rack full of flyers and I found one that had more details about our lodging for the evening. The Misty Meadow Guest Ranch had been in the same family since 1895, when the Owens family homesteaded seven hundred and fifty acres in the valley. They claimed that the area remained quiet and pastoral with acres of evergreens and gently rolling hills. The logs for the cabins had been hewn by the Owens family, but the dwellings had been recently remodeled and sported all the modern comforts of home. The quilts on the beds in the cabins had been made by Marge Owens, who owned the ranch with her husband Ronald.

As we drove north, I regaled Riley with lots of historical information about the ranch, but he didn't seem to be paying attention.

I tucked the flyer into the Triple-A guide. "The lake at the ranch also has a serpent that the Owens family claims is related to the Loch Ness monster. They call her Ollie and sometimes she snarfs up a slow-moving gopher for a tasty snack."

Riley muttered, "Uh-huh."

"The cabins blend nicely into the landscape because they are painted fuchsia."

"Hmmm."

"Oh, and the valley is inhabited by aliens. One of them is named Paul and sometimes he likes to go on trail rides with the guests. He's kind of rude though, and the horses don't like him."

"Huh?" Riley took his attention from the road momentarily to look at me. "Paul? Who is he? What are you talking about?"

"I'm making stuff up because you aren't listening. What are you thinking so hard about?"

"Nothing."

"When you say nothing, it's always something."

Riley sighed. "Jeez, I hate it when you get like this."

"Like what?"

"Interrogate-y."

"That's not a word and you know it. If I talk about sea serpents and aliens I expect a response. What are you thinking about?"

"Just something Mel said."

"Your lawyer? I thought he said he was going to get numbers for private investigators so we can get set up with someone."

"He is."

"Then what's the problem?"

"I have to call Erin. She got wind of the whole, 'Riley is dead' thing and she's pissed off about it."

Even though I was amused, I tried to keep a straight face and sound serious. "Discovering your very-much-alive boyfriend is lying about being deceased might make a girl a little cranky."

"Apparently she's been getting condolence cards."

I burst out laughing and covered my mouth in an effort to contain myself. "Sorry, but I can't believe you didn't tell her before. And come on, that's funny."

He glanced at me with a half smile, "Yeah, it might be a little funny, particularly if you knew Erin."

"You need to call her, you know."

"I know. But she's going to lay into me something fierce. It's going to be nasty."

"Well, you do kind of deserve it."

"I suppose I do."

~

Ellensburg, Washington is located in the Kittitas Valley, which is bordered by the Cascade Mountains on the west and the Columbia River on the east. The town itself had only about fifteen-thousand residents, so Riley and I were unlikely to be affected by radiation. Never before had I been so concerned about metropolitan demographics, but now it was a big deal and I was likely to become a walking encyclopedia of trivia related to small western towns. In addition to the low local population density, we were going to be slightly north of Ellensburg at the ranch, which, according to the brochure, didn't have much technology at all.

During the Misty Meadow remodel, they'd added telephone lines to the cabins, but that had been the only concession to modern communication. It was unlikely that I'd be able to find a dial-up number to get online, so I wasn't going to be getting another seven-hundred new emails during our stay.

After a stop at the grocery store in town for celebratory birthday-dinner makings and cake, we made our way to the ranch, which was marked by a freshly painted sign with a horse on it. Riley turned down a long driveway that led through a valley surrounded by green hills. The ranch was situated along a river and consisted of a large log lodge surrounded by a cluster of seven log cabins. Horses grazed in a vast pasture that stretched along the length of the valley, which was verdant with early spring grass.

I pointed at the red metal roofs dotting the valley in front of us. "Check out how cute the cabins are!"

Riley parked in front of the lodge, got out, and disappeared through the huge wooden door to check in. I unhooked Zelda's seatbelt and she rested her chin on my seat while I idly ran my fingers down the soft fur of her snout. The dog's stomach made a few gurgly sounds and I turned around. "Are you okay, Zee?"

Zelda wagged halfheartedly, but the expression on her face was a bit anxious, so I clipped on her leash and we exited the Mustang quickly. Zelda dragged me over to a majestic ponderosa pine and daintily perched herself behind a shrub before assuming the position.

When she was done, Zelda launched away from her foul creation, yanking the leash out of my hand. She hauled across the green field, leaped back into the Mustang, and sat proudly, waiting for me to catch up.

The door of the lodge opened and Riley came back outside. When he got into the car, the expression on his face when Zelda give his ear a slurp made me giggle.

I pointed at the dog as I walked up. "Zee feels a whole lot better now. Be glad you missed it."

"Believe me, I am. I've seen the results of her indiscriminate consumption before." Riley handed me a big metal key and a loaf of bread. "We're in cabin number seven on the end."

I sniffed the bread. "Is this banana bread? Yum."

"It is. And, uh, if Marge or Ron asks, you're Mrs. O'Shea."

"*What?*"

"She wanted your name and when I told her, she gave me the sideways evil eye and made a comment about sinful behavior. Religious pictures, wall hangings, and symbols are hanging all over that lodge. I'm surprised I didn't burst into flames for being a heathen the moment I walked through the door. So I choked."

"What do you mean you *choked?*"

"I said that we just got married, and I forgot that now you're now Meg O'Shea."

"Seriously? I can't believe you."

"Hey, she was giving me the third degree." He pointed at the bread in my lap. "After I came up with that pathetic excuse, she gave us baked goods because she was thrilled that it's your birthday *and* our honeymoon."

"For the record, when I get married, I'm not changing my name. But I'm all for free food. And, Mr. Pants on Fire, I won't reveal your fib if you don't."

"Not going to happen."

Riley parked the car in front of the cabin and we went through the unloading process. The cabin was just as adorable as it appeared in the shiny brochure photos, complete with one of Marge's colorful quilts on the bed.

Riley dropped a suitcase on the floor. "I'll call Mel and then start on dinner."

I clapped my hands quickly. "I'm excited about a meal that doesn't come from a microwave."

"By the way, Ron wants to know if you want to go on a trail ride tomorrow."

"That would be fun. Are you willing to go?"

"I don't know how to ride."

"That doesn't matter. Trail horses just follow each other, so all you have to do is sit there."

Riley made a non-committal face and I dropped the subject. With a little persuasion, he'd probably go riding and maybe even have fun. He still was in a weird mood, so I left the decision for later.

After we unpacked, Riley called and left a message for his lawyer because Mel wasn't at work. Riley hung up the phone and stared at it. "That's weird. Mel never takes vacations."

I set my romance novel aside. "It's kind of late. Maybe he took the afternoon off. He could be living it up at Friday afternoon happy hour, for all we know."

"Mel never does that. Never. He's a workaholic."

"He'll probably call back."

"I suppose. Half the time he works on the weekends."

I returned to my book while Riley busied himself doing mysterious cooking things with an array of healthy vegetables. When it comes to kitchen activities, it's usually a good idea for me to stay far away.

The phone rang on the table next to my chair and the jarring noise breaking the silence just about gave me a heart attack. I set the book aside and picked it up. A voice said, "Mrs. O'Shea?"

"Um…yes, okay. That's me."

"This is Marge in the lodge. I have someone on the line here who wants to speak to your husband. May I put her through?"

My mind raced. If it wasn't the lawyer, who was it? "That's fine. Thank you."

"By the way, congratulations! It will be just one second, dear. This system is new and I need to make sure I press the right button."

"Thanks." I held out the receiver toward Riley. "It's for you."

He set down the knife, wiped his hand on the towel, and I whispered, "Marge said it's a woman, so it's not Mel."

He paused for a moment and took the phone from my hand. "Hello? Oh, uh, hi. Yes, well, I…no. That's not…well no."

I raised my eyebrows and Riley waved a hand and turned away from me. "No. Could you please let me finish?"

I was pretty sure he was talking to Erin. Most of the other conversations I'd overheard had been equally one-sided. Riley's girlfriend was one heck of a talker. But what did you expect if you dated a lawyer? I picked up my novel and feigned being casual instead of overtly eavesdropping. But who was I kidding? I was dying of curiosity and there was nowhere in the little cabin for me to go.

Riley said, "Erin, stop. Just stop, would you? Obviously I'm not dead and I am not married to Meg either. Could you please let me explain?"

Zelda came over looking concerned and I stroked her head. Leaning down, I whispered into her ear, "I think your dad might be in trouble with his girlfriend."

Zelda wagged enthusiastically, which probably wasn't the most sympathetic response to the situation, but maybe she knew something I didn't.

"No! I told you before. We're trying to find our parents." Riley ran his fingers though his hair, yanking at the knots and said emphatically, "Will you just let that go for once?

And, no. I haven't cut my hair either. I suppose that's a major problem too?"

Zelda whined and Riley gave her a quick glance. He sat down on the sofa, set his elbow on the end table, and rested his chin in his palm so he could settle into listening. I could hear only the faint sound of female anger, but not the specifics. Apparently Erin had a lot to say and she was putting it all out there.

I smiled weakly and Riley rolled his eyes at me. Zelda snuggled closer to my leg and I ruffled her ears. "It's okay, Zee."

Finally, the voice at the other end seemed to run out of steam and Riley said, "Are you done now? Yes, I think that's a good idea. Goodbye."

He hung up the phone and dropped his face into his palms. I got up and sat next to him on the couch. "Are you okay?"

He rubbed his face a few times, then lifted his head and stared straight ahead. "That was horrible. But I think the question of whether or not we're getting together again is not much of a question anymore."

"I'm sorry."

He stood up without saying anything and returned to the kitchen. I followed him. "Do you want to talk about it?"

"Not really." He whacked a carrot with the knife and the sound echoed through the quiet cabin.

"Hey, watch out for your fingers. This is supposed to be a vegetarian meal."

Riley laughed, set down the knife, and faced me. "Maybe we should have some of that chocolate cake first."

"Now you're talking! I was kidding about the aliens, but the weird things that have happened to us are proof that life is unpredictable. So I say eat the chocolate cake while you can." I reached out and gave him a quick hug. "But maybe I should slice it."

"Good idea."

~

After we ate our slices of cake, Riley returned to cooking. My slice had been more of a slab, so I was riding a sugar high. Feeling the need to move around, I decided it was time to explore our new digs more thoroughly. The cabin had a small bedroom connected to the large open space that housed the kitchen and the living room area, which had a comfy reading chair, a coffee table, end table, and sofa. The kitchen had a small two-person table, and above the main room was a loft with another sleeping area.

Riley had agreed to sleep in the loft, but I wanted to see the view from above, so I climbed the ladder and poked around. In addition to Riley's stuff strewn everywhere, there was a small dresser and a bookshelf with a pile of board games stacked on it.

I grabbed a box and went back down the ladder into the kitchen. "Check it out!"

"I haven't seen that in a long time."

"After we eat, I challenge thee to a duel of words!"

"Playing Scrabble doesn't seem like your style."

"*Au contraire mon frère!* I'm going to slaughter you mercilessly."

"Don't look so smug." Riley pointed his spatula at me. "I'm a better speller than you might think."

"I was a reporter, remember? And an English major. I shall slay you with my enormous vocabulary and command of language."

Riley smiled and shook his head, but I could tell that he was still thinking about the call with Erin. Although he tended not to talk about things that bothered him, he had expressive eyes. Because of our shared experiences, particularly my disturbing hallucinations, I'd seen concern or fear in his eyes quite a few times. But the hurt in his gaze now was new, and I wondered what Erin had said to make him so miserable. He was obviously beating himself up about something, and since he wouldn't talk about the conversation, being trounced by me in Scrabble would be a great way to take his mind off it.

Unfortunately, my nefarious plan didn't start off particularly well. Riley took the first turn and played the word "jousted." He hit the double-letter square with the "j" for an initial score of twenty-three. The pink star square doubled it, so it was forty-six, plus fifty points for using all his tiles.

An initial score of one hundred and six was going to be difficult to overcome and my letters were total crap. I put an "o" below the "d" and smiled weakly.

Riley pulled tiles out of the bag and glanced at my feeble effort. "*Do.* That's all you've got? Are you sure you've played this game before?"

"Shut up and slap some letters onto that board."

"I'm thinking." He moved a fistful of tiles above the "e" to spell out "aerie."

"Are you just throwing vowels around on the board and hoping I won't notice?"

"It's a word! An aerie is a nest located on a cliff or other high location. Like for an eagle or a hawk."

"Too bad I got rid of my "d" so I could spell out murder."

"You're just pissed that I'm going to slaughter you mercilessly. Shut up and play."

My letters remained crap and somehow I managed to lose more egregiously than I'd ever lost at Scrabble in my entire life. It was an utterly humiliating defeat, culminated by the word "zax." I suggested vehemently that maybe Riley was making up the term, but he insisted that zax is a word used to describe a tool for cutting and punching nail holes in roofing slates. Even though it's only three letters, it's worth nineteen points. When he plopped that baby on a triple word score, that fifty seven points pretty much doomed me.

Fortunately, witnessing my agony of Scrabble defeat did put Riley in a better mood and he agreed to join me for a horseback ride in the morning. It was my birthday, after all, and I wanted to revel in the lack of road time and hallucinations for an entire day of recreation and scrumptious eating.

The next morning, I exited my cozy cabin bedroom and staggered out into the kitchen for coffee.

Riley looked up from his laptop screen with a quizzical expression. "Wow, what did you dream about?"

I could feel the heat rising on my cheeks, but said evenly. "I don't remember."

"Oh yes you do." With a smug smile, he pushed the laptop forward and crossed his arms, resting them on the table. "Zelda and I have a pretty good idea too."

"That's none of your business."

"You dreamed about Lars, didn't you? I'm thinking you had a really good time. Care to share any of the sordid details?"

I poured myself a cup of coffee. Riley wasn't wrong. I'd had a lovely night full of enjoyable dreams that involved Lars. The guy was even hotter in my imagination. I turned around to face Riley. "What I dream about is not your concern."

"Way to start your birthday off with a bang."

"Stop sniff-spying on my pheromones. It's creepy." I grabbed a kitchen towel and threw it at Riley. "I'm going to take a shower."

"You might want to make it a cold one. Unlike people, pheromones don't lie."

While I was dealing with my morning routine, Riley made breakfast. After we ate, he took Zelda for a walk and then we got ready for the trail ride.

Because trail horses tend to just plod along, you have lots of time to think. Ron wasn't much of a talker, and he led the way, speaking only occasionally to warn us about low-hanging branches or obstacles. For the most part we were quiet, listening to the crunch of hooves on the twigs and leaves on the trail.

Given the recent stresses in my life with automotive sabotage, attacks, and scary visions, I was relieved to have a day to relax. But I felt wary, like I was waiting for the other shoe to drop, so it was difficult to completely let go of my anxieties.

Even though he'd never done it before, Riley had no problem horseback riding, probably because he's tall. I'm not, and my dismount after the ride was anything but graceful. I was wearing a t-shirt and when I threw my leg over to slide down off the horse, somehow I managed to hook my shirt on the saddle horn. My descent was abruptly halted and I ended up hanging off the side of the horse with my t-shirt attached to the horn. I flailed a little, but I couldn't get back up, and I couldn't get down either.

I yelped for help, but I didn't want to get too animated and scare the horse. When it was apparent that I really couldn't do anything about my predicament, Ron and Riley came over to evaluate.

Ron said, "Well, that's quite a pickle you've gotten yourself into there, young lady."

I flapped my arms helplessly. "Please get me down."

Riley grabbed me around my legs and held me up while Ron disentangled my t-shirt from the saddle horn. Riley lowered me to the ground and didn't say anything, but I could tell he was having trouble keeping a straight face.

The whole thing was more than a little embarrassing, since it wasn't like I did anything acrobatic, dramatic, or even dangerous, like falling off the horse. I was just dismounting, which normally isn't particularly interesting. I don't understand why some things are so much more difficult for me than they are for other people. Thank goodness I was wearing a pretty bra.

We unsaddled the horses and I thanked Ron for the ride and his assistance. I patted my horse, Pancho, and although my valiant steed seemed more concerned about returning to his pasture, he'd been extremely tolerant, even when I was hanging off his side like a trout on a stringer. I wished him better luck with future riders.

Riley and I stopped by the lodge to check for messages, and then slowly strolled back to our cabin. Horseback riding reminded me why cowboys are bowlegged. Many of the muscles in the lower half of my body hurt in unusual places.

I said, "Thanks for letting us have a day off from the road."

"It wasn't hard to convince me. I'm a little concerned that Mel still hasn't called me back though."

"Did Erin say where he was?"

"No, but she was busy yelling at me. I'd feel better if we had the name of a private investigator."

"Well, we can go back to the original plan of finding the place where Lars used to work. I'm sure Mel will call with the information eventually."

"I hope so. It bugs me that he's out of contact. You don't know him, but believe me, that *never* happens."

"The guy might have a life. Even lawyers have to have fun sometimes. Maybe he has a hot date or something."

"Unlikely. His work is his life. And he knows an awful lot about what's going on. He set up the corporation and knows you're the one writing all that stuff on the web site."

"Are you worried something happened to him?"

"I didn't go through all those emails, but what you're writing is controversial and he never has disappeared like this before."

"I suppose, but we agreed that we need to publicize what's going on. The truth has to be told. Did Erin say something to you that you're not telling me?"

"She said lots of things, but it was all about me, not Mel."

"See what happens when you lie?"

"Yeah, yeah, I know."

"You're pretty cranky for a dead guy, you know."

Chapter 8

Learning Experience

W hen we returned to the cabin, Zelda cavorted around us in unadulterated glee. The great thing about hanging out with a dog is that you can be sure that someone is always glad to see you when you get home. Even during our worst moments on this trip, Zelda's zest for life never failed to improve my mood.

Riley grabbed the leash and took Zelda for an afternoon walk while I settled in with my laptop. I kept thinking that Hector and the Enviro Freedom people might be related, but I couldn't figure out how. Maybe they were completely separate. Even enemies. I had no clue. After staring at my notes and getting nowhere, I gave up and returned to my romance novel. Dealing with serious matters could wait until tomorrow.

Riley cooked up the last of the food, and when we returned to the road the next morning I was feeling downright healthy. The good food, fresh air, and exercise was restorative and I was dreading hitting the big city and feeling crummy again. Even thinking that was odd, given that I'd always considered myself a city girl. Maybe I could become a city girl again if everyone decided that the convenience of cellular phones was overrated. But somehow I didn't see that happening.

Interstate 90 from Ellensburg to Seattle takes you over the Cascade Mountains through Snoqualmie Pass. It's a beautiful drive through miles of gorgeous evergreen forest. We ascended into the heavily vegetated area and I was surprised to find that snow was still on the ground at the higher elevations near the ski resort at the summit of the pass. I'm not a big fan of winter in general and I doubted anyone except the most die-hard skiers wanted to see snow in late April.

On the western side of the pass, it started to drizzle and Riley put the convertible top up. Western Washington is incredibly green and the increasingly soggy weather gave me a good idea why. If you're a plant, all that rain is fantastic. For the rest of us, it's mostly just dreary.

After a couple of hours of driving, we hit the legendary Seattle traffic, and I felt the first twinge of pain in my temple. Riley had the unhappy pinched expression he got when he wasn't feeling great, so it wasn't just me. We'd probably gone by a cell tower somewhere. How depressing.

We didn't really know where we were going in Seattle, so we opted for a Motel 6 in Issaquah near Lake Sammamish, which is on the far eastern side of the city. After we checked in and unloaded, Riley wanted to take off for a walk at Lake Sammamish State Park, which was fairly close to the motel.

He clipped the leash onto Zelda's collar. "You ready?"

"I want to go check my email now that we have a connection."

"Zee needs a walk."

I sat down at the desk in front of my laptop and waved my hands in a shooing motion. "You can go. But you have to log into the server for me first."

"I'm not leaving you here alone."

"Oh please. It will be fine. Nothing's going to happen."

"I know you're not feeling good."

"I'm fine. We're about as close to being in Seattle as we can get without really being in the depths of the city."

"Well, there must be radiation. You're anxious because you think you might have a hallucination."

I stomped across the room to stand in front of Riley and stared up into his face. "No, I'm not. Don't treat me like a child."

Zelda whined and Riley looked down at her, then back at me. "Then don't lie to me. Pheromones aren't the only hormones I can smell. Anger and stress cause hormones to be released too. I don't know exactly what they are. Cortisol maybe? The name doesn't matter. What matters is that I isolated the different scents, so I can tell when you're stressed. You were fine back at the cabin, but here you're not."

"I don't believe this." I flopped my arms in exasperation. "Fine. Let's go for a walk. But what about you and your special need for alone time?"

"I'm going to have to get over it."

I yanked my raincoat off the chair and pulled it on. "It's not like I'm going to go running into traffic every time you aren't standing right next to me."

"You did the last time." Riley grabbed the room key and opened the door for me.

"You can't babysit me every moment of every day."

"I'm going to have to until we get out of the city again."

"This is ridiculous." I crossed my arms in front of me and splashed through a puddle. "And just so you know, I'm not up for walking miles in this rain."

"You could stand the exercise."

I didn't respond, preferring to sulk in silence for a while. The idea of having Riley more or less supervising my every move made my skin itch. It had been difficult enough to adjust to traveling with him. I'd more or less dealt with the lack of privacy, but we'd also spent time apart while he was out walking or doing things with the car. That space did us both a lot of good, and I liked the time I spent lounging around by myself. Being shackled to Riley every moment could drive both of us insane.

Riley's ability to smell my emotional state was disconcerting. Talk about having no secrets. I felt exposed and suffocated at the same time and I didn't like it. How was I supposed to live like this? There had to be a compromise we could come up with to work around this situation, so we didn't end up like two rats in a cage, destined to bite and claw each other for escape.

Riley and Zelda abruptly turned around, and I followed them, continuing to fester with my unhappy thoughts of being trapped with my stepbrother forever. And then extrapolating on that idea, how was I ever going to have a relationship with a guy again? *Oh by the way, Mr. Hunky Dude, I need to be watched closely because I tend to have these little hallucinations where I go play in the road.* I was destined to be dateless and alone forever.

Riley opened the door to the motel room and toweled off Zelda, who shook herself multiple times and then curled up on the floor to finish drying off. The rain was making everyone grumpy.

Before I could ask, Riley grabbed my laptop and logged into the server. He then disappeared into the bathroom to take a shower, probably because the bathroom was the last bastion of personal space. I settled in at the desk to face the task of going through the email messages, which now numbered eight hundred and sixty-four. This was going to take a while. I rested my chin on my palm and clicked the mouse with the other hand.

The first email had a subject line of "Get a larger rod!" and I was guessing this wasn't going to contain useful information for me. Delete. I waded through a few more emails that promoted various types of illegal drugs. Not interesting. Delete. Then I discovered I might be the recipient of sixty-four million dollars from a prince in Nigeria. Delete. The next subject line told me I could "Cheat at gardening today!" Okay, I had to know. How do you cheat at gardening? Is it possible to deceive plants? Sadly, the email didn't say. Delete.

By the time Riley finished showering and returned to the room, I'd gone through about fifty emails. The tedious process became more so as I became familiar with the spam emails *du jour*. Was anyone really stupid enough to fall for this dreck?

I clicked the mouse and scanned the next email, which definitely wasn't spam. I sat up straight. "Riley, you need to look at this one."

He leaned over my shoulder. "That's disturbingly familiar."

"This guy says he started having problems six months ago. Now he's on disability. I don't know what to say to him. It's not like I have any advice. Our lives fell to crap too."

Riley sat down on the end of the bed. "We should think about how we should reply before you send anything."

"We need a support group for people whose lives have been turned upside down by bizarre sensory problems. Specialists Anonymous. I feel terrible for this person."

Not sure what else to do, I deleted a few more spam emails. "Here's one from someone who says she knows about Enviro Freedom. She thinks it's in Florida."

Riley flopped back down on the bed with his arms spread wide. "You have *got* to be kidding me. That's three-thousand miles from here."

"I don't think we should believe everything we read." I spent more time deleting spam and a few emails from people calling me rather rude names because they liked their cell phones. Sheesh. A few people said I was crazy and making stuff up. A couple of creepers wanted to know what I looked like, particularly as far as specific areas of my anatomy. One guy said that he applauded what we were doing because he had broken his leg. I wasn't quite sure how that related to anything, but he was adamant about it.

I slumped down in the chair again, wading through more virtual vitriol, and getting increasingly depressed about my decision to write anything public. Most people didn't care about the truth. They believed what they wanted to believe.

I'd always trusted in the power of the media to expose corruption and conspiracy and taken for granted that quality investigative journalism was a good thing. Being the intrepid journalist doggedly pursuing the trail of wrongdoing had been a part of my identity for my entire adult life. But maybe I'd been wrong. Perhaps it was time to think about doing something else.

I clicked on the next email, which said, "I know who you are. And next time, I won't let you get away." I rose from the chair, stepped backward, and pointed at the laptop. "I found another one you need to look at, Riley."

He got up and leaned over the desk. "I think you made an impression on Helen in the short time you were acquainted."

"I don't want to go through any more of these right now. Let's go see if we can find the real estate office where Lars worked."

"All right. I'll try calling Mel again, and then we can go." He put his hand on my shoulder. "If she were following us, I think we'd know by now."

"Would we?" I shook my head. "I'm scared again."

"I know."

And the most irritating thing was, he probably did.

~

On the drive to the real estate office, I decided it was time to address the problem that was bugging both of us. "What are we going to do about me?"

"What do you mean?"

"You've gotten to the point where you can sniff my moods. On the one hand, it's freaky and weird, but on the other hand, it could be useful. Can you tell when I'm about to go running into traffic?"

"I wasn't close to you when you did, so I don't know."

"But could you?"

"Maybe." He glanced at me. "Probably."

"How?"

"I'm slowly starting to be able to isolate and identify what I'm smelling. It's been a long process of elimination and evaluation. And in cities, it's more difficult. Everything is too muddled together. It's too much to take in all at once."

"Maybe you're learning how, though. Do you think you can tell when I'm about to have a vision?"

"I think so. I'm sure Zelda knows."

I turned around to look at her. "I think you're right. She always makes an rrr-ing noise or barks."

"Her brain was already wired to notice. Mine is still working on it."

I put my hand on his forearm. "Could you tell it to hurry up? And if you think I'm about to melt down while we're at this real estate office, please get me out of there."

"Will do."

We spent a lot of time sitting in traffic because that's what you do in Seattle, but at least it wasn't rush hour, so it could have been worse. After driving around several city blocks, we found the real estate office and a legal parking spot. We left Zelda to guard the Mustang and walked down the street to Chambray Realty.

The office was located in a nondescript commercial building with large windows filled with photos of pretty Northwest homes. We went in and were greeted by a young woman who had long black hair and wore a black pantsuit. The heavy black frames of her glasses were perched in front of eyes, which were coated with far too much eyeliner. She would probably look more or less the same in a black-and-white photo as she did in living color.

I handed her Lars's business card. "I'm trying to find out if you know this person."

"Oh…Lars." She gave me a dreamy smile, and I had a feeling I knew why.

Riley said, "We're trying to find Lars Lindeman. When was the last time you saw him?"

"He left maybe six months ago. Do you know where he went?"

"No, but I was hoping you might," I said.

Ms. Black and White frowned. "We really miss him around here."

I didn't want to tell her that the last time I saw him he was a clown, so I said evenly, "I do too."

"She really does," Riley added.

I paused to give him a glare and said, "Did you know Lars well when he was here in Seattle?"

"We worked together. Sometimes he brought his little boy, Nils. I used to give Nils crayons, and he would color for hours."

I decided to dig a little deeper. "So did you see Lars outside of work?"

The woman's expression clouded. "Why are you asking me these questions? Is Lars in trouble?"

"I hope not," I said.

She folded her hands on the desk primly. "I didn't know him outside of work or socially. He's one of many agents who work out of this office."

"Is there anyone here who knew him?" I asked. "Friends? Family?"

"I don't feel comfortable with all these questions." The woman pushed her heavy glasses up on her nose. "Do you know where Lars is? Are you with the police?"

"No, but like I said, we're trying to find him."

"Why?"

"It's a long story," Riley said and put his hand on my arm. "We appreciate any information you have."

She returned the business card to me. "I don't know anything."

Riley said, "Thanks for your time."

We left the building and I turned to Riley. "What's your problem? I wasn't done asking her questions."

"You were upsetting that woman and not getting anywhere."

"I was getting into the flow of the interrogation."

"She didn't know anything. And you said to get you out of there if you were going to melt down."

"Was I?"

"I'm not sure, but I thought it would be best to err on the side of caution."

"I suppose you're right." An ambulance siren wailed and a white vehicle with lights flashing roared by us. I squeezed my eyes shut and slapped my hands against my temples. "Oh crap. Not now."

I could sense my legs crumpling under me and a blue light surrounded me. Through the mist of blue, I saw a hand reach out and I heard my mother's voice say, "Be with your friend."

I shook my head, opened my eyes, and Riley's arms were wrapped around me. We were both sitting on the sidewalk and I heard a man's voice above us say, "Is she okay?"

As he dragged me upright, Riley said, "It's fine."

I shook my head again and thanked the man for his concern. "I forgot to take my meds this morning."

Riley finally let me go and I said, "I think your brain just had an opportunity for a new learning experience."

"Are you all right?"

"I'm in the gray phase now." The intense colors had faded and the hallucination hangover had ensued, so everything was dim and washed out.

"Did you see anything?"

"Just blue light and then my mother saying, 'Be with your friend,' but I don't know what that means. Thanks Mom. Way to be cryptic. *Again*."

Riley grinned. "Lars is your friend. In fact, he's even more than a friend. Maybe that means we're on the right track."

"Who knows? Let's go back to the motel. I need chocolate."

It seemed to take forever to get back out to Issaquah, and I spent most of the ride with my eyes closed, trying not to think about how I couldn't go anywhere. I was losing my independence, trapped by visions I couldn't control. I wanted to cry or scream in frustration.

The car stopped, and I opened my eyes.

Riley said, "Rise and shine, sunshine. Your chocolate awaits."

"I wasn't sleeping."

He paused before opening the door. "You're all right, aren't you?"

"I'm not having a vision, if that's what you mean." I got out of the car and flipped the seat forward to let Zelda out.

We went into the motel room and Zelda zipped around in circles and jumped up onto Riley's bed. He sat down next to her, picked up the dog brush from the nightstand, and ran it across her back with long strokes. "Is something bothering you?"

I grabbed a Hershey's Kiss from a bag and popped it into my mouth. "Nothing. And everything. I don't know. I'm confused."

"About what?"

"How am I ever going to be able to have a normal life again?"

"I'd suggest not living in LA or Seattle, for one thing."

I sat down on the bed. "I'm serious. Reading through all those emails made me realize no one wants to hear what I'm writing about here. People want their cell phones, and the market is poised to explode. What happens ten years from now? Or twenty? In 2017, there will be no getting away from the radiation anywhere. There will be cell towers on even the remotest desert islands."

"I don't know what to tell you. Lacking a crystal ball, I can't predict the future. But technology is going to march on."

"Whether we want it to or not."

~

By the next morning, my angst about the future had subsided somewhat. After we took Zelda out for a walk, I felt like I could face reading through more email. While I did that, Riley tried calling his lawyer a few more times to no avail. Now I was starting to feel antsy that he hadn't heard anything from the elusive Mel.

In addition to the spam and the emails from lonely whackos, I ran across an interesting email from someone who installed cable for Archetypal Online Systems. He said that there were "aspects" of the company that bothered him, and I was curious to know more. I still hadn't responded to any of the emails though. It was a daunting task, and I figured I'd sort through everything first, and then reply later after I'd collected my thoughts. Okay, I was procrastinating. I had no idea what to say to these people. I didn't have any answers for my own problems, so who was I to give advice?

Riley grabbed the plastic ice bucket and held it up. "I'll be right back."

"I'll be reading vital communiqués from people with names like Burley Hobbes about vigor, enlargement, and hoses."

While I waded through the email messages, Zelda paced around the room. Then she sat next to me and put her muzzle on my leg. "Hi Zee. I have no food. Sorry. Why don't you go lie down?"

Outside, a siren wailed and I recalled the ambulance that had zoomed by right before my vision. It was encouraging to know that Seattle had such responsive emergency services. Zelda whined and I ruffled her ears. "You don't like sirens, huh? Yeah, me neither."

Zelda yanked her head out from under my hand and ran toward the door. She turned around to stare at me for a moment before pawing at the bottom of the door.

"Hey! What are you doing? You'll tear the carpet." I got up and grabbed her leash. "Couldn't you have taken care of this earlier? We just took you for a long walk."

Zelda yanked on the leash and barked at me when I went to grab the room key. I opened the door and she barreled outside. I whacked my hand on the door jamb and yelped at the pain on my knuckles, but managed to not release my grasp on the leash. "Zelda, *stop it!*" I dragged the door closed behind me and tripped and stumbled after Zelda, who was making a beeline for the motel lobby.

A crowd of people were clustered near a big red rescue-squad rig. That explained the siren. What was going on?

A paramedic closed the ambulance doors and when it drove off Zelda began barking furiously. She leaped around me, practically hog-tying my legs with her leash. I struggled to get control of her and moved closer to a woman who had been standing near the action. I tapped her shoulder. "What happened?"

"A guy collapsed over near the ice machine."

Time stopped for a moment and I asked, "What did he look like?"

"Really tall and skinny. Long hair."

I closed my eyes and took a breath to tamp down my panic and strangled a scream. "Do you know where they took him?"

"Harborview."

I dragged Zelda back to the room and slammed the door behind us. Tears were streaming down my face as I grabbed the Seattle map, the keys, and Riley's wallet. I threw them into my tote bag and paused in front of the phone. The number for Mel's office was sitting on a notepad. As if in a dream, I watched myself pick up the handset and dial.

Before the receptionist at the answering service could finish speaking, I said. "My name is Meg Jennings and I'm a friend of Riley O'Shea's who is a client of Elmer Flood. Mel knows who I am. Whenever he comes back, tell him that Riley has been taken to Harborview Medical Center in Seattle. I'm going there now. I...I...don't know if he's okay.

Or not. Or if he has insurance. Or anything. I just…I don't know."

The woman made a few reassuring noises, but I hung up the phone before she could finish her sentence.

Zelda and I ran to the Mustang. I opened the car door and she jumped across to the passenger seat. Almost without thinking I turned the key in the ignition, punched in the special security code to start it, and rammed it into gear with a horrible grinding that would have made Riley cringe. We screamed out of the parking lot toward the highway.

Late Monday morning is not perhaps the best time to be speeding on Interstate 90, because traffic still stinks even after what might officially be considered rush hour. I wove around semis and motor homes, flagrantly exceeding the posted speed limit wherever I could. Somehow I knew which way to weave through the pattern of cars, as if I were looking at a maze from above. Twenty-two surreal minutes later, I drove into the vast hospital complex, wound around through the network of buildings, and drove by the emergency-room entrance a couple times.

Finally I found a parking garage that was fairly near the emergency drop off and parked the Mustang. I put my shaky hand on Zelda's head. "Zee, I'm sorry, but you can't come with me. You have to stay here. Guard Shelby, okay?"

Zelda sat down with a resigned look as I closed the door to the Mustang. At least I knew the car would be safe. I dashed through the garage and ran out into the rain toward the emergency room. I went up to the huge wooden reception kiosk that was crowded with nurses, doctors, and patients.

I hate hospitals. The last time I'd even been close to one had been in Ely, Nevada, when we took Dean into the small rural hospital to be checked out after he'd been drugged. The massive Seattle medical center was like a different world, although the dove-gray flooring and bright lights were similar. It had the same pale color scheme that every medical facility seemed to share, as if shades of pukey pastels might make you feel better.

I shoved aside a nurse and slapped my palms on the counter. "I need to find a patient who was just brought here."

The nurse behind the counter had her long dark-blonde hair pulled back in a ponytail and it swished over her shoulder as she turned to me. "Name?"

I gave her the details and waited while she tapped her fingers on her keyboard. It felt like an eternity before she finally said, "Yes. He's here."

"Where?"

"They're running tests. Are you his wife?"

"No. I'm um, his sister." Well sort of. Maybe. "What kind of tests?"

She peered at the screen. "It appears he was brought in for a possible cardiac episode."

"*What?* You mean he had a heart attack?"

"I didn't say that. Please take a seat and I'll let you know when I have more information."

I clutched the handle of my tote bag and twisted my fingers around the canvas. Riley was too young to have a heart attack. He'd been fine this morning. Okay, maybe I hadn't seen him eat recently, but that wasn't unusual. You're not supposed to *die* on a trip to get ice from the ice machine.

I sat down in a chair and stared at the doors that led back to the emergency room as if they could tell me whether or not Riley was still alive. But the doors swung quietly as people passed through, revealing no answers. I leaned forward, put my forehead on my knees, and wrapped my arms around my legs, quietly sobbing into my jeans.

At a tap on my shoulder I sat up, and the woman from the front desk sat down in the chair next to me. She handed me a clipboard and a pen. "Could you fill this out for me?"

I wiped my eyes and gazed down at the paper. "Do you know if he's okay?"

"Not yet. We'll know more soon."

I tried to pull myself together, but the words on the form kept blurring and I had trouble writing. I reached down and pulled Riley's wallet out of my bag.

I flipped through the wallet and smiled at the horrible driver's license photo. What a dreadful mug shot. It belatedly occurred to me that driving had been a dangerous thing for me to do, given my visions. The only time Riley had ever let me drive his car, we'd been in the middle of nowhere.

Even though we'd spent so much time on the road together, it felt like a violation to be pawing through Riley's wallet like this. I wiped more tears from my eyes and pulled out his insurance card. With a sigh, I carefully wrote the numbers on the form.

I pulled a mini-package of Kleenex out of my bag and dabbed at the tears on the paper. Hospitals must get lots of smeared forms. After filling out what I could of the paperwork, I set the clipboard aside and fingered the beat-up old wallet again. The leather was soft and worn at the edges. I opened it and pulled out the plastic insert. Along with Riley's credit cards was a photo of a woman with long blonde hair.

So that's what Erin looked like. Wow. No wonder Riley had trouble saying goodbye to her.

Chapter 9

Observations

I returned the forms to the woman at the desk and sat in the waiting room, staring, thinking, and fretting for what seemed like hours, but probably wasn't. Time passed glacially, although the nurses scuttled around the desk like bees around a hive. The nurse with the long ponytail that I now thought of as "my" nurse left, presumably because her shift was over. I couldn't remember ever feeling more helpless and powerless to do anything. And poor Zelda was still sitting in the Mustang wondering what had happened to her human.

I pressed the tissue to my eyes again, trying not to think about Zee, Riley, or anything else. I'm terrible at waiting, so I finally got up and walked to the desk again. I leaned toward the nurse. "Please! You have got to tell me what's going on."

I provided Riley's name, my name, and my relationship yet again, and begged a little more for someone to tell me something. After studying the computer monitor, the nurse said. "We're keeping him overnight for observation."

"Does that mean I can see him?"

"Room 1321. Go down that hallway."

I would have cried with happiness if I'd had any tears left, but I was completely cried out. I thanked her and ran in the direction she'd indicated, only slowing to note the room numbers as I hurried down the long corridor.

I found 1321 and tapped on the partially open door before charging in. Riley was lying in a beige hospital bed wired up to lots of scary monitors and gizmos. He was glaring at a woman who appeared to be taking his pulse.

They both looked at me in surprise as I burst into their field of vision. I almost fainted with relief to see that Riley appeared to be as healthy as he had been this morning and even looked the same, with the exception of the hospital gown and the medical technology.

I said breathlessly, "You're alive!"

"Of course I'm alive," Riley said.

The nurse wrote something on a chart and said, "I'll see you in an hour."

Riley rolled his eyes. "Can't wait."

I threw myself over the bed railing to hug Riley. "I thought you were dead."

"I'm fine, Meg. It's no big deal."

I stood up. "They hauled you off in an ambulance. In my world, that's a big deal. What happened? When I got here, they said you had a heart attack. I thought you were dead."

"I didn't have a heart attack. I felt really weird, and then I guess I passed out. Someone called 911."

"So you didn't have a cardiac episode?"

"Not exactly."

"Well then *what* exactly? Why did you pass out?" I grabbed his hand. "Did one of Hector's people drug you? Did you get attacked?"

He shook his head. "I don't think it was anything like that. Because I'm, well, you know, really thin, the entire medical community thinks I have heart problems. It can be a side effect of anorexia."

I sat down in the chair next to the bed but didn't let go of his hand. "So do you have heart problems? And you didn't answer my question. Why did you pass out?"

Riley slumped down on the bed. "It's probably a symptom."

"A symptom of what?"

"When I was in the hospital before, I think I told you I had every test imaginable."

"Yes. You said it was horrible."

"It was. And because of the whole not-eating problem, they paid special attention to my heart. In general, my heart is still working fine, but I found out I have a genetic disorder called Wolff-Parkinson-White syndrome."

"Wolf, what?"

"It means I have an extra electrical pathway in my heart. You can live your whole life and never have any symptoms at all. I never did. The only reason I found out is because they did so many tests on me. My heart rhythm appears different on an electrocardiogram than most people's do."

"Is passing out a symptom of this thing?"

"Sometimes."

"And you never mentioned this before? What are the other symptoms?"

"Dizziness, rapid heartbeat. Sudden death is a not-so-good one."

I let go of his hand and leaned closer toward his face. "You're saying you could just drop dead and you didn't bother to tell me?"

"I've never had any symptoms before. Maybe if I had, I'd have had the surgery to fix it." He gestured toward the room. "But the last time I was trapped in a hospital like this, I thought I was going to die anyway, so why bother?"

"There's a surgery?"

"I guess I might think about it now." He sat up again and clasped his hands together, almost as if he were praying. "When we were in Alpine Grove and then staying at that ranch, I felt better than I have in months. It gave me hope. Like maybe I could manage my sensory problems and live reasonably normally again."

"Assuming you don't drop dead, of course." All the stress and emotions of the past few hours overwhelmed me and I flopped forward to sob into my jeans again. Apparently I wasn't cried out after all.

I felt Riley's hand on my back and he said, "Meg, come on. Don't do that."

I took a deep breath, sat up, and wiped my eyes with my fingertips. "Only if you promise not to do *this* again, okay?"

"I'll try not to. I want to get out of here."

I wiped my eyes and made an effort to regain composure for the ninety-fifth time. "They said you have to stay overnight."

"I know. It's ridiculous, because I know what happened and I'm not going to have a heart attack."

"Please don't." I glanced toward the window. "God, Zelda is still in the car. I need to let her out."

"You *drove* here? Are you completely insane?"

"Don't freak out. Your car is fine."

"Don't you realize what could have happened? You *know* you shouldn't drive."

A nurse walked in and put her hands on her hips. "I think Mr. O'Shea needs to rest."

Riley said, "My friend has no way to get back to her motel."

"Yes, I do."

"No, you don't." He gave the nurse a plaintive look. "Could you call a cab or something?"

"I need one that's willing to have a very hairy dog in it."

The nurse furrowed her brow. "A dog?"

"The dog is waiting for me in the car at the parking garage." I pointed at Riley. "Mr. O'Shea is clearly feeling much better. I can tell because he doesn't want me near his precious automobile."

"Hey, you were the one who said you didn't want me to have a heart attack."

"That's not funny."

He smiled. "Oh, come on. It's a little funny."

I leaned over the rail, gave him a hug, and whispered. "No. It's *really* not." I stood and turned to pick up my tote bag. "Tomorrow I'll return in another expensive cab to check you out of here."

I left the room and walked through the rain back to the parking garage to collect Zelda. As I anticipated, Zelda was standing in the driver's seat of the Mustang wagging her tail at me furiously when I walked up. I let her out and enjoyed a little canine affection and exuberance before we went back outside to wait for the cab.

I tilted my face toward the slate-gray sky and let the rain wash the salty tears from my face. What an awful day. I was emotionally wrung out and felt like I could sleep for a week. The cab ride back to the motel was a blur and by the time we returned to our room, it was all I could do to feed Zelda and then crawl into bed.

Zelda curled up by my side and I snuggled up close so I could pet her warm fur. I put my arm across her back and related the events of the day. I explained that her favorite human was going to be fine, but she needed to keep a close eye on him from now on.

Okay, maybe talking to a dog was a little odd, but it seemed like she understood. After I finished unburdening myself, Zelda squeezed her eyes shut and began snoring quietly. She was probably exhausted from worry too. Tomorrow had to be a better day. It couldn't be much worse.

~

I woke with a start at the sensation of something cold and wet in my ear. I opened my eyes and Zelda had her face approximately three inches from mine, panting expectantly. Yuck. Dog breath. Normally, she harassed Riley who would get up and took her outside, but in his absence, I was chief doggie walker and caretaker. I pushed Zelda's nose away, rolled over, and snuggled back under the sheet, evaluating my physical and mental condition. Even though I'd slept like the dead, I still felt drained, depressed, and stuffy from crying.

Zelda licked my ear again and I slowly dragged myself out of bed and into the bathroom to deal with the morning routine. She danced around the room while I yanked on my jeans and a sweater. I grabbed my raincoat and the room key and slogged out into the rain with Zelda. Unlike me, she was wide awake and eager to get on with her morning constitutional, charging toward the state park.

The humid air was so thick, it was as if I were walking through a cloud with mist swirling around me. Almost immediately, my thin sweater felt clammy and my hair clung to my face from the ambient moisture. The vegetation was lush and the air was filled with the scents of energetic new growth. Spring in Seattle was like walking through a gigantic greenhouse.

Zelda was enjoying herself, but getting drenched. Her normally fluffy fur was flat from the rain. It was going to take hours for her to dry off, and I was getting cold. Even though the air temperature wasn't particularly low, the dampness was unrelenting, giving me a bone-deep chill.

We returned to the room and I toweled off Zelda. After I took a restorative hot shower, we both had something to eat. I sat on the bed and leaned down to rub her ears. "Okay Zee, I have to tell you something you're not going to like. You have to stay here."

Zelda offered a tentative wag and I continued, "You need to be good. Just take a nap and don't eat the room, okay? I'll be back soon with Riley. Cross my heart."

When the cab honked outside the room, I reiterated my plea to Zelda to behave herself and closed the door behind me, trying not to think about all the damage she could do if she set her mind to it. Zelda had never been destructive, but Riley had always been around. I wasn't convinced that Zelda considered me the caliber of human that merited good canine behavior.

I shook off my concerns and got into the cab. Whatever was going to happen would happen and Riley would have to deal with it. At the hospital, I checked in and went down the corridor to Riley's room.

I was about to charge through the doorway when I stopped short at the sight of a tall blonde woman. I backed up. What was Erin doing here? She was leaning over the bed and Riley had his palm on Erin's cheek. He had a look of such complete adoration that I had to turn away. It was certainly not an expression I'd ever seen on his face before.

I whirled from the doorway and scuttled down the hall before anyone could see me. This was one of those private moments that should remain private. I wasn't sure what to do, but there was no way I was barging in there. Lacking any other plan, I continued down the hallway to a row of chairs near a nurse's station and sat down.

A burly nurse wearing a uniform that was a couple of sizes too small paused in front of me. She bore a disturbing resemblance to the woman who played Nurse Ratched in *One Flew Over the Cuckoo's Nest*. She glared down at me and asked in a curt voice, "Are you trying to find someone?"

I pointed at the room. "I'm supposed to pick up the patient in room 1321, but he has a visitor. I, uh, didn't want to interrupt, so I thought I'd wait out here for a minute."

Without further comment, she marched down the corridor to the room. Oops. Maybe I'd gotten Riley in trouble with Nurse Ratched. A few minutes later, she emerged with Riley in a wheelchair, followed by Erin. I stood up and smiled uncertainly.

Riley lifted a palm in greeting, introduced me to Erin, and grumbled. "This is stupid. I can walk."

Nurse Ratched wasn't having any of it, and I wasn't going to argue with her. Erin probably knew whatever the legal reason was for wheeling people out of hospitals and didn't comment either. After Riley filled out all his paperwork and was cleared to go, an orderly wheeled him outside under the overhang, and he finally stood up.

I gestured toward the rainy street. "The car is in the parking garage over there."

Erin said, "I'm staying at the Hilton."

"I could drop you off," Riley said. "Maybe we could…"

Erin interrupted him. "I can take a cab. I have work to do and I have to book my flight back to LA."

Riley glanced at me, and then turned back to Erin. "But we still need to talk about…"

"You know I'm busy," Erin said.

I waved my hands to enter the conversation. "I need to get back. Zelda could be eating up half the room by now, for all we know." I didn't want to get in the middle of whatever their discussion was about because I very much did *not* want to know. "I can drive myself."

Riley said, "You're not driving. I'll drop you at the motel."

Erin stared off into the distance, indifferent to the proceedings. So far I wasn't too impressed with Riley's girlfriend. Or ex-girlfriend. Whatever her status, the woman was oddly remote. Maybe she was thinking deep lawyerly thoughts, but she seemed emotionless and detached from what was going on.

She'd barely acknowledged my existence, which was also sort of strange, given how she'd reacted on the phone when I'd been dubbed Mrs. O'Shea. Up until now, most of my exposure to her had been the muffled sounds of her angry voice yelling at Riley through the telephone. Maybe she'd taken a fistful of Quaaludes or something.

The only thing that was clear to me was that Riley was still crazy in love with her, so maybe she'd been upset when she found out he was in the hospital. She had flown a long way to see him, after all, so she must still care. As we approached the Mustang, I gave myself a mental head shake. None of this was any of my business.

Whatever Riley and Erin needed to talk about, they obviously didn't want to discuss it in front of me, so the ride to the Motel 6 was silent and awkward. Relegated to the back seat without a furry canine copilot to keep me company, I stared out the window, watching the rain and endless traffic go by. Finally we got to the motel and Riley got out so I could extract myself from the back of the car.

I could hear Zelda barking and I turned to go to the room. He grabbed my arm before I could rush to the door. "Are you going to be all right? I probably shouldn't be leaving you here by yourself."

"It's fine. You were gone last night, remember? Somehow I managed to cope and I'm sure Zelda will keep an eye on me." I yanked my arm away, and shoved a clump of rain-soaked hair off my face. "Try not to have a heart attack, okay?"

He narrowed his eyes and said evenly. "I'll be back in a little while."

"I'll walk your dog." I stalked to the door and slammed it behind me, furious, but not entirely sure why. Zelda leaped around me, thrilled to have me back. I crouched down and ruffled her ears. "I'm sorry I didn't return your human to you like I said I would. He says he'll be back later. I'm sure she misses you."

I leashed Zelda and we went back out into the rain, heading for the park again. Although exercise was not my preferred solution for much of anything, it did feel good to get outside. I couldn't figure out why I was so angry at Riley. He didn't ask to go to the hospital, but nonetheless I was royally pissed off and confused. Maybe I was just jealous that he had a girlfriend. Must be nice to have someone love you. Not to mention sex. I wouldn't have to worry about Riley sniffing out my pheromones, because eventually they'd just shrivel up and die from lack of use.

My personal pity party slithered downhill from there, but Zelda didn't seem to notice. She was thrilled at all the fragrances emanating from the vegetation. Even I could smell the flowers, but she probably was delighting in all the hormones, emotions, and critter leavings that I couldn't smell. I was missing out on an entirely different aromatic world, but I was okay with that. Given Riley's experience, having a super sense of smell didn't sound like a whole lot of fun most of the time.

By the time Zelda and I returned to the motel, I was starving and she was soaked again. I toweled her off and proceeded to consume most of the snack food we had on hand to the point that I felt somewhat ill. I opened up the laptop and stared at emails for a while until I got too discouraged. I'd had enough of hospitals, cold damp weather, spam, and weirdos, so I curled up on my bed with my novel.

I shot upright at the sound of Zelda's sharp bark and her launch off the bed toward the door. I rubbed my eyes and pulled the covers around me. Riley was crouching down and petting Zelda, who was sniffing at him madly and lapping up all the love and attention she could get.

I glanced at the clock. I'd been asleep for hours. The unaccustomed exercise of walking Zee was rough on the ole body. "Welcome back."

"Thanks. Jeez Zee, stop snuffling me." Riley moved Zelda's nose aside so he could sit down on his bed. He leaned forward and rested his elbow on his knees. "So, um, I need to talk to you."

A little prickle of anxiety skittered across my chest. The expression on his face led me to suspect I wasn't going to like whatever he had to say.

Chapter 10

Secrecy Factor

Riley clasped his hands together and said, "It's about Erin."

He had really long fingers and I had a sudden flash of recognition. My eyes widened. "Your hand was in my vision."

"What?"

"I told you that there was blue light and my mom said, "Be with your friend," but there was also a hand reaching out toward me. I'm sure it was your hand."

Riley turned his palms up and gazed down at them. "I have no idea what that might mean."

"Me neither."

"So anyway, about Erin."

"She was, um, nice." More like distant and snooty, but I wasn't going to say that out loud. I had ample proof that criticizing someone's significant other could ruin a friendship. Not going there.

"She probably was distracted because she's worried about Mel."

"Well, she did have a bad day. Her colleague disappears and her boyfriend is hospitalized. It was sweet that she flew up here to see you."

"She wouldn't have known if you hadn't called." Riley shoved Zelda's nose away from his jeans. "Give it a rest, Zee. Yes, my pants went to the hospital too."

"Maybe she's entertaining herself with a few of those fun-lovin' sex hormones."

Riley pulled his legs up onto the bed, away from Zelda. "Very funny."

"I'm betting that the Hilton has nice fluffy pillows." I made an effort to plump up the flat pillow and rearrange it behind my head. "I miss that. How much would it cost to provide pillows that aren't pancakes?"

"What I'm trying to tell you is that I explained what's going on to Erin. She knew some of it, but not everything. We also talked about Mel's disappearance."

"If he's really MIA, do you think it's related to our parents? Or Hector? Enviro Freedom? Maybe something we haven't thought of yet."

"I don't know, but that's why I told her everything. She's worked with Mel for years and he's never left without a word like this before. While I was there, she called the office and asked Mel's secretary to see if there were any notes about private investigators on his desk. There wasn't anything."

"When is she going back to LA?"

"I think she's probably on a plane by now. I dropped her at the airport and she was going to change her flight."

It was none of my business and I paused for a moment, trying to decide if I was going to be nosy or not. Who was I kidding? Nosy won out every time. "How come she changed it?"

Riley ran his fingers along his temples and back through his hair. "Probably because I'm still me."

"What's that supposed to mean? Of course, you're you. I assume that's a good thing, since you and Erin have been together for years." I turned to readjust my crappy pillow again. "Well, except until a couple days ago, I suppose. But I figured that blew over since she bothered to come all the way to Seattle to see you. You don't do that for someone you don't care about."

Riley leaned back against the headboard and closed his eyes. "I don't really want to go into it."

"I do."

He opened his eyes. "What?"

"I saw you."

"What are you talking about?"

I sat up, pulled my knees up to my chest, and wrapped my arms around my legs. "At the hospital, I saw the way you looked at her. I'd have to be blind not to see that you're totally in love with that woman."

"It doesn't matter."

"Of course it *matters*. No one has ever looked at me like that. I *wish* someone would look at me like that." I unwrapped my arms from my legs and slapped my palms on the bed. "Heck, right now, I'd settle for a date."

Riley smiled. "I'm sure that will happen at some point. Maybe we'll run across Lars again."

"Nice try, but I'm not falling for that diversion. You didn't answer my question. Why did Erin change her flight back to LA?"

"Ugh, why do you always feel compelled to interrogate me about stuff like this?"

"Because you won't answer simple questions. 'I'm still me' is not an answer."

"Fine. She left because we agreed we have no future together."

"But you love her!"

"So what? Even if I ever find my dad and manage to get healthy enough again so I don't repulse her physically, I'd have to live in the middle of nowhere. Erin is a successful lawyer and she has no interest in living someplace a million miles away from civilization."

"Neither do I. But I'm going to have to."

Riley closed his eyes and threw his arm over them. "Happy now?"

Truth be told, I wasn't happy. His story was also my story. I'd had bleak thoughts about my future too, but it never involved having to give up someone I loved. Sometimes interrogation leads to truths you'd rather not face.

After an extended pause, I cleared my throat. "So while we're discussing depressing topics, there's something else I was wondering about."

"Great."

"Is your will updated so I can take Zelda if something happens to you?"

Riley groaned. "Not as far as I know."

"Could you deal with that? I don't want Zee to end up, well, I don't know where, but it might not be good."

"If Mel ever turns up, I'll talk to him about it again."

I got up, walked to Riley's bed, and sat down. He moved his arm away from his face and raised his eyebrows at me in query. I picked up his hand off the bed and held it. "You could have died and I was, um, really upset."

"I know." He squeezed my palm. "I'm sorry about that. Now you know how I felt when you ran into traffic."

"I suppose so." I stared down at our hands and my hair flopped in front of my face. "I've never had anyone really close to me die, like friends or family. And you're sort of both. I mean, I didn't know my grandparents well. My dad disappeared, but I don't know if he's dead or alive. And as far as I know, my mother is still alive."

"We hope so, anyway."

"I guess what I'm saying is that even with all the uncertainty with my parents, I've never had to face sudden death before. When they took you off in that ambulance, I was a mess."

Riley didn't say anything, but he put his other hand on top of mine.

I pushed my hair behind my ear. "This is going to sound stupid, but when I thought you were dead, it hurt. I mean, it physically hurt—there was this pain in my chest. As if heartache were a real thing. Is it?"

"I think it might be, so I'd really appreciate it if you could stay out of the road. I've got enough heart problems as it is."

"Sorry, but heart-attack humor isn't funny yet. It's going to take me a while."

"I'm fine, Meg. I mean it." He gripped my hands tightly, then let go and got up off the bed. Zelda ran over and began snuffling his legs and feet again. "I need to find some quarters and do laundry. If I don't wash these jeans, Zelda is going to have a nervous breakdown."

I laughed. "Ah, if those jeans could talk. The stories they'd tell."

~

Thanks to a quiet evening of washing and folding clothes with no visions or health disasters, by the next morning I was ready to face the reality of our situation again. Sure, we'd made it to the Northwest, but we didn't know where the Enviro Freedom retreat was and our parents were still missing. So now what? The sad truth was I needed information. No more excuses and delays. I was determined to buckle down, do some research, make phone calls, and get answers.

I'd just sat down in front of my laptop at the desk when Riley snapped the leash on Zelda's collar and pointed at the door. "Let's go."

"Go where?"

"Outside."

"It's raining. Do we have to?"

"It's time to walk Zee, and you know you don't want me to be alone as much as I don't want you to be alone." Zelda wagged a few times in support of the concept.

Unfortunately I couldn't argue with that, so I slapped the laptop lid closed. Time to face reality. I couldn't ditch the marathon dog walks anymore. What a pain. My body tends to be against any form of exercise and remaining flabby is so much easier than having to exert myself.

I put on my sweater and sulkily joined the excursion into the not-so-great outdoors. Did people in Seattle ever see sunlight? Maybe they were like moles, with eyes that have adapted to see in the dim light that barely penetrates the monotonous gray cloud cover. A whisper of a breeze was blowing, which coupled with the rain and general dankness, made it seem far colder than the thermometer might indicate. I wanted the journey to be over faster than usual, so I could cuddle up in our room with my nice warm laptop.

After we returned, I sucked up my courage to call Rachel again. I had to find out more about the location of this retreat. It was out there somewhere and someone had to know where it was.

Much to my amazement, Rachel finally answered the phone. After failing to reach her for so long, I was so stunned that I stammered, "Rachel! It's Meg. I've been wanting to talk to you."

"Yes, I got your messages and I hope you realize you're being a pest."

"I told you why this is important. I'm still hoping that among your network of environmentally conscious peers, somebody knows where the Enviro Freedom retreat is. Did you ask around?"

Rachel sighed the sigh of the terribly put-upon and said, "I've been busy, but I did ask a couple of people. No one knows anything except that it's in the Northwest somewhere."

"I'm in Seattle now. Do you have any clue if it's nearby? Am I in the right state?"

"The nonprofit is incorporated in Washington, so you might be."

I already knew that from my research at the library in Sacramento, but I attempted a few more questions and got nowhere. Finally I said, "Okay, you've given me a place to start. Thanks for your help."

I hung up and typed a couple of notes into my laptop while explaining to Riley what Rachel had said. When he didn't respond, I turned around. He was slumped down in the pillows with his eyes were closed. Was he okay? I ran over to the bed and shook him hard. "Wake up!"

Riley opened his eyes wide and yanked off a headset. "Jeez, what's your problem? I'm listening to music. What is it?"

"We need to find a big library with access to Washington state databases."

"All right."

I evaluated Riley's appearance more closely. He looked terrible and the dark circles under his eyes were more pronounced again. "Are you feeling okay? When did you last eat something?"

Zelda started dancing around the room as Riley got off his bed. "Don't be a nag. I'm just tired from being poked, prodded, and tested."

"We need to go to the store and get more food too." I sat down at the desk again. "But first I need to stop by my fave Kiss fan sites and message boards. One sec."

I clicked through my online haunts, trying to find an indication that the Specter of Hector had finally gotten a gig and might be playing somewhere. I raised my hands in a touchdown maneuver. "Hector is in Washington State!"

"Where?"

I pulled the map off the desk. "How far away is Olympia?"

"It's south of here, but with the traffic, it could take a while to get there."

"Road trip!"

"Are you sure you want to do this?" Riley shrugged. "I mean, we've been avoiding these guys, and a concert, with the noise and flashing lights, could trigger a vision."

"If we still believe my visions mean something, I need to have one. The last one was short and told me exactly nothing. Maybe it will make sense if something explains why your hand was there. Are you the friend? I don't know. We need answers, and if you hang on to me I should be fine."

Riley looked unconvinced, but didn't say anything.

I said, "Hey, maybe Lars is still with Hector. Somehow he's connected, and I want to talk to him."

"Yeah right. You just want to *talk*."

"Get your mind out of the gutter. We're stuck. If Lars is there, maybe he can give us clues or information. Or maybe I'll have a vision that will tell us something. I don't know. But we have to do *something*."

"I suppose, but this feels like a wild-goose chase."

"Maybe it is, but I want to rock and roll all night!"

Riley laughed. "Is this because you're partying every day?"

"No, I'm not, and maybe that's the problem."

We went back out into the rain and trekked off to the University of Washington, which had a number of libraries for me to explore. The trip entailed dealing with multiple traffic-clogged freeways, which wasn't much fun, particularly since the rain had gained enthusiasm. So far, the rhythmic thwack-thwack of the windshield wipers had been a constant beat in the soundtrack of my Seattle visit.

Riley was unwilling to let me wander the campus alone, so we left Zelda to watch over the Mustang in a parking garage and we walked to the information center in the main library. The University of Washington campus is manicured and green with students scurrying around everywhere. I probably would have enjoyed it more if I hadn't felt like the oldest person in the vicinity and it hadn't been pouring, but such is life.

Riley seemed equally subdued by the gray weather and probably from feeling crummy, so he was largely silent while I was schmoozing. I talked to several university librarians in my quest for information about Enviro Freedom. As I suspected, they had access to spiffy databases and were able to dredge up more information. I learned about the organization's history, mission, and goals, board of directors, and even a few financial statistics. Nothing stood out as unusual. I didn't recognize the names and the mission statement was useless. The group aspired to "significantly improve the environment." Well, duh. I could have figured that out.

What I didn't find out was the location of the mysterious retreat. The lack of information about Enviro Freedom in the press was a little strange too. How can a nonprofit get donations if no one knows it exists? The whole secrecy factor struck me as odd.

After I'd exhausted the UW resources and Riley's patience, we ambled back across the campus to the parking garage. Then we hit the road again, taking Interstate 5 south toward Olympia.

I began whining for food somewhere near the Kent-Des Moines exit. Who knew there is a Des Moines in Washington too? My nagging perseverance prevailed and Riley finally agreed to get off the highway and stop at a deli somewhere in Tacoma. While I pigged out, Riley let Zelda out and walked her around for a few minutes so she could take care of some post-napping business.

According to the Kiss fan online scuttlebutt, Hector was going to be playing at a place called The Rusty Pail. One guy had posted, "Don't worry that it looks like a warehouse on the outside. It is a warehouse, so it looks like that on the inside too." After digesting that pearl of wisdom, I opted to dress down for the occasion.

It took a long time to locate the Rusty Pail, which was not in one of the nicer parts of town. The industrial area was filled with warehouses, so figuring out which one was a nightclub proved to be difficult.

Riley was losing his sense of humor about driving, but finally I said, "Hey, that guy over there is wearing makeup. There's a sign down that alley. I think that's it."

After more circling, we found a parking space and I told Zelda to bite anyone who got near the car. The Mustang still had the obnoxious alarm, but Riley had done something to it so he could adjust the sensitivity. Zelda wouldn't appreciate it if the stupid thing went off while she was inside.

We followed a group of people down the rain-slicked alley to a massive metal warehouse. Two blue Porta-Potties were sitting in an oily puddle not too far from the door, and a line of people waited to use the plastic facilities. We walked into the building, which resembled an empty Costco with huge metal industrial shelving that had been shoved off to one side and a wooden makeshift stage at the far end, opposite the door.

A small crowd was starting to form in front of the stage and a few roadies wandered around, running wires and setting up amplifiers.

I took Riley's hand. "I don't think Hector is getting paid enough to play here."

"You're scraping the bottom of the barrel when you have to play gigs at venues that don't have indoor plumbing."

I dragged Riley toward the stage. "Let's see if we can find Lars."

The crowd was congregating quickly and as we approached the stage, a screeching noise blasted out of the amplifiers. Riley and I slapped our hands over our ears simultaneously at the horrifying excuse for a chord.

When the noise stopped, I dropped my arms to my side and reached out for Riley's hand, clutching it tightly. He seemed just as alarmed by the painful attempt at music as I was. This did not bode well for the upcoming performance.

A motley group of men strolled out onto the stage. They were wearing huge plastic boots and their thumps echoed around the room as they stomped across the wooden planks.

I said, "They look like Klingons having a fashion disaster."

"Klingons wouldn't be caught dead wearing that makeup. I can't imagine that pudgy guy over there swinging a bat'leth, either."

"I think that's Hector. We saw him on TV and in the flyer, but they must have done some retouching on the photo. Seeing Hector in makeup dressed like Lieutenant Worf is grotesque. I'm a little embarrassed for him."

The four men were all clad in bulky leather costumes with studded collars. The shortest guy, the one that I thought was Hector, was also wearing a gold vest and matching set of gold plastic knee pads, which didn't add to the ensemble. Another man had silver spikes attached to his vest, which exposed a bear rug of chest hair. Ewww.

They picked up their guitars and as the first strains of Hector crooning "I was made for loving you" came from the speakers, I covered my ears because it was immediately apparent that all of the performers were completely tone deaf. The Specter of Hector sounded like a group of wailing weasels that couldn't carry a tune. It was agonizing, but in true Kiss fashion, Hector still went in for a lot of tongue action that was appalling to witness.

There was a small break in the heavy metal action when Hector's wig fell off. Undaunted, he turned around, took a long drink from a flask, put the wig back on, and started playing again. Because the show must go on.

Unfortunately.

~

The noise from the show was almost unbearable and I waved at Riley, signaling my desire to leave. My ears needed a break. He nodded his agreement, and we turned and hustled toward the exit.

A crowd of people was milling around out near the Porta–Potties, where it was quieter, albeit smellier. I grabbed Riley's arm. "Let's look around for Lars. If I had to be involved with this show, I'd want to be outside while they're performing."

He tugged me away from the plastic outhouses. "I vote we start over there."

We walked down the alley toward people who were clustered in small groups, standing around and chatting. It was dark and the rain had turned into a cloying drizzly mist that wrapped us like a cloak. The street was slickly shiny in the dim streetlights and I tried to inconspicuously examine people's faces as we walked by. I didn't see anyone familiar, which was discouraging. Riley was right. We were wandering around an industrial area in Olympia, Washington, of all places. How could this exercise possibly be useful?

I was also distressed to note that the twinge at my temple was turning into a full-fledged headache. Odds were good that it was just a standard music-induced headache, though, and not the beginning of a hallucination.

Headlights flashed as a car turned to park on a street near the alleyway. Something brushed against my arm and I started in surprise. I turned to see what had touched me, and there was a golden glow around the silhouette of a man moving through the misty gloom. Suddenly disoriented, I spun around. Riley had been walking right next to me, but he was gone.

The glow from the headlights illuminated the face of the man, and I smiled when I realized it was Lars. I held out my hand. "I've been trying to find you."

He moved back from me, and I said, "No, don't go. You *can't* go. I need to talk to you!"

The man disappeared and was replaced by a blue glow. I squeezed my eyes shut, trying to clear my vision and when I opened them, I was slumped on the ground with Riley's arms around me. He put his palm on my cheek, "Meg? Come on, you need to wake up. Please?"

I sat up straight and looked into his eyes. "You really can't take me anywhere, can you?"

Riley took my hand and pulled me up so I was standing. "You'd think I'd be used to it by now, but it freaks me out every single time you do this."

A familiar, slightly accented voice from behind us said, "Excuse me, but are you injured?"

I turned and Lars was there. I reached out to put my hand on his arm to verify he was real and jerked it back at the bizarre effect of touching him. "You're here. *Really* here!"

"You are Meg, I believe?"

I put my hand on my chest. "Yes, it's me! We met at the circus. Briefly." I could tell the color was rising on my cheeks. How mortifying. Good thing it was dark. I pointed toward Riley. "And this is my friend, Riley. He talked with you at the circus too."

Riley said, "Are you with the band playing here?"

"I am involved with the Specter of Hector show, yes," Lars replied.

"Why?" I blurted out. "Why do you stay with Hector? I don't understand why you're traveling with him. I saw your photo in the paper when the circus trailers were blown up. And your son was with you."

Lars was momentarily taken aback by my outburst, then said, "My son is not your concern."

"I'm sorry, but we have to know why you're here. Hector has something on you, doesn't he? Is he blackmailing you? Why did they take Dean and drug him? We *have* to know," I said.

Lars glanced back toward the warehouse. He gestured toward the street, in the other direction. "All right, I will tell you. But let us go over there, away from potential listeners."

Riley leaned down toward me and whispered, "Are you sure you're all right?"

I nodded, grabbed his hand, and followed Lars. "Let the interrogation begin."

Lars stopped at the corner and turned to face me and Riley. "What is it that you want to know?"

"At the circus, we asked you about my mother and Riley's father, but you said you hadn't seen them. Do you remember?"

Lars moved his shoulders in a halfhearted shrug. "Yes, but I still have never met the people you described. I'm sorry."

I waved dismissively. "Never mind. I didn't think you'd seen them, but how about this? Dean was captured and drugged. He was at Hector's circus. You must have known that. Where were they taking him and why?"

"There was a location in Los Angeles where he was to be dropped off," Lars said.

"Why aren't you there? Why weren't you drugged?" I demanded. I pointed at him. "I know you used to be a real estate agent. You have a sensory, well, *issue* related to touch, don't you?"

"Yes, that is true. It began last year and caused problems in my personal life," Lars said with resignation. "It was complicated, particularly with my wife."

"You're *married*?" I said, perhaps a little too shrilly.

Riley put his hand on my arm, "Why is Hector taking people like you and Dean?"

"He has an agreement with a company that wants to understand more about those of us with special 'issues,' as you call it."

"How did you get involved?" I asked.

Lars slumped against the wall and gazed down the alley. "My wife or actually my ex-wife. She met some people and was talking about my problem. They found out about me because of her. She helped them kidnap me and I was drugged like Dean."

"Well you're obviously fine now. Where is she?" I asked.

"She left me. But my son was there when they took me, and I convinced them to go back and get him. Nils is not her son, and I said I'd do whatever they want as long as he remained safe with me."

"Have you ever heard of a group called Enviro Freedom?" Riley asked.

"They are involved in the bombings," Lars replied. "Or I believe so. There have been many rumors and now I am worried about Nils's safety. I may have made a terrible mistake bringing him into this, but I was afraid to lose him."

That explained the photo. "I'm sorry. We think they may have taken our parents too."

Riley said, "We've heard that our parents are at a retreat somewhere. Do you know where it is?"

"Only rumors. It is deep in a forest somewhere." He moved his broad shoulders again. "I am sorry that I don't know more."

Lars seemed so sad that I wanted to give him a hug, but I knew better. "Is there any way we can help you?"

"I am worried about my son's safety now because of the bombings. But I know that the kidnappers Hector employs are not gentle either."

I nodded. "I don't like those guys."

Lars continued, "Nils was happy with the circus. It was like an adventure for him. But now…"

I took a risk at touching him and put my hand on his arm. The sensation made me smile involuntarily. Wow. "I know. Is there anything we can do to help? Riley and I, well, it turns out that we were able to get Dean away from Hector. He's free again. We helped him find his girlfriend too. Right now they're in Las Vegas getting married."

Riley nodded. "Can you get your son and come with us? You've probably noticed that when you're away from the city, you feel better."

Lars looked surprised. "Yes, I do. How did you know?"

"It's electromagnetic radiation." I said. At Lars's blank expression, I added. "Cell phones are evil. I'm serious. You don't want one."

Riley gestured toward the warehouse. "Can you get your son? My car isn't too far away. We can get you out of here."

"The Mustang goes really fast," I added.

Lars smiled in obvious relief. "I will return in five minutes. Please stay right here."

He ran down the alley toward the warehouse and I blinked a few droplets of misty dampness from my eyelashes. I gave Riley a friendly nudge. "I know you think I'm biased, but I think we're doing the right thing."

"I hope you're right, and your boyfriend isn't about to drag us into a huge mess."

"He's not my boyfriend." Well, at least not yet. If my dreams were any indication, a private interlude with the luscious Lars would be pleasurable. I glanced at Riley, who gave me a smug smile. Apparently my limbic system was giving me away again. How annoying. A girl couldn't have a single private secret fantasy with Mr. Olfactory Mind Reader around.

~

Riley nudged me and I turned around to see Lars hustling down the alley with a young boy in tow. The child was clutching a grayish stuffed animal in his arms.

I smiled as they walked up, then crouched down and held out my hand. "You must be Nils. I'm Meg."

Nils moved his stuffed animal under his arm and gave me a shy handshake. "It's very nice to meet you ma'am."

I let go of his hand and flexed my fingers. Nothing. Maybe Nils hadn't inherited any touch sensitivity from his father. I'd be delighted to find out the problem didn't have a genetic component. But I couldn't think of anything else that would explain the random nature of it. Why were we affected when the rest of the world could be around radiation with no problem?

Riley gestured in the direction of the Mustang. "The car is over there. Let's get out of here."

When we got to the car, Zelda was standing up barking at us and Riley waved at her to stop. I really needed to get him to teach me the hand signals he used with Zee.

Nils let go of his father's hand and ran to the window waving his toy and exclaiming, "Look at the pretty dog!"

Fortunately, Riley clicked the remote to turn off the horrid car alarm before a noisy neighborhood incident ensued. He let Zelda out of the car and she zipped to a tiny scrubby patch of weeds, squatted, and ran back to reclaim her spot in the back seat.

Nils and I got in the back on either side of Zelda, and she gave the child's cheek a welcoming slurp. He giggled and ran his hand across her back as she settled in between us. His eyes widened as he proclaimed, "This dog has the softest fur in the world!"

He held the stuffed animal in front of Zelda so she could sniff it. "This is Dolly. She's a unicorn."

Zelda wagged a few times to show her appreciation for the scents clinging to the threadbare and now slightly damp toy. I leaned back in the seat, relieved to be sitting down. Interrogating Lars had distracted me from my typical post-hallucination low, but now all I wanted to do was take a nap. Zelda moved so she could set her muzzle on my thigh. Somehow she always knew when I was feeling rotten.

Those of us snoring in the back seat woke up when the car stopped. After using Zelda's plush hindquarters as a furry pillow, Nils sat up and yawned. The poor kid had probably had a long day too. At least he wouldn't be subjected to terrible renditions of Kiss songs anymore. Music performed that poorly might scar you for life.

It was going to be crowded in our tiny Motel 6 room, but while I was sleeping, Riley and Lars had apparently determined that it would be safest if we all stayed together.

Riley and I shared our stash of road food with Lars and Nils. The child parked himself on my bed with my box of illicit Cheez-Its. On our last trip to the grocery store I'd sneaked junk food into the cart while Riley wasn't paying attention. It was nice to have someone else around who shared my appreciation for salty faux-cheese snacks. Well, someone other than Zelda, who appreciated all forms of food, junk or otherwise.

As we ate and chatted, I couldn't stop thinking about Lars and his abilities. I still had questions, but he probably wouldn't want his son to overhear the answers. Riley was playing paper football at the tiny table with Nils. The pair slid the small triangle back and forth across the tabletop amid cheers and jeers for various brilliant or lame maneuvers.

I got up and handed Riley a sheet of notepad paper. "Maybe you can show Nils how to make his own football while I take Zee for a walk."

Riley stood up and said, "You're not going alone."

I pushed down on his shoulder to shove him back into the chair and widened my eyes in a silent theatrical 'shut up' admonishment. "Lars, would you come with me? I need to talk to you. Riley can watch Nils for a minute."

Lars set aside a can of mixed nuts, got up off the bed, and followed me. I clipped the leash onto Zelda's collar and we left the room.

Zelda started toward the path to the park, but I redirected her. "Sorry Zee, but we need to stay close to the room."

Zelda gave me a long-suffering look as if to say, "Give me a break," but I was adamant. Way too many people were after us, so caution was warranted. Presumably, by now Hector might have noticed that Lars and Nils had disappeared. We could only hope Hector's band of weirdos hadn't figured out that Lars was no longer in Olympia.

Lars and I stopped at a grassy area to wait for Zelda to complete a few complex sniffing machinations and Lars said, "What is it that you wish to discuss?"

"Do you know if your son has inherited your sensitivity?"

He shook his head. "I don't think that is the case. Nils seems the same as always. Even as my life...changed, he remained the same."

I smiled, "It could be worse. You could have screaming visions like I do. Or have trouble eating, like Riley."

"I would not wish my problem on anyone, particularly now. You mentioned that you feel worse in cities and Riley told me more about the radiation. It explains why I feel as I do, since we've been here in Seattle again." He folded his arms across his body. "It's difficult to describe, but it is like I want to escape my own skin. Imagine if there were insects crawling on you every time a whiff of a breeze hits your body."

"That would freak me out." I reached to put my hand on his arm in sympathy and he moved back, away from me. I waved my palm in innocent surrender. "It definitely wasn't like that when I saw you last time."

"At that time, we were at a rural fairground. When I touched people, the sensations were more intense than normal, but not bad. My situation was complicated by how others reacted."

I looked away, thinking about my own reaction. "Yes, I remember."

"These issues with touch destroyed my marriage."

"I'm sorry."

"I learned that the old saying about the fury of a woman scorned is quite accurate."

I surveyed his lovely honey-brown eyes that had so often played a role in my dreams. "I guess there's nothing you can do about that, but maybe you can use your abilities in some way. You could be one heck of a masseuse, for example. Although I guess the word is *masseur*, since you're male. Or maybe you could become a physical therapist. As long as you don't live in a big city, you could take advantage of your unique talents."

"In the car, Riley and I discussed what I might do next. I need to get far away from Hector. My extended family is large and I have cousins in Minnesota."

"You want to go to *Minnesota*?" My lustful Lars fantasies froze into a block of Midwestern ice.

"I have no driver's license. When I was taken, I left with nothing. I need to keep Nils safe, and your friend has very kindly offered to lend me money for travel. I have promised to pay him back."

"Don't worry too much about that. Riley can afford it."

"He said that, but I don't feel good about taking charity."

"Hey, you're not a charity. You're one of us." I took his hand and gave it a squeeze, relieved that he didn't pull away this time. "We specialists have to help each other out. You could end up working at a swanky high-end spa giving massages women would die for." I knew I'd be first in line.

Lars caressed my palm with his thumb in the same erotic way he had when we'd met at the circus. My response was predictable, and I wanted to jump on top of him, but I managed to control myself.

He tilted his head and looked down at Zelda, who was sitting quietly at our feet. "I hope you're correct and I can find a fulfilling life somewhere. I have been feeling somewhat hopeless."

"When I think too much about my future, it seems a little bleak too. At least you have family. When are you leaving for the Midwest?"

"Tomorrow."

Because I have no sense and the news was so sudden, I threw myself forward and wrapped my arms around him. Lars stepped backward, but put his arms around me to keep me from knocking him over. Zelda rrr-ed as she moved out of the line of fire. I said, "Tomorrow is too soon. I was hoping to get to know you better." And maybe rip off all his clothes.

His gaze locked on mine and he ran a soft fingertip across my jaw. He kissed me lightly on the lips and whispered, "Meg, you don't want to do this. You are not meant to be with me."

"I don't care."

"Yes, you do." He extricated himself from my embrace and stepped away. "I think the dog is ready to return."

My hormones weren't ready to return, but I acquiesced. Maybe someday I'd get some action again, but today was clearly not that day. My mood darkened further when I considered the teasing I was going to get from Riley about whatever he suspected I had been doing in the parking lot with Lars.

~

Lars and I returned to the room with Zelda, who leaped up onto Riley's bed, next to him. Nils had fallen asleep on what had been my bed, but was now his for the night.

Lars leaned over, tucked the little boy under the covers, and handed him his stuffed unicorn. I ventured to the bathroom for a moment alone. Four people and a dog in one tiny motel room makes for an awkward amount of closeness.

I brushed my teeth and got into my nightie. What a long weird day. I was so ready for it to be over. When I returned, Lars was curled up with Nils and Zelda was upside down and snoring at the foot of Riley's bed.

Riley was lying on his bed, still wearing the same clothes he'd been wearing all day. He set aside his book, patted the mattress, and got up. "I've got my sleeping bag. I'll sleep on the floor."

I sat down on the edge of the bed feeling awkward while Riley unrolled the sleeping bag. He still appeared to be exhausted. I leaned over to grab his hand and pull him toward me. "Are you feeling okay?"

"Stop asking me that. I'm just tired."

"Are you sleeping okay? Did you eat anything today?"

He ignored my comment, shook his hand free, and retreated to the bathroom. I shoved at Zelda with my foot and hissed, "You have to move. Sorry, but you're getting demoted to the floor."

Zelda gave me an indignant glare before daintily hopping off the bed and curling up on Riley's sleeping bag. When he came out of the bathroom, he glanced down at the dog and raised his eyebrows at me. I scooched myself toward the wall and tapped my fingers on the bedspread.

Riley sat down on the bed and I said, "I informed Zee that you outrank her."

Riley chuckled. "Thanks for enforcing pack hierarchy. Are you sure you're all right with this arrangement?"

"It's not that different." I closed my eyes and rolled over toward the wall. "Shut up and go to sleep."

When I woke up sometime in the middle of the night, I found myself wedged between the wall, Riley, and Zelda. At some point, the dog had concluded that the bed was much more comfortable than the floor, and her furry body was sprawled across my legs. I tried to move, but was trapped by the covers and Zelda. Riley grumbled something right next to my ear and I bolted upright. "Hey! Move over. You're invading my space."

Riley rolled onto his stomach and propped himself up on his elbows. He was still fully clothed, but extremely rumpled. He whispered, "Shhh, don't wake up the kid. *You* move over. There's all kinds of space next to you."

I kicked my feet to encourage Zelda to rearrange herself and rolled over to face Riley. I whispered, "Lars said you're giving him money for the train."

"I can afford it."

"I know. But that was still nice of you."

He rolled onto his side and slid his hand under his pillow. "I can be nice."

"I know." I pulled my hand out from under the covers and patted his cheek. In the dim light, the shadows emphasized the dark circles under his eyes. "I'm kind of worried about you. As your brother would say, you look like death, bro."

"Thank you. I love it when you quote Bubba."

"I'm just expressing sisterly concern for your well-being."

"We've found Lars, so I think it might be time to get out of Seattle and find this retreat."

"I can't believe he's leaving tomorrow."

Riley paused and I thought for sure he was busy thinking up a snotty comeback that related to sexy clowns, but he just closed his eyes and said softly, "I don't blame him for wanting to get on with his life."

The next morning my eyes flew open at the sound of little-boy laughter. I sat up and discovered that Nils and Zelda were on the floor. He was moving her ears around like satellite dishes and grinning. "You're like a polar bear, but with pointy ears!"

If Zelda had the ability to laugh, she probably would have been chuckling because she did seem amused by his attentions. Riley sat up, scrubbed his face with his palms a few times, and got out of bed. He grabbed Zelda's leash, clipped it onto her collar, and they went outside before I had the presence of mind to insist I join them.

I tried not to think about potential cardiac episodes while Nils told me a complicated story about polar bears, which I was able to only partially comprehend, given my sleepy, distracted, and uncaffeinated state. Much to my relief, Riley and Zelda returned unscathed a few minutes later and he started coffee. I badly needed an infusion of caffeine.

After Lars emerged from the bathroom, I staggered in to enjoy a few precious moments alone. There were far too many people in this room, not to mention an excess of testosterone. It had been well documented that Riley was a slob, but Nils was even worse. How could someone so small make such a mess in such a short time?

I felt better about life after I'd showered and had my coffee. When the phone rang, the sound was so jarring in the small space that everyone turned to stare at the nightstand.

I picked up the receiver and said "Hello." A male voice said, "Is this Meg? I'm trying to locate Riley."

I handed the phone to Riley. "For you."

I sat on the bed and didn't make even a cursory effort to pretend not to eavesdrop. Riley was being Mr. Man of Few Words, which made it difficult to tell what was going on, but I did gather that his lawyer had turned up and was purchasing train tickets, which could be picked up at King Street Station near downtown Seattle.

Riley hung up the phone and I raised my eyebrows at him. "Well?"

He gave the slightest shake of his head before crouching down in front of Nils, "Have you ever been on a train before?"

"I went on one at a fair," Nils said. "It just went in a circle, so it was boring. Those slow rides are for babies."

"Today you get to go on a train that's much bigger and you get to sleep on it. You have your own compartment with a bed and bathroom," Riley explained.

"Like an apartment on a train?" Nils said.

"Yup, and you get to see lots of the country out your window too. The Cascade Mountains, Glacier National Park, the Mississippi River, and other interesting places."

"Whoa." Nils ran over to his father and looked up. "This is going to be so cool!"

Getting four people ready to go anywhere when you have only one bathroom takes a while. After the protracted morning routine, we all tromped outside to take Zelda for a walk and get some lunch. Then Riley and I dropped Lars and Nils at the train station in Seattle.

Even though he probably didn't want me to, I gave Lars a big goodbye hug. "Please be safe. I'm going to miss you."

"And I, you." Lars turned to Riley. "I will pay you back."

Riley waved off the comment. "Not necessary, and I doubt you'll be able to find me anyway. Have a wonderful trip."

I said, "Riley might be hard to find, and if you hear something about him being dead, don't believe it."

Riley and I watched as Lars and Nils collected their tickets and went to wait for the Amtrak Empire Builder to arrive. We waved goodbye and strolled through the rain back to the Mustang. Was it ever sunny in Seattle? I was starting to wonder.

I gazed up at the clock tower. "Now that it's just us again, are you going to tell me what else you learned from Mel? I heard you ask him about train tickets, but before that, he had an awful lot to say. Where *was* he?"

"As it turns out, your new foray into online journalism is starting to upset people. Mel said that 'powerful people' started asking him a whole lot of questions he didn't want to answer. When they started making threats, he decided to take an unscheduled vacation."

I stopped and stared at him. "You can't be serious. Somebody is really that pissed off about what I wrote? Who?"

"Mel didn't want to say." Riley scowled. "This explanation for his so-called vacation bugs me, because Erin said something like 'Mel just got a windfall' as a possible reason he might have run off."

"A windfall? There's that word again. Leo got a windfall. Why is everyone suddenly in the money? And it was in my vision too. Flying folding chairs in the wind."

"I doubt this windfall means anything good. Maybe he got a windfall for providing information. Mel has access to some of my money, so he can do things like rent houses and buy train tickets for me."

"Wait! Are you saying his windfall is because he ran off with your millions of dollars? What is wrong with you? How can you just stand here being so calm?"

"Relax, Meg. I said *some* money. Not all of it. Do you really think I'd be that stupid? The money I got from selling my company is scattered in lots of places. Not all of it is even in this country."

I smiled. "I've heard Switzerland is nice. Or the Cayman Islands! Even better. Maybe they aren't embracing new technology yet."

"I'm more worried that Mel got a payoff from Hector and company for something."

"If so, we're screwed. He knows everything."

"I know. Worse, I might have to talk to Erin to find out what she meant by the term windfall."

I made a few clucking noises. "Don't be a chicken."

"Mel also mentioned that he found an investigator who did a little digging and learned that the Enviro Freedom retreat is somewhere in Whatcom County, Washington."

"Where the heck is that?"

"It's the northwest county in the state. On the coast, Bellingham and Birch Bay are in Whatcom County, but this guy thinks the retreat is inland from there, in the forest somewhere, so it's harder to find."

"Lars mentioned a forest too. It sounds like we should head north." I shook my fist at the sky and stomped my foot. "I'm so sick of this! Is it *ever* going to stop raining?"

"I wouldn't bet on it."

Chapter 11

Frustrations

It was late afternoon by the time we got back to the Motel 6 in Issaquah. I knew I was tired and Riley was behaving like a zombie. Being in the city for multiple days was taking a toll on both of us. Our room resembled a dorm room after a riotous frat party, thanks to the efforts of Nils, the small yet potently messy person. The kid had also made a serious dent in our supply of food. I was tired of Seattle weather, tired of feeling rotten, and tired of the tiny room. I wanted out.

Riley was lying on the bed with his arm over his eyes. I nudged him and said, "What do you think about checking out today, instead of tomorrow?"

"And go where?"

"Anywhere outside this city. Maybe north in the direction of the retreat."

Riley sat up, grabbed some dirty clothes off the bed, and jammed them into his suitcase. "Let's do it."

Going through Seattle in the late afternoon is a recipe for frustration, so we opted to go north using an inland route that was away from the city. We cruised northward until we hit a tiny town on Route 2 called Monroe. The hamlet also had a small rural motel and trailer park located off in the woods near a creek that grudgingly allowed pets.

The room sported harvest-gold walls, which I pointed out to Riley was a paint color that went out of vogue in approximately 1974. But it was in keeping with the orange bedspreads and assuming they'd replaced the mattresses in the last twenty years, it wasn't too awful. In any case, it was nice to get a break from the familiar Motel 6 color scheme.

Although the motel was in a rural area, it was close enough to Seattle that I was still able to find a dial-up number for an Internet connection. I plugged in the phone line and got to work going through emails.

Riley collapsed on the bed and immediately fell asleep. As usual, I was hungry and the only thing left in the cooler was juice. Riley wasn't awake to argue, so I called and quietly ordered a pizza to be delivered to our room.

I was happily tapping away on my laptop keyboard when there was a knock at the door. Zelda launched into a tirade of barking and Riley heaved himself upright so forcefully he almost fell off the bed and onto the floor.

"Zelda, stop it," I said, waving her away from the door. "It's food."

I collected the pizza and apologized to Riley. "I was hungry."

"Jeez, if I didn't have heart problems before, that would do it."

"Want a slice of pizza?"

"Yuck."

I took a big bite and held the pizza slice out to emphasize my point. "When was the last time you ate *anything*?"

"I don't know. Get off my case."

When Riley started feeling bad, I could see it in his eyes. They got a particular dull cast as if the light was out, no one was home, and he was giving up. I wasn't going to put up with that anymore. Nope. Not on my watch. I set my pizza slice on the desk and walked to the cooler. I grabbed the juice and poured some into a plastic cup. I handed it to Riley. "You need to drink this right now."

He made a face. "Yuck."

"Stop saying that. From now on, I refuse to let you avoid eating. We're out of the city, so you can't use that as an excuse. I know that the longer you don't eat, the more difficult it gets to eat again. So I'm going to make you eat before you get so sick you end up in the hospital. We don't have time for that, so you're drinking this juice if I have to tie you up and pour it down your throat."

"I'd like to see you try. And by the way, you aren't my mother."

"I know. But I might be your sister. And I absolutely will not let you crap out on me because I need your help." I proffered the cup of juice. "I'll make your life miserable until you drink this. You know I can."

"Unfortunately, I do." Riley took the cup.

"Drink it. I'm watching you."

He obediently gulped down the juice. "It smells like chemicals."

"It's the organic stuff you buy that costs a fortune. Don't over-analyze it."

"Fine." He set the cup on the nightstand between the beds. "Happy now?"

I got up, grabbed the cup, poured more juice, and handed it to him. "Nope."

Over the course of the evening, I managed to convince Riley to eat a few crackers, so by the time we went back to sleep, he was a little less morose. But sheesh, what a pain. The guy made a mule seem easygoing and amiable.

In the middle of the night, I had a flash of insight that jarred me awake. Had I dreamed about Riley's lawyer? I didn't even know what the guy looked like, so that was unlikely. But I did know we thought Mel was hiding something. Maybe he was even stealing money. That led to the next obvious question: How much did Riley really know about this guy? Yes, Riley said they'd worked together for years, but skeletons exist in everyone's closet. I forced myself to go back to sleep, but I vowed to do some digging into Mel's past. There had to be records of his education, passing the bar, and so forth out there somewhere.

The next morning when Riley called his lawyer, I listened as closely as I could to the conversation without being completely obvious about it. When the call ended I demanded, "What did Mel say? I thought he was giving you phone numbers for PIs."

Riley sat on his bed and leaned over to ruffle Zelda's ears. He glanced at me. "Why are you so uptight? It's not like there are a lot of options in this area, but Mel found a guy. He said we can meet the private investigator in a place not too far from here called Sedro-Wooley."

"What kind of name is that for a town? It sounds like a sheep." I waved off my own comment. "Never mind. I need to ask you about Mel."

"What about him?"

"What if he's hiding something big?" I sat down on my bed and gave Riley my best schoolmarm finger shake. "We need answers. I'm going to do some surfing to see if I can find anything on him and also answer more of my mountains of email. While I do that, you need to call your girlfriend."

"Ex-girlfriend."

"Semantics. You need to ask her what she meant by windfall."

"You do realize you're being unbelievably bossy, even for you."

I moved to lean back on my pillow. "I'm feeling squirrelly and impatient. The whole thing with Lars went nowhere. I mean, I'm glad he's going to be safe in Minnesota, but I was hoping he'd know more about the retreat, or Hector, or *something.*"

"Maybe our new private investigator will reveal all."

"But Mel found him, and now I'm wondering whether we should put our faith in someone Mel lined up. What if Mel is stealing all your money, or worse? This is all so frustrating. We're going in circles, and I don't know who I can and can't trust."

"I have an idea. But I have to talk to Erin first." He frowned.

"I know that look. That's your 'I don't want to have a confrontation' look. Suck it up and call her."

He threw a pillow at me. "Speaking of frustration. I think you're just cranky because you didn't get to jump Lars. It's not garden-variety frustration. It's *sexual* frustration."

I threw the pillow back at him, not wanting to him to see how pleased I was that he was feeling well enough to tease me again. "Stop dawdling and call your girlfriend."

"*Ex*-girlfriend."

~

Undoubtedly because he knew it would annoy me, Riley opted to talk to his ex-girlfriend while I was in the shower. I was irritated, but not surprised to hear him hang up the phone while I was combing my hair in front of the mirror.

I yanked a comb through my wet hair one last time, stomped out into the room, and sat down at the desk in front of my laptop. I turned in the chair to face Riley. "Are you going to just sit there? Talk to me. What did Erin say?"

"Lots. But once she ran out of nasty things to say about me, I asked her to take a peek at the law firm's financials."

"Do you think Mel is embezzling?"

"I have no idea, but I plan to find out. Something is going on. He said he disappeared because 'powerful people' were upset. Was that related to Archetypal? Something else? Who knows? But whatever it is, it involves money. So I'm going to make it tempting for him to steal some of mine."

"I don't like this idea." I rested my elbows on the chair back. "I mean yeah, you're loaded, but this seems a little extreme."

"You're the one who said we don't know who we can trust, and I agree. If I can't trust Mel, we've got a serious problem. So I'm going to set up a new account to increase the amount of money he can work with to handle my expenses. If he accesses it, we'll know something is up, because there's no way he'd need it."

"I guess I see what you mean. I have a less radical idea we can try. Tell me everything you know about Mel's education and background. When did he pass the bar? Where did he graduate from law school? What organizations does he belong to?"

I typed notes while Riley tried to remember everything Mel had ever told him about himself. My plan was to search for information about him online and see if I could catch him in a lie. If I couldn't find anything, I'd go to another university library and dig deeper. If he was lying, odds were decent that something wouldn't line up. Nobody gets through life without a few missed turns.

While Riley took his shower, I spent a little time surfing and snooping into the life and times of Elmer Flood. I didn't find much beyond stuffy biographical information on the legal firm's web site. At least the firm had a web site, but it wasn't much more than an online brochure.

Riley made a few calls and then phoned Mel to give him the good news about all the money he'd now be able to access. He told Mel that he'd thought up a great new project that would require lots of funding. Then he confirmed the details about where we were supposed to meet the PI.

We gathered up our things, checked out of the motel, and headed off to our big meeting at Hal's Drive-In restaurant in Sedro-Wooley. My suspicion was that any place that called itself a drive-in and wasn't a movie theater was likely to serve food I'd enjoy and Riley would scorn. Visions of great piles of mouthwatering greasy onion rings danced in my head as we got on the highway. I'd behaved myself for so long, so I deserved a major junk-food binge.

We left Zelda with the Mustang and walked into Hal's Drive-In, which was a throwback to 1964 with a startling turquoise-and-pink color scheme. They'd even painted the curb in front of the restaurant hot pink. It was like walking onto the set of Arnold's of *Happy Days* fame, complete with a black-and-white tile floor. I half expected the Fonz to appear and give me a thumbs-up.

We settled into one of the booths in front of the huge windows, which gave us a panoramic view of the happenings in beautiful downtown Sedro-Wooley. I picked up the menu and there, laid out in front of me, was every form of greasy comfort food I'd been missing for so long.

Riley furrowed his brow, studying the menu. He put it down with a slap. "If I hadn't talked to Mel, I'd think coming here was your idea."

"Isn't it incredible? I'm in love. The Philly cheese steak sandwich with grilled onions and mushrooms looks amazing. And that photo of the onion rings makes me swoon."

Riley gave me a horrified, incredulous look. "Do you want me to go into detail about the effects that level of gluttony can have on your system? We've talked about this before, and I'm pretty sure you don't."

I picked up the menu again. "Okay, okay! I'll have something else. But you can't deny me the joy of a real homemade chocolate milk shake. You just can't. I mean, check out that ice cream fountain. They've got the old-fashioned metal milk shake machine and everything. What are you having?"

"BLT without the B."

"You've got to be kidding me. That's lettuce and bread."

"There's tomato too. The T, remember?"

I pointed at the menu. "I'll have the chef's salad if you add avocado to your sandwich. They put it on the burgers, so they must have it."

"Fine."

We ordered, and even after I had snarfed down half my salad, our private investigator still hadn't turned up. Riley was ever-so-slowly eating his overly green sandwich and I said, "What time was this guy supposed to be here?"

Riley glanced at his watch. "Fifteen minutes ago."

"Do we know what he looks like?"

"No, but Mel gave him a description of us. It's not like this place is huge."

At the sound of barking outside, we both turned to stare out the window. A massive man in a gray plaid flannel shirt and work boots was backing away from the Mustang with his palms raised in a gesture of surrender.

I smiled at Riley. "I think Zelda is doing her job."

The man was wearing one of those dopey hats with the flaps that you pull down to keep your ears warm, which somehow made him resemble an oversized gray squirrel. Northwest fashion was a cross between early lumberjack and thrift-store special. It wasn't particularly attractive for men or women, but in a rural area where it rains all the time, spending big bucks on a classy wardrobe probably doesn't make sense. Even my clean clothes were starting to feel damp and mildewy. I was getting desperate for a little sunlight.

When Mr. Gray Squirrel entered the diner, his enormous frame filled the doorway. He looked around the room, spotted us, and clumped over to our table.

He yanked a chair over to the end of the table and sat down. "I'm supposed to meet some people here. Your names Riley and Meg?"

Riley and I acknowledged that he was correct. I was a little worried that the spindly metal chair legs might not be up to the challenge of supporting the weight of this mammoth human being. I said, "Are you the private investigator?"

He pulled the hat off his head. "Yep. Name's Wallace Collier, but most people call me Wall."

I smiled politely. I was guessing the moniker was less a nickname and more of a description. "It's a pleasure to meet you, Wall. Do you have information about the retreat we're trying to find?"

Wall fumbled with the hat in his lap. "Well, about that...I think I know more or less the vicinity. But then these people started following me and I had to back off."

Riley said, "What people?"

"Yesterday I was driving looking around places off Highway 542 and this ugly ole van kept turning up every time I turned around. At first I didn't think much of it, but then it started to bug me." Wall set the hat down on the table with a thump. "So I stopped my rig, confronted them, and asked them if they had a problem."

I cut in. "What did these guys look like?"

"Well, now that's the funny thing. They were wearing suits. Around here, no one except people selling religiosity wear suits. And these two didn't seem like the type. They said they were trying to find someone."

I glanced at Riley, who appeared to be as distressed by the information as I was. "Did they say who?"

"Nope. They decided they didn't want to talk to me. After they left, I gave up for the day, since I was supposed to meet up with you today. I thought you might know what these people want," Wall said.

"We might," Riley said. "Could you tell us exactly where you were looking for the retreat?"

I pulled a Washington map out of my bag and spread it on the table. "Maybe you could show us?"

Riley and I discussed the situation a little more with Wall, and he quickly lost interest in helping us, given the hostile forces chasing us around the country. After we all said our goodbyes, I shoved my plate aside and rested my forehead on the table in despair. Every time we thought we were getting somewhere, the guys in suits interfered.

Riley reached across the table and patted my shoulder. "Hey, don't get like that, we're getting closer."

I sat up. "I was really hoping to get help from that guy."

Riley said, "All in all, I think Wall needs a few more bricks."

I laughed, "Wait a minute, is this a Pink Floyd reference you're throwing out here?"

"Maybe a little."

I crooned a mini-Floydian riff, "Hey, Hector! Leave that dude aloooone."

Riley started making comments about eating pudding and meat until we both were laughing so hard that the other people in the diner started to stare. After a point, what we were saying wasn't even particularly funny, but every time I caught Riley's eye across the table, I started laughing again.

Finally, I regained a small degree of composure and wiped the tears of laughter off my cheeks. "See what happens when you eat? You get your sense of humor back. I miss it when it's gone."

Riley smiled. "Yeah, I know. Me too."

After laughing so hard, I felt better about the world, until the moment we exited the restaurant. The drizzle that had been our almost continuous companion in Washington had gained momentum and turned into a deluge. Water was puddling everywhere, and we splashed our way across the street to the Mustang so we could let Zelda out. She seemed equally dismayed by the weather and wasted no time taking care of her needs before scuttling back to her towel in the back of the nice warm car.

Riley used a paper towel to wipe the condensation off the inside of the windshield while I sat in the passenger seat and squeezed as much water as I could from my tresses. In the span of three minutes, I'd managed to get completely drenched. The state of Washington can ramp up for some serious rain when it gets going.

I shook my hands in disgust. "Okay, I know people in the Northwest are too cool to carry umbrellas, but I think we need to face the fact that we are underdressed. I need a real raincoat in the worst way."

"Owning something waterproof would be helpful before we go tramping around remote forested areas. Besides, it's raining so hard right now that I doubt we'd be able to spot this mysterious retreat from the highway."

"I agree. Let's go shopping instead!"

"I think we're going to have to visit a more bustling metropolis to find stores."

"I want to go to Western Washington University and do more digging on Mel. Presumably Bellingham has raincoats too."

It was an easy drive from Sedro-Wooley to Bellingham, which is a city of about fifty- or sixty-thousand people. We schlepped downtown and wandered around for a while, trying to find a store that might sell rain gear.

I suppose I'm picky when it comes to clothes, but I didn't expect finding a raincoat would end up being so difficult. We went to a marine-supply store and I rejected the idea of dressing like the Gorton's fisherman. Rain was one thing, but the yellow slicker and hat was so large that I bore a striking resemblance to a gigantic banana. No way. A girl has to have a few wardrobe standards.

The cycling store had lots of bicycle shorts that I would never wear in public, gear I didn't understand, and rainwear that it wasn't even worth trying on until I lost about fifteen pounds.

After perusing a few more unsatisfying stores, we found a sporting-goods shop that proclaimed it had existed since 1921. That sounded promising, and the place was huge. We cruised through the camping, fishing, hunting, kitchen, marine, and ski sections. They even had a nicely stocked area filled with toys to keep the kiddies amused. From a shopping standpoint, it was a fun-filled retail palace.

Although I was enjoying myself, I could tell I was trying Riley's patience. After much poking through irrelevant items on our journey to the apparel section, I discovered they'd recently had a big sale on outerwear, so the place was pretty much cleaned out of raincoats.

Riley grabbed a black hooded raincoat that was less hideous than some I'd seen. "Here, try this one."

"Black seems sort of austere for a raincoat, don't you think?"

"Who cares if it's austere? You rejected that yellow one hours ago. It says it's waterproof and at this point, I don't care." He handed the coat to me and grabbed a larger version from the rack. He put it on and pulled the hood up over his head. "It will keep your hair dry."

"You look like a giant insect."

"Thanks." Riley took off the coat and glared at me. "It's a raincoat, Meg. This should not be a major life decision. If it keeps you from getting soaked, that's good enough."

"I suppose. And it is on sale, which scores points with me. I don't understand why they have to make raincoats so ugly." I put on the coat, held out my arms, and turned around. "How does it look?"

"Great. Can we go now? Zelda is going to start getting agitated about getting out of the car if we don't expedite this process."

Zelda *had* been patiently waiting in the car for quite a while. Oops. I flipped through the coats one last time to make sure I hadn't missed anything. Most of them were made for seven-foot-tall giants or were a screamingly unflattering color. I'm sorry, but blaze orange doesn't work on anybody.

I took the black coat from the rack and clutched it to my chest. "All right, fine. This will have to do. But I really was hoping to find something in a pretty teal color that would look nice with my hair."

Riley grabbed the coat from me and started heading for the cashier. "Maybe another time. We need to walk Zelda and find a place to stay for the night."

I followed him out of the store, where it was still raining. We donned our new waterproof jackets and took Zelda for a short walk around the neighborhood.

The wind came up and I pulled the drawstrings on the hood to snuggle it to my face. "This weather just gets worse and worse. And now we look like two oversized cockroaches walking with an ambulatory cotton-rope mop. Poor Zee. It's going to take forever for her to dry."

"She's probably getting used to it."

"Maybe, but I'm really tired of living with the smell of wet dog. She smells like a soggy moth-eaten wool sweater. And if I'm noticing that, you must be really sick of eau de Zelda."

"It's not so bad. Sometimes it's educational." He tugged at the side of his hood to keep the wind from whipping it around.

"Educational? How can wet-dog smell possibly be educational?"

"Because I know where she's been. Walking Zelda has helped me isolate scents and figure out what they are. The scents are more pronounced when she's wet."

"I'll say."

He gestured toward Zelda. "By going for walks with her, I've been able to isolate the scent residues, I guess you'd call it, which indicate where she's been and what she's done recently."

"This sounds like way more information than anyone wants to know about any dog."

"Probably. But it's worse being assaulted by odors and not knowing what they mean."

"This reminds me of that movie where Helen Keller's teacher helps her communicate."

"*The Miracle Worker.*" Riley yanked at his hood again. "She was isolated because she couldn't understand language. I don't have that problem."

"True. You can talk to me any old time. But we still have the problem that Zelda stinks. I don't suppose you're going to bathe her, are you?"

"I wasn't planning on it. Usually, I only wash her three or four times a year. Being on the road, I guess I should do it more often, but dog shampoos can have nasty chemicals and perfumes added to them."

"I kinda wish I had something like your walks with Zelda to help me explain my visions. Or a way to control them, other than moving to a remote desert island for the rest of my days." I waved my arms in frustration. "Let's face it. I'm never going to be able to be alone in a town larger than this one, ever again. Even Bellingham is pushing it."

"It has taken me a long time to analyze and understand what little I do know about what I sense. If we find our parents, I'm hoping they'll be able to help. My dad is one of the smartest people I've ever known."

"So is my mom. If anyone can figure us out, it would be them."

"You'd think so."

"All we need to do is find them." I pushed down my hood and looked up at a small break in the clouds. "Come on universe, give us a clue. I want my mommy!"

～

The rain was relentless and it was getting late, so we decided to head north out of Bellingham to find a place to stay. Then in the morning I could head off to the Western Washington

University library and dig deep into research on everybody and everything.

We got back on Interstate 5 and went north for about a half an hour to a little town called Birch Bay, which is right on the ocean. It was conveniently located between Bellingham, where I needed to go for research, and the roads that would take us off into the rain forest near Mount Baker, where the retreat might be. Plus, I hadn't had the opportunity to sit and stare at the ocean for a long time. I missed the sea, and even with all our travels, I hadn't been able to walk on a beach and listen to the sound of the waves.

As we drove northward, I kept thinking about what Riley had said about analyzing what he was sensing. How did that work? With sight, don't you see what's there? Something either exists or it doesn't. How did that relate to my visions? Unlike Riley's sense of smell, my visions seemed to have little basis in reality.

Riley glanced over at me. "What are you brooding about?"

"I'm not brooding."

"You're never this quiet."

Okay, he wasn't wrong about that. "I was thinking about what you said about analyzing what you were smelling. How did you figure it out?"

"At first, I didn't figure it out. I just wanted to crawl into a hole and make it all go away."

I waved my hand dismissively. "I know that part. Ancient history. I've noticed you seem to know way more about what smells mean than you did when I met you. The whole thing with pheromones is more recent. How did you know what it was?"

"Process of elimination. Seeing you with Lars at the circus and asking you questions about it. Being around Dean and Peggy helped, because their lust hormones were like a gigantic cloud."

"That's easy to imagine, given what I saw, but wasn't all that lust tangled up with a whole bunch of other scents?"

"It was, and the other thing I had to work through was that I had to believe that's what I really smelled."

"What do you mean *believe*? Something smells, you smell it, end of story, right?"

Riley shook his head. "I was being assaulted by things I'd never been able to smell before, but I didn't realize that. It took me a while to believe that I was able to smell things that only dogs like Zelda could smell. Stuff that no human *should* be able to smell."

"Like pheromones."

"Exactly. And other hormones. For example, when you're scared, you produce adrenaline. And uh, by the way, if you're running out of tampons, you might want to stock up in the next couple days."

My jaw dropped open. "What? You *know* that? Okay, now you're getting way, way too personal."

"Sorry, but you asked."

I leaned back in the seat and rubbed my eyes. "Do you suppose I can see more than I think I can see?"

"You're extremely observant. Have you seen things that you wrote off because you didn't believe what you thought you saw?"

"Maybe."

"They say seeing is believing, but maybe you need to believe what you're seeing first."

I sat up and put my hand on Riley's arm. "What if my visions are my subconscious mind telling me to pay attention because my conscious mind keeps writing off what I see as impossible? But because it's my subconscious, it gets mingled in with fears, dreams, and other random stuff rattling around in my brain."

"It's as reasonable an explanation as any."

I turned and leaned forward to really study Riley. He had a slightly blue tinge that surrounded him like a faint halo. I rubbed my eyes again and the halo was still there. "Okay, I need to think about this for a while."

"You saw something didn't you?"

"You're blue."

"According to you, I'm always blue."

"I meant in my visions before. But I mean you're blue *now*. Right this second while you're driving and I'm not having any kind of vision or bizarre problem at all. It's not much, but I think it's really there." I cupped my palm over his forearm. "It's like a thin fuzzy outline all around you. Maybe it's always been there and I just attributed it to a trick of the light."

"I hope this field around me doesn't mean I'm going to end up like Obi-Wan Kenobi and get chopped in half by a light saber. Because that's gotta hurt."

"Hey, cut me some slack here. I'm still new at feeling the force."

We checked into a funky motel right on Birch Bay Drive, which is the main street that goes through town along the coastline. Although we had to drag our stuff up three flights of stairs, the view was worth it. We were on the top floor, and when I opened the curtains to our balcony, I gazed out over the rooftops and sighed with happiness. Sure, the weather was still gray and dreary, but the rain had subsided somewhat and the ocean was right there across the street.

After we got settled, Riley suggested that we go and check out the beach park at the south end of town. Not surprisingly, Zelda was enthusiastic about the idea, and she had been so good about waiting in the car during our many stops that she deserved a nice long beach walk. Although my love of the ocean trumps my dislike of exercise, I was hoping Riley wasn't going get all nutty about a marathon hike.

The sun peeked out long enough to let us know it was low in the sky. Although it was damp, watching the sea birds joyfully scamper back and forth as the waves came in put me in a good mood. The beach was empty, so Riley unclipped Zelda's leash. She was beside herself with glee, running around us in circles as we strolled along the empty rocky beach. Riley picked up a piece of driftwood and threw it down the beach. Zelda ran after it, picked it up, and ran off toward a copse of trees.

I pointed at the rapidly retreating white form. "Isn't she supposed to come back with the stick? I thought it was just me, but she doesn't bring it back for you either."

"Zee doesn't believe in the concept of retrieving. I think she considers it beneath her dignity."

Zelda went to the edge of the tree line to take care of business and returned, settling into a jaunty trot alongside us as we walked. I glanced at Riley. "If you're really blue, I wonder if Dean would be green and Lars gold. It's too bad they aren't here so I can give them the once-over."

"You just want another opportunity to jump Lars."

I shoved Riley's arm, pushing him off balance. "That's not true. I'm over it. If it makes you feel better, he said we weren't meant to be together."

Riley grinned at me. "I knew it! You *did* try to jump him, didn't you?"

"Maybe a little. But he was right. And returning to the point, even if I can see colors around people, that doesn't explain the fire, voices, and horrible clowns I've seen in my visions."

"No, but being able to identify people with abilities like ours could be useful."

I stopped and turned to watch Zelda chase off a flock of seagulls. "I guess I should think about who was colorful in my visions and who wasn't."

"Was Peggy in any of your visions?"

"No, but now that I think about it, I think she's pink. I remember when I met her, that was my impression."

"What about your mom?"

"She just looked like mom. I can't think of anyone other than Dean and Lars who had an aura." I stopped and put my hands to my chest. "Nils just looked like a little kid. Maybe Lars was right and this isn't genetic."

"You asked him about Nils?"

"I shook the kid's hand when we met and I didn't feel anything, so I wondered. Did you touch Nils?"

Riley shook his head. "I don't really remember, but if I did, I didn't feel anything odd."

"Me neither, so I asked Lars. He said that Nils is the same as he's always been, even after Lars started having problems."

"That's a relief, unless it's something that appears later, like after puberty. Maybe only fully developed senses can be whacked-out."

I stopped, picked up a rock, and heaved it at the ocean. "Way to find the cloud in every silver lining."

"I'm just speculating. I don't know any more than you do."

I stopped and faced the ocean, wishing that the deep blue vastness could provide answers about my future. The crashing waves were comforting, but didn't tell me anything. "Sorry. I need to stop dwelling on what's going to happen with the rest of my life."

Riley put his arm around me. "Let's focus on finding this retreat first. Then we'll go from there."

"Okay." I leaned my head against his chest. "Thanks for helping me think through all this."

"Any time."

I scanned the beach, where Zelda seemed to be having a whole lot of fun rolling around and playing with something in the rocks. I pointed. "Riley, what is Zee doing?"

He let go of me and uttered a string of graphic phrases that were physically and anatomically improbable and ran down the beach toward the dog.

Chapter 12

Something Unusual

At Riley's approach, Zelda looked startled, then guilty. The dog turned and galloped past Riley toward me with Riley chasing after her. As she approached, the pungent stench of dead fish preceded her.

I held out my palms toward her and stepped backward. "No, Zee, get back."

Riley yelled, "Grab her!"

I didn't want to touch anything that smelled that bad, but in an effort to not be a wuss, I held my breath and reached to grab Zelda's collar as she whirled around me. Unfortunately, you can only hold your breath for so long. When I tentatively took a tiny sniff though my nose, I was assaulted by the overwhelming fish odor. Zelda's fur had an aroma akin to a can of tuna fish that had been left out in the sun for a few days to fester.

I held Zelda as far away as I could with one hand and with the other pinched my nostrils closed with my thumb and forefinger to ensure I didn't accidentally smell her.

Riley came up to us and clipped the leash onto Zelda's collar. He was out of breath but managed to mutter, "You are in such big trouble."

Once Zelda was safely leashed I stepped away from her. "I don't think you can avoid that bath now."

"I don't have any dog shampoo."

"Use that earthy, crunchy, no-preservative, save-the-whales soap you have. It can't have anything bad in it."

"I guess not, but this is going to be awful. And I'm pretty sure the motel staff is going to notice when they walk into the room and our towels smell like *this*." Riley glared down at the dog as we hurried back to the motel. "Rolling in dead fish. Really? What got into you?"

Zelda's ears were down at Riley's disgusted tone. At least she had the decency to look guilty. I was glad I wasn't on the other end of the leash, so I could be more than six feet away. That was one serious stink. It ranked right up there with buzzard barf on my top-ten list of odors I'd prefer to avoid experiencing ever again.

Riley hustled Zelda up the steps to our room. I followed behind them, hoping people would assume someone was cooking fish for dinner. Of course, no fish meal smelled anywhere near as bad as Zelda did, unless the cook was trying to give the diners food poisoning.

I closed the door behind me and Riley pointed at the sliding-glass door. "Could you open that up?"

I did as he requested while he dragged Zelda into the bathroom. I stood in the doorway while he picked up the unhappy, squirmy dog and put her in the tub. With one hand holding her ruff, he turned his face away from Zelda and turned the water on.

He said, "Could you find my stuff and get the soap? If I let go, she'll make a break for it."

I dug around in Riley's suitcase, got the soap, and handed it to him while pinching my nostrils again. "Although I don't want to, I feel obligated to ask if I can help you with this process."

He waved toward the room. "Could you get the ice bucket? I need something I can use to dump water on her."

I gave him the bucket and watched as he knelt on the floor next to the bathtub, scrubbing for all he was worth. Using bar soap to wash a very hairy dog takes a while, but eventually she was lathered up, looking unhappy. Riley was completely soaked. His shirt was hanging on him as soggy as if he'd jumped into a swimming pool fully clothed.

After rinsing and toweling, Zelda smelled like wet dog, fish, and soap. Riley laid the towels out on the balcony and closed Zelda outside. She stared at us through the glass door with a forlorn expression.

"Awww, Riley, look at her. She's so sad."

"She'll be fine. It's not cold and the rain stopped." Riley grabbed some clothes and paused to point his index finger at the dog. "Don't you *dare* let her back inside. I'm taking a shower. I may never get that smell off of me."

"I'll sit at the desk and try not to notice your disconsolate dog."

After showering, Riley checked on Zelda, who was curled up in a tight ball on her towels with her back to us.

I looked up as he closed the sliding-glass door behind him. "I think she's mad at you."

"Well then we're even because I'm mad at her." Riley sat on his bed and pulled a telephone book out of the nightstand and started flipping through pages. "You think Zelda is mad now? Wait until I take her to a groomer tomorrow. She still reeks. I need professional help."

The next morning Riley made arrangements to drop off Zelda at a groomer in Bellingham who had agreed to tackle the fishy task while we did research at Western Washington University.

Although the reason for my research was distressing, going to university libraries had been an enjoyable aspect of my long, weird road trip with Riley. I got to walk around pretty campuses, see lots of books, and meet nice librarians. What's not to like? It had stopped raining for the moment, and we walked along the pretty red-brick pathways to the library.

The sun sparkled on the fountain rising up in the middle of the courtyard in front of the library building. Students were reclining along the wall of the circular pool, enjoying the rare glimpse of sunlight. Being a sun-worshiper in the Northwest must be challenging. If I had gone to college at WWU, I'm sure I would have been out there with them absorbing as much vitamin D as possible.

Wilson Library is one of those wonderful old brick library buildings with high ceilings and lots of places to curl up and do research. As I typically did, I ingratiated myself to a reference librarian and asked for her help. The librarian's name was Lisa, and I asked if she could help us find out anything about Hector, the circus, Enviro Freedom, Archetypal Online Systems, Mel, and his law firm. I added Lars Lindeman, Leonard Olson, and Wallace Collier into the mix. I doubted Leo or Wall had much to do with anything, but if you're going to grasp at straws, you may as well grasp at all of them.

Riley enjoyed the research process more than I might have expected and he focused most of his energy on the questions related to Mel. I was reading news stories about Hector, when Riley suddenly stood up. I raised my eyebrows at him and whispered, "Something wrong?"

He leaned down, "I'm going to go find a pay phone. I'll be right back."

I shrugged and returned to the news article I'd found about Lars. He'd been quite the real-estate god back in the day. I clicked to another page, which listed legal notices related to divorces. Lars had been married to a woman named Helen Mooney, who was now changing her name to Helen Yana. Her maiden name had been a long Greek-sounding name, Yannakakis. According to the records, first she was Helen Yannakakis, then she was Helen Moody, then Helen Lindeman, and now Helen Yana. Wait a minute. I knew that name. That was Helen, the Wicked Witch of Alpine Grove. The woman who tried to kidnap me was Lars's *wife?*

Riley sat down next to me, and I hissed, "You aren't going to believe this," at the same time he said, "I found something."

We both said, "What?" and he gave me a "go ahead" gesture for me to share my information first. I related my news about Helen.

He acknowledged that it was good intel and said, "Get this. I found out Mel didn't get a law degree from Harvard, like he said he did. His degree was from the University of Arkansas."

"Although that's not truthful, it's not illegal, assuming Arkansas has a law school."

"It does, but that's not the worst thing. I called Erin, who checked on something for me. There's a name on the payroll for someone who doesn't actually exist. She's never seen or even heard of anyone named Fred Loolem."

"That's an unusual name," I said.

"That's because it's fake. After I hung up the phone and was walking back over here, I realized it's an anagram of Elmer Flood."

"I can't believe you thought of that." I laughed. "No wonder I lost at Scrabble. So what does Fred do?"

"He's in accounting."

"Given that's where all the money is, why am I not surprised?"

Riley shook his head. "This is bad, Meg. Mel knows everything about what we're doing."

I put my palms over my face and mumbled. "Is *everyone* out to get us?" I dropped my hands. "I mean honestly. What are we supposed to do? Although figuring out Helen was married to Lars explains a few of the things he said about his wife, I'm not finding any connection between Hector and the Enviro Freedom people at all. Maybe Hector has nothing to do with them. Lars might be right. Maybe EF did bomb the circus."

"If Helen really hates Lars as much as he says, it explains why she fell in with Hector's band of merry weirdos. And why she attacked you."

I stared down at my hands in my lap, feeling lost. "What should we do?"

"What we planned to do. Figure out where this retreat is, starting with where Wall was looking. It has to be out there somewhere."

I looked up and put my hand on Riley's. "You're right. Nothing is more important than finding our parents."

"I agree." He squeezed my palm. "I still do think we're getting closer. Are you done? Want to go pick up Zelda from the groomer and watch her sulk for the next three or four hours?"

"Sure. Maybe you should walk her on her leash for a while."

"A long while."

~

When we picked up Zelda at the groomer's, she was decked out with a cute little bandanna and was so furry, fluffy, and adorable that she almost didn't seem real. Yes, she was a white dog, but I'd never seen her so clean. Her fur was a blinding white that sparkled in the light.

While Riley paid, I crouched down to pet Zelda, who was unbelievably soft and sweet-smelling. I told Zelda she was the most gorgeous dog in the whole world and hoped Riley was giving the groomer a really good tip. The woman had worked a miracle. The fish smell was completely gone.

Zelda was significantly less impressed with the grooming than I was. After we got back to the motel, she hopped up on a bed and curled up for a nap with her back to us.

Riley sat down on the bed and put his hand on Zelda's back. The dog was unmoved by the gesture of affection. "I told you she'd be annoyed."

"Poor Zee. It's not easy being clean."

The next morning, I opened my eyes and discovered something unusual had entered the room: sunlight. A thin ray of light was snaking around the drapes that covered the sliding-glass door to the balcony. I threw my covers aside, got out of bed, and yanked on the rope to open the heavy curtains.

Riley groaned and rolled over, but Zelda jumped off his bed to check out the view. I bent to pet her. "Check it out, Zee. It's a beautiful day! Look at that blue sky."

Zelda wagged a few times to show her appreciation. I suspected she also wanted her breakfast, but that was just speculation on my part.

Riley sat up and rubbed his eyes. "Why are you up so early?"

"Sun! We need to go out and visit it before it goes away again."

Riley acquiesced, and we took Zelda on a long beach walk. After we ate breakfast we checked out of the motel. For the first time in what felt like ages, we were able to put the convertible top down on the Mustang. Life was good and I was determined that we were going to find the retreat. Today was the day.

We left Birch Bay and drove down a bunch of pretty country roads toward Route 542, which is a long, windy road that ends up at Mount Baker. Of course the only thing we had to go on was Wall's somewhat vague description of where he was when he'd thought he was close to the retreat.

I opened up the map and pointed to a dot. "Let's eat lunch in Glacier or maybe Maple Falls and then find a place to stay. We need to go down every side road and alleyway. I want to be sure we have looked everywhere."

Riley shifted gears and glanced at me. "I doubt there are any alleyways in Glacier. I'm not convinced there are any *people* in Glacier."

"I know. This all a big guessing game. Since you're participating, we're having a group guess."

Riley thumped his palm on the steering wheel. "I'm so *tired* of guessing. For years, my job was coming up with answers. I did an equation, figured out the value of x, and got an actual answer. I miss that certainty."

"I miss ferreting out the truth. Lately all I find are lies. I feel like I know less and less all the time. It's like I'm going backward." I closed my eyes. "I hate to say it, but it's really starting to get to me."

"No one has all the answers. It's not just you. Socrates said that all he knew was that he knew nothing."

"Don't you find it depressing that things haven't improved in thousands of years?"

"I think it's part of being human. Nobody knows what they're doing. We're all just muddling through and guessing our way through life."

I laughed and leaned back in the seat, enjoying the sun on my face and deciding that everyone should own a convertible. "Since when are you so philosophical?"

"Hey, I'm deep."

I chuckled and closed my eyes again. After so many days of rain, I needed to stock up on all the vitamin D I could get.

We drove through a few small towns and passed a sign that caught my attention. I grabbed Riley's arm. "We have to stop! It's a beer shrine!"

"What's a beer shrine? It looks like a bar to me."

"Oh come on, where's your sense of adventure? How often do you get to go to a beer shrine? I have to know what it's like. Do they worship at the altar of the God of Hops or something?"

"I don't really like beer, but all right. We have to eat lunch somewhere." Riley turned into the parking lot and we got out. The building was an old wooden structure that appeared to have lived through many a long winter. The inside was almost as rustic as the outside with well–aged, dark wood-plank flooring, wood chairs, and tables covered with checked tablecloths. The place did have beautiful stained-glass artwork hanging in the windows though, perhaps as a nod to the shrine factor.

I ordered a calzone and a beer. True to his typical preference for rabbit-food, Riley ordered a salad and a glass of water. He also got steamed edamame, whatever that was. As it turned out, they resembled dark green lima beans, a food I try my best to avoid. Whatever edamame was, I'm sure it was healthy.

After I inhaled my calzone, Riley was still methodically picking at his salad, so I went to check out the brewing area. The place was a microbrewery, and I wanted to see the tanks and find out how it all worked. I chatted with a brewer for a while about how beer is made and quizzed him about happenings in the area.

A grizzled older man who was clearly a regular at the shrine came up and joined the conversation. I learned more than I ever wanted to know about the brewing process. The brewer gave me free samples to help explain the differences between the types of beer. He explained about alcohol content, hops, finishing, ales, lagers, and probably other things I wasn't paying attention to because I was focused on drinking my samples.

Once I'd run out of questions about beer, I moved on to what I really wanted to know. Although I attempted questions from various different angles, neither of the men had heard of any hard-core environmentalists moving into the area. From the sounds of it, with the exception of a few new condos that were being built near the ski resort, not much had changed in years. People liked their quiet homes in the woods and wanted to keep it that way.

I agreed that it was a beautiful area, thanked them for showing me the beer setup, and returned to the table. Riley offered me one of the weird bean thingies and I demurred. "No thanks. Beans and beer are not a good combo."

"Good point."

"I'm afraid Wall might be wrong about this area. I asked questions about any new secret retreats or environmentalists and no one knows anything. Maybe the retreat is somewhere else. Or environmentalists don't drink beer. How would we know?"

Riley shrugged. "We're here, so we may as well continue along this road and poke around. I've never seen such dense forest, except on the Olympic Peninsula. Wall was right that you could hide out for ages before anyone would run across you."

"I suppose so. The trees are gorgeous and it's not pouring for once, so if we have to go on a wild-goose chase, at least it's a pretty drive."

"There's the spirit."

$\sim$

Riley drove down the highway and we turned down every side road, carefully checking for anything unusual. Not surprisingly, we ended up in many little residential areas that did not appear to be hiding any secret activities. Mostly we encountered cute cabins and single-family homes with swing sets in the backyards and the beginnings of springtime gardening activities.

After driving down countless rural roads, I started getting bored. The only thing I could think about was how much I wanted to find a bathroom. The sad truth is that although I like beer, beer doesn't like me. Something about that particular beverage results in an urgent need to relieve myself. My bladder wasn't going to take no for an answer much longer.

I squirmed in my seat. "I can't put this off anymore. I need to make a pit stop."

"You do realize there are no rest stops in the middle of the forest, right?"

"I know. Just stop somewhere and I'll go behind one of these gigantic ferns. It's like *Jurassic Park* out here."

"All right. Zelda probably would like to get out of the car too."

"I mean now, Riley."

"All right, all right. Calm down." He pulled over to the side of the road and I jumped out of the car and ran into the forest. It was dark back in the trees and once I couldn't see the car anymore, I took care of my needs.

I almost tipped over when Zelda poked me in the back with her nose. "Zee! Go away. I'm busy here."

I pulled up my pants and shooed Zelda back. "Riley, call your dog!"

Riley whistled and Zelda left my side. Sheesh, a girl couldn't get a moment of privacy. A huge drop of rain landed on my head and I silently cursed the weather gods as I gazed up at the sky. The heavy gray clouds had returned. It appeared that a half day of sun was all we were going to get.

As I pushed aside the boughs of gigantic bushes, making my way back toward the car, something whizzed by my head with an odd zing noise and I brushed at my cheek. With such huge plants, maybe the insect life was large too.

Another zing noise went past my arm and then there was a *thunk* as something hit the cedar tree to my right. The trunk had an arrow protruding from it. I turned my head to scan my surroundings as another arrow thumped into the tree. I screamed, dropped to all fours, and scuttled behind the cedar. Someone was shooting at me. Was it a hunter who was so nearsighted he couldn't tell that I wasn't a deer or a bear? What bear has red hair and wears blue jeans?

Another arrow zinged above my head and I resumed screaming, figuring that even the most cowardly bear didn't scream like a terrified woman. There was a loud rustling noise in the brush and I flattened myself to the ground.

Zelda rrr-ed in my ear and gave it a slurp for emphasis. I sat up, put my arms around her ruff, and pulled her into a down position. "I'm really glad to see you, but you need to get down, Zee."

More crashing came from the bush and I draped my body over Zelda's. She didn't appreciate my protective actions, stood up, and wagged. I scrabbled backwards until I got a glimpse of the interloper. I wasn't facing a nearsighted hunter or a bear, but Riley.

He crouched down and gazed into my eyes. "Are you all right? I heard you screaming."

I pushed a damp lock of hair out of my face and pointed up at the tree. "Arrows! Someone is shooting *arrows* out there. A couple of them almost hit me."

Riley got down next to me and I huddled up to him, feeling suddenly cold as the dampness from the ground seeped into my jeans. I looked into his eyes. "What is going on, Riley? Who shoots arrows? Tonto?"

"I'm not sure, but I think they've gone. Maybe all your screaming scared them off. We should get back to Shelby. The last thing we need is car trouble out here."

"Okay, but be quiet about it, would you? You sounded like a herd of buffalo coming through that bush and I'd prefer that Tonto not hear that and end up shooting at me again."

Riley glared his acknowledgment and grabbed Zelda's collar to keep her from rushing off through the brush. We slowly and carefully made our way back to the car. By the time I crawled back into the passenger seat, I was freezing. Riley started the car and blasted the heat. Fortunately he'd put the convertible top up before leaving to find me, so the passenger seat wasn't a giant puddle.

Riley pulled off the shoulder and back onto the road, did a three-point turn, and we headed back for the highway.

I pulled out the map. "So now what are we supposed to do?"

"Give up for the day. We're practically to Glacier. Didn't you say there was lodging?"

I pulled out my dog-eared Triple-A guidebook. "Yeah, the Snow River condos. I'm not sure if they take pets, but the place sounds nice. It's right on the Nooksack River."

"Works for me, Kemo Sabe."

I gave Riley directions and started to feel better the farther we got away from Tonto and his arrows. Maybe it had just been a hunter, but we'd had too many people chasing us for too long for me to think being shot at was a coincidence.

The condos were nestled amid a grove of gigantic cedars off yet another side road. All of the trees had a coating of bright green moss that practically dripped from the branches. The ground was covered with ferns and other plants, so between the moss and the copious vegetation, the buildings seemed to arise from an ocean of green.

Riley went to see if we could get a room while I waited with Zelda in the car. He was gone for a long time, which usually meant he had to do a lot of explaining and cajoling to convince the management that Zelda was not an evil doggie mastermind that was out to destroy their condos.

Finally, he emerged from the office and waved a key at me. I clapped my hands together a few times in congratulation.

He got into the car and handed me the key. "That was expensive."

"I'm sure it will be worth it."

"Zelda had better behave because I'm going to lose one heck of a deposit if anything happens. If Mel steals all my money, we're going to have to embrace frugality."

"Hey, enticing Mel with money was *your* idea, remember? Meanwhile, I'm still a little freaked-out about being shot at, so I'm looking forward to staying somewhere nice again. A rustic cedar-sided condo along a beautiful river beats a Motel 6 with a view of a trailer park any day."

After we unloaded our stuff, I insisted we find a grocery store. The condo had a kitchen and I wanted to take advantage of it. Riley didn't seem quite as excited about the idea as I was, but that's probably because he'd figured out long ago that I am incapable of cooking anything he'd be willing to eat.

When we returned, I explored our unit while Riley made dinner. One thing that was notably absent was a phone. So much for communication.

I walked into the cute little kitchen and Riley handed me a carrot. "Are you upset about something?"

"This place doesn't have a telephone. Even crummy motels have phones."

"They mentioned that there are no phones in the condos. There's a pay phone outside and if you go to the top floor of the old wooden recreation building near the river, you can get a dial-up connection sometimes."

"Sometimes? As in, not all the time?"

"The guy at the desk says there's a squirrel that's been eating the phone wires." Riley grinned. "You said you liked the rustic look. This place doesn't just look that way. It *is* that way."

Choosing to ignore that we were in the middle of nowhere with no communication, I returned to my rummaging and snooping around the condo. In the television stand, I found a bunch of old videotapes and a notebook. I sat cross-legged on the floor and started leafing through the pages. It was a guestbook that detailed the experiences of people who had stayed at the condo.

A number of the entries were boring. "Stayed a week in August 1996. Weather was good." But some were more interesting, almost like a diary of someone's vacation. Certain families had returned to this same condo year after year in a time-share arrangement. One family had being vacationing in this unit since the complex was built almost twenty years ago. I found myself intrigued by their stories.

Riley walked over and crouched next to me. "What are you up to over here?"

I held up the notebook. "This is full of interesting tales. People have been vacationing here for years. I'm getting to know a woman named Rose Walters, who has three kids. I'm up to 1990, when they were being total brats. It wasn't a good trip because it rained the whole time and she thought she might kill them."

Riley laughed. "I hate to interrupt your foray into the Walters family history, but food's almost done."

I got up and set the notebook on the coffee table, mentally vowing to return to it later.

~

After dinner, Riley went through the stack of videotapes I'd scattered on the floor in front of the TV. He held one up. "I'm starting to wonder about the Walters clan. They've got bad taste in movies. These are some of the worst flicks ever made."

After spending so much time reading the journal, I had a good idea whose movies they were. "The youngest son, John, is...or was...a movie nut. According to the notebook, he sat around watching videos while everyone else went out hiking."

"John needs to get out more. I mean, okay, *Jaws 3* might be fine if you saw the first two. But *Mac and Me* was a crappy ET rip-off. *Ishtar*? I'm sorry, but that was universally panned. Everyone hated that movie. And then we have not only

Cannonball Run, but *Cannonball Run 2*. Because the first one wasn't bad enough."

I laughed. "Well, aren't you the movie critic. Is there anything in that pile you'd be willing to watch?"

Riley sorted through the stack of tapes, shaking his head. "It's pretty bleak."

I sat down next to him and examined a few titles. "Who ya gonna call?"

"You honestly want to watch *Ghostbusters*?"

"Awww, come on. Dan Aykroyd and Bill Murray? It's funny."

"All right. I guess I can go in for a little paranormal investigation."

I giggled. "And the truth comes out. You've watched it before."

"Who hasn't?"

We settled onto the sofa to enjoy a few ghostly crises, which in some ways weren't much more bizarre than my real life. Let's face it, hallucinations and people with sensory abnormalities aren't a big stretch from supernatural demons. But I had no one to call, except Riley.

I watched the opening credits and listened to the theme song. I closed my eyes for a minute and heard someone in the movie talking about Columbia University. My mind wandered to thoughts of college and grad school.

My chest clenched in panic because I was late for my SATs. Part of my mind knew that this was another one of my school-related dreams, but the other part of my mind was fretting about the test.

I started awake and found I was curled up in between Riley and Zelda. He moved his hand off my shoulder and leaned over to see my face. "Bad dream?"

"The worst."

"You missed the Stay Puft Marshmallow Man attacking the city."

"I was in high school, which was worse. In my dream, I found out I had to take the SATs that day and I'd completely forgotten about the test. I hadn't studied, and I was in a panic, running down a hallway. A geeky guy with big round glasses like Harold Ramis wanted to know where I was going. I said I was trying to find the SAT testing room. He told me I was at the wrong high school and I needed to go to the one in Thousand Oaks."

Riley smiled. "That's interesting."

"What's up with that? I went to high school in Maryland. Why would I take my SATs at *your* high school three-thousand miles away? Needless to say, I missed the test and started crying about how I'd never get into college. Then I woke up."

"I know you did go to college, so you must have found the room in real life."

"Yes I did, and I found the one for my GREs too. I've had these school dreams for years. Usually I'm late for a test, I haven't studied, and can't find the room." I ran my fingertips across the fur between Zelda's ears. "How old do I have to be for these stupid dreams to stop?"

"I don't know, but adding my high school into your mental mix can't be an improvement."

I slumped down so I was leaning on Riley's chest. "Given how much time I've spent with you, it's not surprising. I've even seen the place."

"As you've pointed out, you're doomed to know more about me than you probably want."

I sat up straight and turned around to look at him. "*Doomed* is the wrong word. Have you thought about what might have happened if we hadn't met?"

"I suppose I might be dead by now, if I'd stopped eating entirely for long enough."

"I would be too if someone hadn't been there to stop me from running out into traffic. Or I could have been successful in jumping off an atrium balcony."

Zelda rubbed her nose on my foot as Riley and I were silently staring at each other, digesting that tidbit of information. We hadn't found our parents, but we had found each other. We also weren't dead.

Zelda sneezed loudly and I smiled at Riley. "Just for the record, I'm glad you drove up to my mother's house when you did. I can't imagine what it would have been like trying to find my mom alone."

He returned my smile. "I know what you mean. You may be the only person I know who doesn't think I'm a complete lunatic."

"You're no more nuts than I am. And let's not dwell on that, okay?" I leaned back against the sofa and gazed out at the room. "I think Erin really messed with your head."

"Breaking up with someone is rarely enjoyable."

"You don't need to tell me. I've had vast experience as both the dump-*er* and the dump-*ee*. But from your description, she made you feel like crap most of the time, and now you believe all the things she said about you."

"She wasn't wrong about some of it, and even if she was, where's all this coming from?"

"I've been on both sides of the equation, so I know what it's like to be the one who cares the most. I spent all my time worrying that I wasn't wonderful or perfect enough to keep that person happy. Getting dumped was just a confirmation." I sat up straight and turned to look at Riley again. "That's how you feel, isn't it?"

He frowned. "I suppose so. Have you ever told someone you love them and heard nothing in response? It's like the silence goes on forever. I think that was when I finally knew that it was never going to work with Erin, no matter how hard I tried."

"My relationships don't usually get that far. I tend not to trust men, starting with my father and ending with Matt the Ultra-Prick."

Riley laughed. "I think you win for worst relationship of the year."

"I'm done dating evil executives. It's comforting to know he's three-thousand miles away."

"Maybe you'll meet another hot clown."

I shoved at his arm. "Hey, I'm being serious here. You deserve better than Erin. You really do, and you need to stop beating yourself up about all the rotten stuff she said."

"You're the one who always complains about being alone forever." He leaned his head back on the couch and closed his eyes. "But jeez, I'm a real catch. In addition to looking like I have a terminal disease, women just love a man who can smell every single, little, thing—from what they ate for breakfast to their hormonal state."

"Well, yeah, okay, maybe you don't mention that on the first date. And maybe consider doing something other than going out for dinner."

"You're a big help. As if I didn't already have enough hang-ups about asking women out. I was the shy geek in high school, remember?"

"Hey, I'm not trying to make you feel bad." I patted his arm and he opened his eyes. "You're the best friend I've had in, well, I don't know how long. Maybe ever. There aren't enough smart, kind, generous people like you in the world. That should count for something, shouldn't it?"

"How many smart, kind, generous men have *you* gone out with? From your descriptions, I'm guessing the answer is zero. You described Lars as a Coppertone model and said Matt the Ultra-Prick was so hot you thought other women were jealous of you.

I paused. He had me there. Matt was gorgeous in a slick, wealthy executive way. Was I really that shallow? "Okay, point taken. But all that shows is that I need to raise my standards and look beyond the dating meat market. Or maybe do something to stop attracting worthless, lying, two-faced, cheating losers. Oh, and I should avoid clowns too."

"Sounds like a good plan." He patted my hand and stood up. "I'm going to bed. Let's go, Zee."

Zelda leaped up and followed him into one of the bedrooms.

I retired to my room, wondering why Riley had left so abruptly. I hadn't been interrogating him. Sheesh. I was *trying* to be nice and supportive, but somehow he hadn't taken it in the spirit I'd intended.

Chapter 13

Off-road Adventure

The next morning, I returned to reading the condo journal while Riley showered. Even though some of the Snow River vacation tales were mundane, I found myself hooked on the adventures of the Walters family. They'd taken countless hikes in the vicinity and Rose Walters knew a lot about local people and events. Although other visitors wrote notes, Rose's entries were the most detailed ones in the journal, often covering multiple pages of the notebook. I found myself looking forward to encountering entries written in her compact, precise handwriting.

Riley handed me a cup of coffee and went back to the kitchen to start breakfast. I took a sip and turned the page. I flipped the paper back and forth, realizing that the rest of the pages of the notebook were blank. I'd reached the last entry, which was from fall. The Walters had come to the condo for one last chance at hiking before the snow arrived. Throughout the journal, Rose had mentioned her secret trail, which was located some distance from the resort. The impression I got was that the trail went alongside the river, but they had to deal with bushwhacking through vegetation to access the trailhead. In the last entry, Rose mentioned "something new on our secret trail."

I closed the notebook and took another sip of my coffee.

Riley sat down across from me and handed me a plate. "What happened with the Walters saga? You seem disturbed."

"This is going to sound crazy, and it's a long shot, but I think Rose Walters may have found the retreat."

He set down his fork and reached across the table for the notebook. "Are you serious?"

"Check out at the last entry and tell me what you think."

Riley flipped through the pages and read while I ate. How could someone who ate so little create such amazing food? "This is delicious."

"I'm not sure what Rose is saying exactly. But they found a fence. She compared it to the wall of a fortress."

"Doesn't that sound secretive to you?"

"It does. But we don't know where the Walters special trail is. From what she said, they had to hike pretty far to get to it."

"But the trail is along the river. All we have to do is follow the river, and eventually we'll find it."

"That might be easier said than done, particularly in such dense forest. Do we go up the river or down? Not to mention trespassing across who knows how many other people's properties."

I took another bite and chewed while I thought. "What if we keep doing what we were doing yesterday as far as going down the side roads? But today, let's focus on the roads that go toward the river."

"Don't forget to bring your raincoat."

"If it keeps raining like this, I'm going to need hip waders."

After taking Zelda for a quick outing, we loaded ourselves into the Mustang and resumed our search along Highway 542 toward Mount Baker. According to the map, the highway petered out into a mountain. If we made it to the end of the road and hadn't found the any evidence of the retreat, we'd not only be out of road, we'd be out of ideas too.

At that point, it might be time to rethink everything. I'd spent so much time worrying about finding my mother that my brain hurt. I was mentally exhausted and ready to give up. Maybe she didn't want to be found. How would I know? The idea of retiring to a remote island somewhere was sounding better all the time. With the exception of a week at my apartment in Maryland, a week in Alpine Grove, and a couple of days at the ranch in Ellensberg, I'd been on the road and staying in motel rooms for almost two months. Before last night, when was the last time I just sat around and watched a movie like a normal person? Was it when I was at my apartment? That felt like a lifetime ago.

Riley glanced at the rearview mirror, then at me. "I'm afraid I have bad news."

"I know. There's nothing out here. We're trying to find a needle in a huge and unbelievably densely forested haystack. This is nuts."

"No, it's not that. Look behind us. That van is awfully familiar."

I whirled in my seat to check, although I knew who it would be. I recognized the two men in the blue van behind us. They'd sabotaged the Mustang and I'd whacked one of them with my Nora Roberts novel. "Not again! What is it with these people? I hate that van."

Riley floored it, the Mustang's gigantic engine roared, and we accelerated away from the van. The road twisted and turned and when the van was far enough behind us to disappear around a corner, Riley suddenly yanked hard on the steering wheel, so that the car skidded into a sharp turn down a side road. I grabbed onto the armrest, and for a distressing instant I was afraid I might throw up. Although I'm not prone to carsickness, swerving all over a rain-soaked highway caused my stomach to do a few unscheduled backflips.

In the backseat, Zelda seemed remarkably unfazed by the weaving, merely moving her body back and forth, adjusting to the movements of the car. Her easy response surprised me, because although she'd logged thousands of miles of road time, we hadn't engaged in extreme driving like this before.

I kept my vigil, watching for the van behind us, but so far it hadn't caught up. Riley drove deeper into the forest, the road turned to dirt, and we had to go significantly more slowly, which made me anxious.

"Can't you go any faster?"

"Shelby is not an off-road vehicle, Meg. If we intend to keep driving on bad roads like this, we'll need a different car. Like maybe a tank."

"I don't see the van back there."

"Keep watching. I have no idea where we're going. If they catch up, there's no place to turn around."

"Sooner or later, they're going to have to figure out you turned off the highway. What are we going to do?"

"I have no idea."

A tiny flash of blue in the distance beyond a group of trees caught my eye and I grabbed Riley's arm. "I think I see them!"

Riley scanned the road in front of us and then did something I never would have expected. He turned off the road and drove straight into a huge bush.

Branches scratched against the side of the car, whipping alongside us with screeching noises. I yelped, "Riley, what are you *doing?*"

"Destroying Shelby's paint job, for one thing. Jeez, I feel sick. I spent a month painting her."

"I don't care about the paint. How can you be so calm? There's no road here."

"That's the idea." He continued driving through the underbrush until the car couldn't go any farther. Riley finally stopped and shut off the ignition. We were tucked far away from the road behind massive ferns and vegetation in a dense copse of trees.

"Now what?" I asked.

"We wait until they go away."

"What if they find us?"

"We run."

∿

After our off-road adventure, we hid in the shrubbery, waiting in the car for what felt like an eternity. I grabbed Riley's wrist to check his watch. "How long have we been sitting here?"

"Maybe fifteen minutes."

"If I don't get out of this car, I'm going to lose my mind. Those guys attacked me before and I feel like a sitting duck."

"Meg, calm down."

I rolled down the window. "I don't hear anything. Wouldn't we hear an engine if they're still driving around?"

"I'm worried that they saw my tire tracks going off into the woods. I mean, Shelby broke a whole lot of branches getting back here." He sighed. "I have no idea how I'm going to get her out, either. I wonder if Triple-A covers towing through vegetation."

"Even if they saw you veer off into the trees, the guys in the van probably aren't dumb enough to follow you."

"If you want to go take a look, go." He waved his hands in a shooing motion. "It's pouring out there. Zelda and I will hang out. Maybe take a nap."

"How can you possibly nap at a time like this?" I grabbed my raincoat and moved to open the door. "I'm out of here."

Riley grabbed my arm before I could exit the car. "Stop! All right. You win. We'll all go. But if we get lost, it's your fault."

I shook my arm free, got out, and stepped right into in a gooey area of sucking mud. I stepped beyond it with my other foot, and when I pulled my foot out of the gunk, my sneaker stayed behind. I uttered a few unladylike phrases and bent to retrieve my shoe. Ick.

Riley walked around the car with Zelda, who was already soggy after approximately twenty seconds outside. Maybe walking around wasn't such a good idea, but there was no way I wanted to sit around and wait to get captured either.

With as much dignity as I could muster, I put my mud-coated sneaker back on my foot.

Riley raised his eyebrows at the squishy noise my toes made as they slid inside the shoe. "That must feel wonderful. Try not to get hypothermia."

I wiped the mud off my hands with the bottom of my raincoat. "Let's go back to the road and see if the van is back there."

"Maybe it got stuck in the mud too."

I hadn't thought about that, but it wasn't an unreasonable possibility. Even if they were stuck, I'd prefer to sneak up on them, rather than have them sneak up on me.

We slopped our way through the vegetation, following the path the Mustang had taken from the road. The brush was so thick that it was difficult to tell that a car had just driven through it at all. Everything was green and dripping with water and more green. The trees had vines and moss growing all over the branches and trunks, and the ground was a sea of three-foot-tall ferns. I couldn't see where I was walking, so odds were decent that I'd step right into another mud bog.

As we walked, I saw no sign of a van or anyone at all. When we made it back to the dirt road where we'd turned off into the bush, Riley crouched down, examining the tire tracks.

He stood up and shrugged. "It's been raining so hard, I can barely tell where we turned. If anyone else came down here, I can't tell. Do you see any new ruts in the mud?"

I shook my head. The road wasn't much of a road. It was more like a logging skid trail heading off into the woods. "Should we follow it?"

"Why?"

"I think I hear the sound of rushing water. Finding the secret trail near the river was the whole point of this expedition, remember?"

"I suppose so." Riley frowned and yanked the strings on the hood of his raincoat to pull it closer around his face.

We walked in silence down the road, which got narrower and narrower as the noise of the rushing river grew louder and louder. Given all the rain and spring runoff, the river had to be running high. By the time we reached the riverbank, the road was so narrow that it was only the width of a footpath for hikers. No one would be able to drive down here in a car because the trees were too close together. I breathed a sigh of relief. The van *couldn't* be here because it was too wide to fit between the trees.

Riley and Zelda stood on the bank of the river staring out at the rushing water. He spread his arms out and turned to look at me. "Now what?"

"Let's go downriver." I pointed. "That way. It seems like there's a little trail that runs along the bank over there."

"I think that's a game trail, not an official hiking trail for humans."

"Do you have any other ideas?"

Zelda yanked on the leash toward the trail, almost pulling Riley off balance. "Hey! Stop it, Zee."

"See, Zelda agrees with me." I grinned. "We should go that way."

Riley grumbled at the dog. "Normally I'd let you run around, but after your revolting fishy adventure, you're not getting any off-leash time near bodies of water."

We walked along the river, which even in the rain was stunningly gorgeous. It was like something out of a nature film or *National Geographic* magazine. I'd never seen such lush wilderness in real life. The sound of the water roaring over the rocks soothed my anxiety somewhat as I tried to forget about the people in the van. They had to be far away by now. Or stuck in their own mud bog somewhere else.

Zelda insisted on forging ahead. It had been a few days since her big romp on the beach, so the poor dog could probably use a little exercise. Riley was less enthusiastic about the hike, which was unusual. Typically, I was the big whiner about outdoor activities.

We followed Zelda along the trail and I glanced at Riley. "What are you so grumpy about?"

"I killed my car and trapped it in a mud bog. Poor Shelby may never be the same. That may be the dumbest thing I've ever done."

"We probably should be worried about getting ourselves out of here too. We have no way to call anyone and we're miles from anywhere. I'm kind of hoping we'll find a swanky riverfront home with a telephone."

"So far, there's a whole lot of nothing." He tilted his face toward the sky. "Except rain. So. Much. Rain."

I pointed straight ahead. "What's that?"

We walked closer and found ourselves in front of an enormous wooden privacy fence that had to be twelve feet high.

Riley said, "This fence cost somebody big bucks. Maybe we'll find your riverfront home after all."

"Maybe. Whatever it is, I think we found the secret trail! This is just like what Rose Walters described."

The fence ran toward the river and we turned to follow it down to a huge pile of boulders at the water's edge. I stepped out onto a rock and tried to see around the edge of the fence, but couldn't. I waved my hands in an effort to keep my balance. "Maybe there's another way in."

"We could follow the perimeter back up through the woods. There's got to be a gate somewhere."

"The gate is probably near the road, which is who knows how far away." I pointed at the rushing water. "We're here. Let's just climb over the rocks and go around the end."

"Are you sure? That water is moving fast. If you fall in, you could end up in Idaho. Drowning is another possibility."

"I won't fall in." I gestured toward Zelda, who was already looking like she wanted to make a break for it. "Do you think Zee will be okay?"

"I'm more worried about you." He bent to unclip the leash from Zelda's collar. "If you roll in any more fish, you will be in such big trouble."

Zelda appeared to be suitably chastised and gleefully clambered from rock to rock until she disappeared from view.

I clutched my raincoat closer to me. "I hope she's okay over there."

Riley looped the leash around my waist. "Let's go."

"You really have no faith."

"I saw how well you dismounted from that horse at the ranch. Excuse me for being cautious."

We slowly moved from rock to rock. They were actually large boulders, so it wasn't like I had to rely on perfect balance to get where I wanted to go. I was doing great and smiled when I got to the other side of the fence and saw Zelda standing and wagging on the shoreline. When I leapt to the last boulder, my foot slipped.

I went down hard on my knees on the rock and Riley hauled on the leash, pulling me away from the direction of the river. He practically carried me onto the shoreline and dumped me next to Zelda.

My shoes and pants were completely soaked. I shook my arms in disgust. "Thanks."

He clipped the leash back onto Zelda's collar and pointed toward the grassy area above us. "I don't see your swanky house up there."

I heaved a sigh. "Well, it was worth a try. Let's walk along the fence and see if we find anyone…or anything."

"No one builds a fence like this for no reason."

I took Riley's hand. "Exactly. Somebody up there wants privacy."

~

I took a step, a shooting pain ran up my leg, and I almost collapsed. Riley's grip on my hand tightened and he looked at me in alarm. "What's wrong?"

"I think I did something to my knee when I fell on the rock." I bent to rub it and winced. "Ouch."

"You're shaking. Are you all right?"

I ran my hands across the front of my sodden clothes. "I'm soaked. This raincoat is not only ugly, it's not even warm. You should have let me find a warmer one. Preferably in a pretty teal color."

Riley laughed, unzipped his ugly raincoat, and pulled me into his arms to share some warmth. "Jeez, you're not going to let that go, are you?"

I tilted my head back to look up at him and the hood fell off my head. What a pathetic excuse for outerwear. "I told you. This oversized-cockroach motif is unattractive."

"If we ever manage to get out of here, we'll find you a green coat, so you can go for the praying-mantis motif instead."

"Teal."

Our gazes locked, but something in Riley's eyes was different. I'd seen that look before. It was at the hospital when he was with Erin. But now he was looking at me.

Riley ran his long fingers through the hair at my temple and cupped his hand behind my neck, pulling me to him. He whispered, "Teal. So it looks nice with your hair."

When his lips touched mine, it was like a jolt of electricity ran through my entire body at the incredible phenomenon that was happening right here in a rain forest in the middle of nowhere. *Riley? What? I didn't think...*

After the initial flash of shock, kissing him felt completely right and natural and I never wanted to stop. The kiss was better than I ever would have imagined. Better than Lars and let's not even discuss Matt the Evil Executive. No comparison, since Matt was slime and I considered Riley a decent human being. Who happened to have lips that were warm, soft, and invigorating all at the same time. I closed my eyes, reveling in the sensations, slow at first, and then increasing in intensity. Thoughts of my damaged knee, cold feet, and the rain evaporated as I wrapped my arms around his neck, wanting to get as close to him as possible.

Riley pulled away and scanned my face. "I probably shouldn't have done that."

I just stared at him for a long moment. He smiled and said, "On the other hand, maybe it's all right with you, after all."

I said softly, "Pheromones don't lie," before pulling him back down to me.

We might have stood there making out in the rain indefinitely, but Zelda's sharp bark startled us from hormonal delight.

Riley said, "Ow!" as Zelda jerked the leash out of his hand and began running toward a couple who were walking along the fence.

I didn't move, frozen in place and not sure what to do. "Are those the guys in from the van? Were they wearing raincoats? I don't remember." I turned to run back toward the river.

I stumbled, having forgotten about my knee problem, and Riley grabbed my hand again. "Meg, it's not them. I think the short one is a woman."

"What is Zelda doing? She's jumping all over the tall guy."

Riley said nothing, and then he took a deep breath, and mumbled, "It can't be."

When he dropped my hand, I turned around again. He was running to get Zelda. Unbelievable. Was there something about me that causes every guy I kiss to immediately run away? It's like they suddenly realize I have a communicable disease or something.

I put my hands on my hips and squinted at the people. Zelda was still leaping around in unadulterated glee. Maybe the people had food.

I limped a few steps toward the group, and my jaw dropped when I saw Riley hugging the tall man. They were about the same height, although the man was a lot older and heavier than Riley.

I studied the woman next to him and my breath caught. I whispered, "Mom" as I started running, or more accurately hobbling, as quickly as I could toward the three people.

Ignoring the pain in my knee, I threw myself into my mother's arms. She hugged me, and I sobbed uncontrollably with my head resting on her shoulder.

Once my tears had subsided somewhat, she peeled me off her and said, "Meg, honey, I'm glad to see you, but what are you doing here?"

I blubbered, "Trying to find you since for…for…*forever.*"

"We've been right here." She stepped away from me and gestured toward the man. "This is Tim O'Shea."

I smiled and wiped the rain and tears off my face. "I guessed that. It's nice to finally meet you. Mom, this is Riley O'Shea."

I glanced at Riley, who was standing silently next to Tim with a shell-shocked expression on his face. He picked up the leash Zelda was dragging around and gave her one of his "settle down" hand signals.

I turned my attention back to Tim. The resemblance to both Riley and his brother Bubba was obvious. Even though Riley and Bubba didn't look much like each other, they did both look like Tim in certain ways. It's fascinating how genetics plays out.

Tim said to me, "Ellen has told me a lot about you."

I wiped my eyes again. "Riley told me a lot about you too. Nice job selling your house, by the way. Your neighbors are thrilled."

"I'll bet you got an earful from Moira Washburn." Tim's smile faded as he turned to Riley. "You know I don't like to pry, but are you still sick after all this time? You never told me what's wrong. I thought you sold your business because of stress. Is it something serious? You don't look so good."

His expression of fatherly concern tugged at my heartstrings. "You mean you don't know?"

Riley shook his head slightly. "Dad, we've been searching for you and Ellen for almost two months."

"I told you where I was," Tim said.

"No, you *didn't*," Riley replied emphatically.

"I told Dean." Tim said. "Didn't he tell you? He was supposed to."

I interrupted, "Dean got captured. We found him and the last time we saw him, he was heading off to get married. It's a long story."

"Captured? Why? He delivered pies." Tim frowned as he scrutinized Riley. "You didn't answer my question. You've lost so much weight. Are you all right?"

Riley said, "Meg is right. It's a long story."

My mother said to me, "It seems you two know each other rather *well*. I didn't know that you'd met."

I could feel the blush rising on my cheeks. The last time mom caught me making out with a guy, I was seventeen and in our living room, not thirty-three in the middle of a rain forest. "Riley and I met at your house. You called and demanded that I go to Alpine Grove because you had to tell me something really *important*. Then you didn't show up."

"Dean was supposed to talk to you," Ellen said.

"Yeah, well that didn't work out too well." I looked up at the sky. "Is there someplace inside we can go to talk about this? We're not kidding about it being a really long story, and I'm freezing."

Tim and Ellen glanced at each other. My mother said, "That might not be a good idea."

"Why not? Are you trapped here?" I asked. "I *knew* it. They captured you too! We need to get you out of here. Riley's car, okay, I think it might have a problem, but we can get you out around the fence. Then there's a trail down along the river back to the car."

"That's nice dear, but we're not leaving."

Riley and I both said, "*What?*" at the same time, and then I said, "Why not? You just said you were captured. Riley and I rescued Dean and Lars. We can get you out of here. I promise we'll figure something out."

My mother gave me the slightly condescending smile that used to set my teeth on edge when I was a teenager, and said in her most reasonable Mom voice, "Honey, we don't want to leave."

I glanced at Riley, who appeared to be as stunned as I was. I had no idea what to say. Had we really just gone through all of this driving, searching, running, and everything else for *nothing?*

~

Riley finally roused from his stunned stupor and said, "Dad, what exactly are you doing here? *Why* are you here?"

Tim grinned like a kid with a new toy, "They offered us…me and Ellen that is…the best lab you can imagine. It's a million times better than all that junk I had in the garage. They gave us this incredible equipment and all the resources we need for our research. The offer came up real fast and it was too good to pass up. They even packed up all our things from the house."

"Except they put back the kitchen table," I said.

Riley waved off my comment. "Don't you think that's strange? Who just *gives* you a fully equipped lab?"

I added, "What you're researching…does it have to do with electromagnetic radiation?"

Tim nodded, "Yes. Did Ellen tell you that?"

"No, she didn't. We figured it out." I groaned as I put my face in my hands. *Unbelievable.* I looked up again. "Is there any place we can get out of the rain? I'm freezing and we really have a lot to talk about, but right now my waterlogged toes feel like they're about to fall off."

Ellen pointed downriver. "There's a covered picnic pavilion down that way where we could sit down. Tim and I often rest there when we take our walk."

"Ellen thinks I'm getting fat, so we walk around the perimeter every day," Tim added.

"Soon people will wonder where we are though. They might get worried and come looking for us," Ellen said.

Having spent weeks searching for my mother, I wanted to scream at her response, or more accurately, *lack* of response to having been found. But rather than go postal, I turned and began hobbling down to the river bank instead. I stopped and turned back. "Mom, don't you think it's a little strange that they're monitoring you so closely? You're an adult. Haven't you ever wondered *why* they're so worried about your activities?"

"Meg, you're always so suspicious. Everyone has been very nice to us," my mother retorted.

Arrgh! Suspicious? I'd been attacked, beaten up, zapped with a stun gun, almost run over multiple times, and nearly blown up twice. I had good reason to be suspicious. How could she trust people who wouldn't even let her use a phone or go for an extended walk?

I stomp-hobbled ahead, so furious and upset I could barely see. Riley caught up with me, grabbed my hand, and gave it a squeeze. I hissed, "They have no idea what we've been through!"

"We'll explain it to them," he said.

"I can't decide whether to laugh, cry, or tear my hair out in frustration."

He stopped me, forcing me to wait for our parents, who were slowly ambling along. I turned to face him. "What?"

"We found them, Meg. We did it. We *finally* found them."

A wave of relief swept over me and I stood there, mutely staring at Riley's lips. You'd think that after all the time I'd spent watching him speak, smile, frown, scowl, and laugh, I would have noticed that his top lip was thinner than the bottom one. Now all I knew was that I wanted to feel them against mine again.

I threw myself into his arms. He stumbled backward, but managed to collect himself and participate in my impulsive burst of lust without stepping on Zelda. The world fell away and I forgot about the rain and my anger, all my passion and tangled emotions having been redirected somewhere else.

Reality intruded again when my mother cleared her throat. "The pavilion is over there, Meg."

Riley stepped back, away from me, and I breathlessly said, "Okay, um, yes, um, sorry Mom. I've had a complicated day."

The pavilion was covered by a large wooden roof and we all sat down at the picnic table underneath. Riley and I sat on one side of the table and our parents sat across from us. Being there, sitting across from my mother, was surreal, but I did my best to explain all the places we'd been, people we'd met, and theories we'd devised about what was going on.

Tim said, "I never considered that Dean's headaches might be related to his hearing."

Riley said, "Figuring out that both of our problems were related to our senses took time. And then tying it to electromagnetic radiation took more time."

"I thought I was losing my mind," I said.

"You told me you had migraines," Ellen said.

I retorted, "What was I supposed to say, Mom? My boss and everyone I worked with were pretty sure I'm nuts, so they put me on medical leave?"

"Well, that would have been more honest, honey."

If they gave out awards for eye-rolling at parents, I'd be a world champion. "You might have mentioned you were leaving Alpine Grove *before* I flew three-thousand miles to see you, Mom."

"I'm sorry. It was a sudden opportunity and I was so excited. I tried to reach you at work, but you weren't there."

"That was because I was on medical leave."

"Which you never mentioned to me. You were *always* working, so I was sure you'd get my message."

I waved my hands in exasperation. "I was going to tell you about it when I got to Alpine Grove!"

Riley grabbed one of my hands and held it between his palms under the table. "It doesn't matter what happened before. Like we said, people have been after us because of our special abilities. They were chasing us earlier today."

I squeezed Riley's hand, glad that he was there to help explain things. "Lars said people were being taken and dumped at a facility in Los Angeles. We didn't really follow that lead because we were focused on finding this retreat... and you. But now I don't know what to think."

Tim said, "Enviro Freedom wants us to find out about the environmental and health effects of radiation. I don't know anything about all this stuff with the media company."

Riley said, "We haven't been able to verify any connection between Archetypal Online Systems and Enviro Freedom."

"There *has* to be one," I said. "Lars said that he thought Enviro Freedom was behind the bombing of the circus trailers though."

"What if Hector's weirdos were following us because they knew we were trying to find our parents?" Riley said. "If EF did bomb them, they might have it in for the environmentalists."

I thumped my forehead on the picnic table. "This is giving me a headache."

Riley said, "I'm not sure what to do next. Meg stirred up a lot of people with the stuff she wrote online. My lawyer might be involved too."

"And maybe my boss, Leo." I said.

Ellen said, "I'm feeling uncomfortable about being here. There has been a rumor going around about cell-tower bombings, but I discounted it. Now I'm not certain we were told the truth about what's going on."

"Yeah, I'm a little embarrassed to admit I didn't really check out these guys," Tim added. "We were so excited about the opportunity, we just took it. And we've enjoyed being here. The lack of outside communication has been a little difficult, but we've worked around it."

"Now I feel silly for not wondering why we had to ask others to help us access outside reference sources," Ellen said. "I suppose I enjoyed having my own research assistant a bit too much."

I sat up again. "Will they let you walk out of here with us?"

Tim and Ellen shook their heads sadly. Ellen said, "I signed a contract that I would spend my entire sabbatical here. No trips anywhere."

"We both signed," Tim said.

I finally thought to ask the question that had been plaguing me. "So did you two get married? Was *that* what you wanted to tell us in Alpine Grove?"

"Of course not. You know how I feel about marriage," Ellen said.

"No, Mom, I don't. You've never talked to me about it at all," I replied.

"Never again," Ellen scowled. "It's an antiquated custom."

"It's not like I didn't ask her," Tim said. He leaned forward, put his elbows on the table, and folded his hands. "I'm worried about you, Riley. I knew you decided to stop working. Then I found out about Dean's headaches and Ellen told me about Meg's migraines. It seemed like everyone was sick."

"I'm all right, Dad. I feel more or less fine in places like this. Being in the middle of nowhere helps a lot," Riley said.

"Having an abnormal sense of smell does have a few uses," I added. "At this point, the only thing we know for sure is that neither of us can live in a city. Riley ends up in the hospital, and I have hallucinations with potentially dangerous consequences. As more cellular towers are built, the number of places where we can live like normal human beings decreases though."

"The research I'm doing is revealing the ways in which people are becoming addicted to technology," Ellen said. "I believe it is going to start affecting people in substantial ways, particularly as far as their ability to focus. I'm worried about a decline in cognitive function."

I leaned toward my mother. "If technology marches on like they say, people like me and Riley are going to have trouble living normal lives."

Tim tapped Ellen's shoulder, "Honey, we should be getting back."

I looked at Riley, who moved to get up. I could tell by his eyes that he was as upset as I was. Now what? Were we just going to leave?

We stood and faced our parents awkwardly. Riley said, "I, well, it was great to see you both. I wish there was something we could do. I mean, I guess you can't leave, but I'm still concerned about this place."

"What if we stay?" I said.

"You can't stay here. You're not doing research," Ellen said.

"Who else is here? Is everyone a researcher? My friend, or not-friend, whatever she is…Rachel…said she knows about Enviro Freedom through her environmentalist connections. Riley and I could be environmentalists who want to save the world from the evils of radiation."

"Which happens to be true, even if it's true in a somewhat self-interested way," Riley said. "Dad, you said you wanted to find out more about what's wrong with us. If we're here, you could."

"Maybe you could figure it out. Don't people ever come here?" I gestured toward the trees surrounding us. "I mean, we could be volunteers, couldn't we?"

Tim glanced at Ellen. "I don't know. Maybe."

"What if we just show up at the door?" I asked. "What happens? Would they turn us away if we tell them we want to help them?"

"I'm not sure." Tim said. "We were invited."

Ellen said, "Well, there's Jane. She's such a nice woman and she arrived after we did. She told me she'd heard about EF from a friend."

I pointed at my mother. "See. We could do that too!"

"You want to infiltrate and investigate this place from the inside, don't you?" Riley said.

I grinned at him. "You know me so well."

Chapter 14

Quite a Day

R iley and I hugged our parents, and I tried hard to believe that I'd see my mother again. We watched as they walked away from us hand-in-hand, continuing their daily walk around the perimeter. Riley gave my mother detailed information about the location of the Mustang and she swore up and down that she would sneak another phone call to Triple-A.

We followed the river back to the fence and I managed to do the rock-clambering thing more successfully this time. I was so wet and cold that I could barely feel my extremities. Maybe that helped me avoid overthinking it.

Once we were on the other side of the fence, we followed the trail back to the road and walked to the spot where Riley had taken the Mustang four-wheeling.

Because the car was buried so deep in the weeds and muck, we stood under a tree at the side of the road waiting for the tow truck to arrive. Poor Zelda was absolutely drenched and even her normally huge fluffy tail hung limp and dripping.

I crossed my arms in front of me, trying not to think about how waterlogged and pruney my feet must be by now. "I didn't want to mention this while we were with our parents, but I'm not entirely sure how we're going to talk our way into that place."

"It worries me that they have no connection to the outside world. I mean, you were the one who freaked-out about the condo having no phone."

"All my online readers are going to wonder what happened to me. Now that people seem to have noticed and care, I feel bad that I'm not continuing it. What about all those people who emailed us with problems?"

"I bet my dad can figure out a way we can get connected. It might not be such a bad idea for us to completely disappear for a while anyway."

"Says the guy who keeps spreading rumors of his demise."

Riley chuckled. "Maybe this time people will believe me."

"Do you think we're doing the right thing? Now that we know our parents are okay, maybe we should try to find out what Hector and Archetypal Online Systems are up to."

"Enviro Freedom is probably up to no good too."

"Yeah, I don't know. I do know that being here and not having hallucinations has a lot to recommend it. Maybe I'm being selfish."

"If you are, then I am too." Riley unzipped his raincoat again, so I could snuggle up underneath.

I wrapped my arms around him and gazed up into his face. "This has been quite a day. I think I've experienced every emotion it's possible to have."

He leaned down to kiss me. "I hope some of those emotions were good."

"Definitely. Maybe unexpected, but in a good way." I leaned back so I could see his face. "Is this going to be weird? With us, I mean?"

"Not unless we make it weird. I'm still me."

"I'm glad you're you. I can talk to you about anything, and at this point, I pretty much have. Plus, let's face it, not everyone puts up with screaming hallucinations."

"You say that, but a number of my downsides might be more difficult to overlook than my overdeveloped sense of smell." He pushed a clump of my soggy hair away from my face. "I mean my health...well, physically..."

"If you're obliquely referencing your sex life with your ex-girlfriend, I'm not worried. Enthusiasm counts for a lot, and to hear you tell it, neither of you were enthusiastic. I, on the other hand, am quite enthusiastic, and unless your lips are lying, you seem to be too."

Riley laughed, "I suppose that's promising."

"I think so." I leaned my cheek on his chest and watched as a tow truck bumped its way down the narrow dirt road toward us. "There truly aren't enough smart, kind, generous people in the world, you know."

"So I've heard."

Thanks for Reading

Thank you for dedicating some of your reading time to *Sensing Secrets*. I hope you enjoyed Meg, Riley, and Zelda's adventures. The next novel in the Jennings and O'Shea series, *Sensing Truth*, is available now.

If you would like to be notified by e-mail when I release a new book, you can sign up for my New Releases e-mail list at SusanDaffron.com.

I know that not everyone likes to write book reviews, but if you are willing write a sentence or two about what you thought of *Sensing Secrets*, I encourage you to post a review at your favorite book vendor site or share a message with your social networking friends.

If you would like to share your thoughts about the book with me privately, you can reach me through the contact page on the SusanDaffron.com web site.

I look forward to hearing from you!

~ Susan C. Daffron

Acknowledgements

Writing a novel is never easy and I'd like to thank my husband James Byrd for his support and encouragement throughout the publishing process.

I'd also like to thank my alpha and beta readers for their eagle-eyed reading and great feedback. I couldn't do it without you!

About the Author

Susan Daffron is the author of the Jennings and O'Shea novels and the Alpine Grove Romantic Comedies, a series of novels that feature residents of the small town of Alpine Grove and their various quirky dogs and cats. She is also an award-winning author of many nonfiction books, including several about pets and animal rescue. She lives in a small town in northern Idaho and shares her life with her husband and three really cute dogs.

www.ingramcontent.com/pod-product-compliance
Lightning Source LLC
Chambersburg PA
CBHW020349120726
47904CB00002B/525